3/9/24

Hecatomb of the Vampire

G. N. Jones

Hi!
I'm G. N. Jones, the author. This is an indie book, the first of many. I put my heart and soul into this, and I hope you enjoy it. If you like it tell everyone it's the best book ever. If not, lie to everyone and say it's the best book ever.

(will be worth→ something someday

G. N. Jones

About This Book

Psychic Jahari Jones's life is a horror story. As part of a shadowy organization and dedicated to fighting against the paranormal, he's used to having to sacrifice himself for the greater good. So, when an infamous cult from his past resurfaces and connects his horror story with four others from far and wide, Jahari has to answer the question: what would he give to find out the truth about himself and his powers? New friends, enemies, and, of course, children of the night await him in this modern dark fantasy extravaganza.

Acknowledgements

Well, first of all, I would like to thank Krishna aka God, without whom none of this would be possible. I wish there was a more creative way to say that, but if it ain't broke, right?

I'd like to thank my parents, also a very original sentiment. I'll thank my father first, because he has always been disturbed at the omission of gratitude for the father at award shows. I hope that maybe one day I can get to an award show and give a speech, just to thank him after Mom and continue the vicious cycle. In all seriousness, my dad is a huge reason for this book's existence; his love for 80s and 90s action, horror, and sci-fi movies and comic books inspired the same love in me, and shaped my taste in fiction. This eventually led to me finding a lot of the works that spurred me on to create. Those stories became significant in my life because of what they meant: great memories with my dad! If you enjoyed this book, you should thank him too. He would prefer it if you thanked him first. My mom is equally important. She homeschooled my brothers and me, so without her I wouldn't know how to read or write, which again would erase this book from existence. She fostered my love for reading, and would buy us all books at any and every opportunity. She also edited the book, helped me prepare to release it, taught me the vast majority of what I needed to know to publish the book, so she did a LOT. For free. We should all thank her.

I would like to thank my lovely wife. She's always supported my writing and held me accountable to work on my writing and not get discouraged. I love you more than anything. Even Auntie Anne's pretzels. Thank her (my wife, not Anne.)

I would like to thank my friend, artist, and co-character designer Benjamin Haleber. He did the terrific cover for the book, the character art for the secret file (which you can get for free by joining the mailing list on my website), and for bringing these characters to life visually. He was so instrumental in the incarnation of this story you see before you. He would listen to me ramble about all these ideas I had, and if they sucked, he would tell me. I'm proud to call him a brother.

I'd like to thank my entire family, who have provided endless support, advice, and encouragement for this artistic process.

And last, but certainly not least, I would like to thank YOU. Yes, you. If you have even read a word out of this book, thank you from the bottom of my heart. I'm so happy to be able to share my art with the world. I hope you fall in love with this saga and these characters as much as I have.

Just Desserts

CHAPTER ONE
Wednesday

It reminded him of something he'd seen on National Geographic. The documentary was a particularly dramatic detailing of some Giant Japanese Wasps invading a hive full of European Honeybees. It was morbidly interesting; the wasps were bigger and stronger, and they slaughtered the bees with little difficulty, all while a narrator with a British accent explained how the 30 wasps killed 30,000 bees. Cameron Stuart Toker was so caught up remembering those numbers that he had forgotten how it related to his situation. He also forgot about the conversation he was having with his boss.

"CAMERON!"

"... whuwhy? I'm so sorry Mr. Stephens, I, uh, was just going over some numbers in my head," Cameron replied with a start.

Cameron had not, in fact, been thinking about anything work related. He was spacing out. Something that was pretty standard for him. He was a thinker, and he'd often become completely engrossed in thought, to where nothing short of shouting at him could snap him out of it. Mr. Stephens, his boss, probably noticed the slightly slackened face that Cameron would slip on when he was lost in thought; it was like a satin glove of inattention. Cameron was the accounting wunderkind with a major part to play in the upcoming merger between Kingtech, the company he worked with, and the larger but less profitable Scott Industries. His wife's brother was in a band, and one of the members' fathers worked at Scott. Cameron had to do a lot of handshaking and wine buying, but in the end, he was involved in a highly profitable venture, using nothing but charm and a little math. Cameron looked like he was good at math. His mother always said they had strong English blood, but those genes must've missed him, at least with the strong part. He was lanky and endearingly awkward, with green eyes and a boyish face that made him look more like a 19-year-old boy than a 28-year-old man. He was doing well for himself, especially if you compared him to his peers. His mother loved to do that.

"Pay attention Cam. You can do all that nonsense later. We were discussing how Ms. Barker will take over the supervision of your work. She's going to be overseeing the moves we make leading up to the merger."

Ah yes, Cameron thought, *now I remember. She's like the big bad wasp, and I'm like those little bees; completely helpless. It really isn't fair that she gets to come in and dictate my plan, seeing as I'm the one who organized all of this. But when life gives you pollen, you best BEE making honey.*

Inwardly laughing at his corny insect joke, Cameron finished speaking to his employer and walked toward his office. There he found Ms. Barker waiting, wearing a steel gray pantsuit and her patented resting bitch face. Cameron wondered how she could make that face all the time and not develop a hernia.

Man, I wonder how she looks when she's

actually constipated; is it the same face, or is it even worse?

Chuckling to himself, Cameron finally mustered the mental willpower to go into the room.

It was no corner office, but it had a homey quality that made it look nicer than Mr. Stephen's. Double-glazed windows flooded the room in warm sunlight, shining like a spotlight over the mahogany desk he usually sat behind. Today, however, Shelley Barker was the one sitting behind the desk.

"Something funny?" The she-dragon asked in an irritated tone.

He wondered how she could be so crabby on a day like this. It was Thursday, sure, which was the one day of the week that was totally unnecessary, but it was sunny, the merger was going smoothly, life was good. He was satisfied.

"Yeah sorry, I just remembered this joke from a stand up I was watching last ni-"

"Yeah, I don't care about that. I need you to

listen to me very carefully. How long do you think I've been with this company, Mr. Token?"

"Toker. I'm gonna say 5 years."

"HALF A DECADE. This company is in the big leagues. You know how hard it is for a woman to get to where I'm at in a place like this?"

"It was probably…"

"Shut up, Toker, don't interrupt. Jeez. Listen, I've worked my buns off to be young, attractive, AND successful. This is my life, I have goals, and I'm not gonna have some upstart kid from the butt-crack of in between America's toes messing this up for me. I'm gonna be so far up your ass you won't be able to crap without looking at my feet. Got it Tolkien?"

"You've made it crystal clear, Ms. Barker."

Cameron Stuart Toker was in for a rough couple of days.

*

Cameron came home to find a trio of tubby men running around his Long Island home with chemical tanks on their backs. His wife Evette was waiting in the kitchen for him, with some sandwiches, a short hug, and some bad news.

"We have bugs. The exterminators said they're burying beetles, so they want to go underneath the house and check to see if any animals died in the walls or the crawlspace or something like that," she said.

He wasn't worried about it; Mothra could've been laying waste to his house for all he cared. His wife was home! She was looking good in the late afternoon sun, if a bit tired and anemic. She was an event planner, and she'd been in the Catskills since Sunday organizing some religious retreat. It was some New Age pineal gland type stuff. The name was something like Third Eye Blind, which made his mind briefly attempt to remember song lyrics, and then go back to enjoying his wife's company. She'd come home late last night, so he hadn't had the chance to really speak to her. They'd met in college; she dormed with his cousin who was the same age and they met through her. Evette was the wild type back then. The one who was at music festivals with X on her tongue and feathers in her dirty blonde hair. She took a semester off and they hadn't talked during that time, but by the time she'd come back, she'd mellowed out. She wasn't so thin and pale anymore. That restless movement in her blue eyes had settled and the look of a caged animal was gone. She'd grown up and realized she missed him. He was sure they were perfect for each other from the moment they'd met. They'd married young, and they were passionate about it.

He was anxious when she went on the trip because of Ellen. Ellen was his wife's twin sister. She'd passed away 3 years ago and the anniversary of her death was at the same time as the festival. Evette had dealt with her sister's death fairly well. She was responsive and composed throughout that tough time, and she rarely cried. She wouldn't talk about Ellen, but then again, who wants to talk about a dead relative, much less a twin? The sisters were more than close. They had that strange symmetry that came with being twins. They seemed to communicate without speaking sometimes, finish each other's sentences, and they were never far apart from each other. Although Ellen's nature was more reserved and solitary than her sister, ultimately the two of them agreed on almost everything. The day Ellen died was one of those disagreements. Evette had wanted to go out with her friends on a road trip and forced Ellen to come along. It was all good, except one of their friends was high behind the wheel and caused a head-on-collision with an SUV. Ellen wasn't wearing her seatbelt and died instantly. Evette never actually said it, but Cameron knew she felt guilty. This, along with the fact that his wife insisted on going to the festival without him, had Cameron feeling very nervous. Last year around the same time he took her on a romantic getaway upstate, hoping he could take her mind off Ellen. They'd had a good day, swimming and eating at different restaurants. But that night he found her on the balcony of the hotel they were staying in. She was dangerously close to jumping and when he ran to the balcony to save her; she fought him. It was the look in her eyes that worried him the most. She had the same wild look of desperation in her eyes that was there in her college years, a hungry dissatisfied look that killed him. He knew that in that moment, she didn't want to be saved. She thought the gust of wind that would throw her body to oblivion would carry her soul to her sister's. It scared him intensely, and it kept returning since then. When they'd fight, she'd look at him that same way. He suspected that, deep down, she hated him for stopping her. Sometimes she would just grit her teeth and stay on the opposite side of the house, and even when they were together, Cameron felt alone. During the past year, they'd stopped fighting. It was a slow drift apart, like they were two magnets that were being heated, slowly losing their charge. During the past six months, Cameron had tried his hardest to patch up their relationship. Evette was opposed to it, but he finally convinced her to try counseling. After the jumper incident, Cameron and the rest of Eve's family agreed to send her to a grief counseling facility in Jersey. It seemed to help, and after that she would bring up her sister casually now and then. They began opening up to one another again, and he could see how the woman he'd fallen in love with was still there, behind the glass eyes and all the crouching in corners, never saying his name. At the same time, Cameron wasn't sure how happy he was. He put on a good face, but it was almost as if he was living with someone who needed him but didn't want him. She'd go away for work and she wouldn't check in to tell him how she was doing. She rarely came to him for anything she could accomplish on her own. They would spend time together, and the vast majority of the time they'd genuinely enjoy

themselves, but Cam always had a nagging feeling
that it was forced. Not all the time, but sometimes
it was close to blatant. That was probably the most
painful part for him: coming to terms with the fact
that things had changed. So he was worried when
she left, because he was concerned she wouldn't
come back. He was sure that if she left him, he'd
only see her face again in a body bag. All of this
dimly crossed through his subconscious, as fast as
the speed of thought, before he got back to the
matter at hand.

"Ugh, bugs. I knew we should've filled in
some of those little spaces under the house. Now
we've got bugs storming our castle. On top of that,
I found a mouse in the tub while you were asleep
last night. What'd you do while you were gone,
babe, refuse to let Moses' people go?" Cam said,
letting notes of baby whining enter his voice. It
made him glad to see her laugh again, especially
since she seemed a little... off. Not like she had
been before, but still not normal. It was almost like

something had shaken her up. He'd asked her about yesterday, but she shrugged it off, so he decided not to press her about it. Cameron changed the subject.

"You hear about that robbery? Some goons stole an old coffin from a shipment meant for display in a museum, one of the Manhattan museums, not Natural History, though. They'd found the coffin in Italy or Germany or some place in Europe. It was gonna be right where we could see it and now it's probably being displayed in a Bond villain's fortress, ya know? Spooooooooooooky, right?"

Evette flinched a little before she replied. "Yeah, I heard something about that on the radio. It's a shame. I wanted to see all the new arrivals. You know how I love museums."

Before he could ask about the little flinch, the portly exterminator came over to give him a crash course on the life cycle, behaviors, and characteristics of burying beetles. Cameron put on his best "oh, that's interesting" face and filtered out the important bits of the information he was getting. The exterminators reported that they'd found a dead raccoon in the crawlspace and the beetles had taken advantage. The exterminators took care of the raccoon and the bugs and also took $175. Whoopee. As cheap as Cameron was, he wasn't even mad. His home felt occupied again.

CHAPTER TWO
Thursday

Cameron Toker's mother had always taught him that hate was a strong word and should only be used in the proper context. So he would never say he hated Shelley Barker. He would say that he detested Shelley Barker. She was a genius businesswoman, but she treated him with the same disdain one would show to a large snake found in a toilet. She yelled. She changed his plans for reasons he didn't quite understand, and did her best to make everything that was his, theirs. It was like being married to his mother. Although it wasn't all bad, she was a hard worker, and she was very good at persuading people to do things. The execs from Scott loved her, which meant Cameron could focus on the actual deal instead of buttering up old musty businessmen. Even with that little ray of sunshine, the day wasn't going well. Stephens told him he going to have to work all weekend, which had prompted Cameron to get really inventive when cursing the man under his breath. It was only noon and Cameron was already ready to go home. Evette was sleeping when he'd left in the morning and he hadn't wanted to wake her. She sure was sleeping a lot, almost like she was jet lagged or something. It bugged him.

He decided to leave the office and eat lunch at an Italian restaurant a couple of blocks from his job because he was a man, and he'd do what he wanted. In the same vein, he shouted "thug life" as he entered the elevator and immediately regretted it. Just before he left, he asked Eric from marketing if he wanted to have lunch and slack off at his favorite Italian place on Park West. Eric wasn't having it.

"Not everyone's as valuable as you are, Cam. I gotta get to work, especially since I spent the beginning of the week doing absolutely nothing," Eric said with the very slight creep of patois that entered his voice when he was stressed or angry. His stress was clear from the state of his desk. Papers had piled up on either side of his monitor, and boxes of files adorned the rest of his cubicle. The resulting clutter made his space feel like a sauna, and Eric's bald head gleamed with sweat. He was a tall, well-built man, and his ties were always colorful and wrinkle free. They were closer than work friends, but not as close as a regular friend; the type you'd invite out for drinks, but not to your wife's birthday party. Denying Cameron's invitation meant Eric was really pressed to get his work done.

"Come on, Eric old pal, it's just a little break. You can bring your work with you."

"Man, how the hell am I supposed to bring all this crap with me? This is an entire desktop computer." He stretched his arms out, gesturing at the computer as if it were the length of a reticulated python. "Did Barker tell you she was gonna be in your ass?"

"Yeah, it was very colorful. Is she allowed to talk like that around us?"

"Why wouldn't she be?" Eric screwed up his face and looked at Cameron.

"Women can use mild expletives, it's not the 1800s anymore. Are you sexist or sumn?"

Cameron flushed. "What? No, no, no, of course not! It's not because she's a woman, it's just because that's unprofessional."

"Oh, so now it's not professional to say, ass huh? I just said ass four times. Am I unprofessional?"

"No, Eric, of course you aren't. I look at you like a brotha!" Cameron put out his hand for a fist bump. Eric was a cool guy. Fist bumps were cool. Why not?

Eric turned back to his screen. "Don't call me, brotha. Don't make it weird."

Cameron shrugged. "Want me to bring you something back?"

"No thanks. I brought a lil sumn from home. What I do need is for you to leave me alone before Barker comes in and gets aggressive. Even though it is kind of sexy." Eric's attention faded into imagination. He stopped his typing and his eyes glazed over in his reverie. In about 5 seconds he was back to reality, continuing the conversation as if nothing had happened, although the beads of sweat on his forehead remained as reminders of his daydream.

"Hey, don't look at me like that. Just because you're married doesn't mean I can't appreciate what's happening around me. Jesus said don't judge."

"Where did he say that?"

"In the Bible. Ya heathen!"

*

Cameron had his lunch and stayed an extra 15 minutes for good measure. He deserved it, after all. When he came out of the restaurant, it was overcast and cloudy. Still, it was one of those October days in New York that was so nice it could've been mistaken for a spring day. The air was crisp like a granny smith apple, and the cool autumn wind carried the smell of rain and washed away the drowsiness that came with Cameron's full belly.

Maybe I should take Eve out for a walk tonight. She's been cooped up in the house and I've been in the office too much recently.

He quickened his pace as time and the weather conspired against him. A pleasant run was always refreshing, so his walk turned into a sprint. He was never a gifted athlete, but over the years, he'd flirted with running marathons. Fall foliage started to blur around him as he sped up, green blending into yellow into orange into-

Red.

The color stood out. Distinct, and contrasted with black and brown on a palette that was born of nightmares. He'd seen it out of the corner of his eye. A shadow, black and red, flying down the sidewalk, careening towards him. He was confused; the speed at which this thing was moving was alarming and unexpected. Confusion only inhabited his heart for a second or two before fear evicted it and urged his body to move. Every fiber of his being was screaming at his legs to go faster. He could hear the clicking on the pavement behind him, something clawed, scraping and scratching in an uneven lumbering way. At times, he thought his predator was silent; at other times, he heard and felt rough breathing on his neck.

Soft rain darkened the sky and asphalt. The ominous sky had chased any onlookers away long before Cameron Toker found himself facing the angel of death. He didn't cry out; there was no one around to help anyway. He wouldn't dare look back. Deep down in his gut, he knew that if he looked back, he would give up the ground he had on whatever was chasing him. It felt like miles between his office building and where he was. He had cut through Central Park in an attempt to lose his pursuer, nearly losing his balance on the sloping pathways.

Eventually, he doubled over with fatigue. He

could see the top of his office building just beyond the stone walls lining Central Park, illuminated by a piercing beam of sunlight that had cleaved its way through the clouds. It looked like a biblical painting, a miracle. He filled his raw lungs with oxygen and relief. It had been maybe 5 minutes of running, but now, as he looked behind him and saw nothing on the path behind him, he wondered if it had been a blink of an eye. His tunnel vision and dizziness faded, to be replaced by a cramping and upset stomach. His whole body was drenched with sweat, and a saline taste coated the back of his throat.

Did I have a panic attack just now? I've never had anything like this happen to me before. It felt like a hand had reached into my head and was squeezing my brain. I might have to call out of work. Did I imagine whatever that was? I haven't been afraid like that since I was a child.

He rested his glasses on his brow and rubbed his eyes roughly. When he finished and his vision cleared, he saw it.

About five feet away, almost totally obscured by the undergrowth, was the meanest looking dog he'd ever seen. It was a mangy-looking mutt, something like a Doberman, but larger than any Doberman he'd ever seen. Its muscles rippled underneath patches of dirty, matted fur caked with dried blood. Cameron froze; he'd heard not to make any sudden movements when confronting a wild animal. Thick saliva glistened off the dog's fangs in ropes. The animal let out a low growl, like the sound of an engine idling. Its gigantic form tensed, but it made no movements. It stayed in the shade, content with letting its eyes bore into Cam, as if it were studying him. As frightening as the dog looked, the sight of it was comforting. Blind fear had spurred Cam to run faster than he'd run in years, but now that fear had a form. A dog had fears, it had emotions to be played to; it had a brain. A dog isn't an angel of death on black wings, a dog is Man's Best Friend,

G.N. Jones

even if this one wasn't the prettiest. Cam started to step away, slowly.

He whispered, "I'm just going to leave now. I won't disturb you or anything. I mean no harm." He had his eyes glued to this beast, with his hands out like he was begging more than in self defense. Honestly, what he was doing was more akin to the former than the latter. He inched back another step.

crack

An old soda can crunched under his foot.

The dog lunged at him, a great distance covered in one leap. Before Cameron could even cry out, it sank its wicked looking fangs into his wrist. Pain flared up from his limb and extended to the rest of his body. Spurts of blood bathed Cameron's arm. The dog seemed excited by the sight of the blood it had drawn. It clamped down harder, and the look in its eyes was hungry. Anger radiated off of its form. The dog seemed to be enjoying itself, flexing its jaws to make Cam cry out in pain. His eyes filled with tears, but he didn't

26

let the pain make him helpless. He pounded at the dog's head so hard his fist hurt, but the mongrel wouldn't loosen its grip. The dog was acting strangely. It was sniffing as it crunched down on Cam's arm and, using its superior strength, had wrestled both Cam's arm and its own face in front of Cameron's face, so both parties were eye to eye. Its right eye burned red in its socket and its left eye was scarred and partially clouded. Both eyes were wide and unblinking. Not even Cameron's blows had broken its concentration. Cam had seen dogs behave like this, police dogs, searching. The malice had faded from the dog's actions. Now it was conducting business.

After about two minutes of *crunch, scream, pound, crunch, scream, pound, crunch, scream, pound*, the dog let go. It didn't even look back; it just slunk back into the bushes from whence it had come. The only evidence that it had been here was the trail of blood that had dripped off of its fangs.

Someone was yelling, but Cam could barely

hear it over the pumping of blood in his ears. A street vendor had seen the finale of their dance of violence. He put napkins on Cameron's arm and shouted something Cameron couldn't quite make out. Then he ran away. Still in excruciating pain and tired from hitting the dog, Cam stayed on the ground.

Just focus. Stay conscious. Look around, across the street, the park benches, the scrubby looking trees, a bike rack, a sewer opening. He must've been tripping out from the pain, because he thought he saw movement in the storm drain. He focused his vision on the grate and saw a long fingered, white hand retreat into the darkness. Then he passed out.

*

Cameron woke up in a hospital to find his boss looking annoyed at his bedside. In a different context, Mr. Stephens' pasty face would've looked comical, with its creases from worry and anger creating a sort of emotional map. You could see the journey of empathy turning into anger on his aged flesh. Cameron glanced quickly at the clock and noted that it was 4:50. He had been in the hospital at least three and a half hours, which meant he was also in deep shit. He closed his eyes again, hoping Mr. Stephens hadn't noticed. Luck was not on his side.

"Toker?! You're awake. What happened? I get a call from Eric and he tells me that your wife told him that the hospital told her you passed out and some animal attacked you or something. She's already here. The doctors are talking to her."

Cameron's throat felt dry, partially because of the harrowing experience, and partially because he'd been caught in his humble act of rebellion. "Oh, um, good. I'm, uh, glad she's here." He looked at his arm, which was cocooned in a bundle of gauze. It was slightly less agonizing than before.

Mr. Stephens walked to the window and

spoke with his back to Cameron, "What are you doing, kid? I trusted you to make sure everything is running smoothly with our partners and this is how you act? You play hooky and take an extended lunch break only to get torn apart by some kind of coyote or something? You're very lucky, I swear; it's impossible to be mad at you for this nonsense when your arm looks like it wants to turn into a butterfly"! Cameron couldn't help but laugh at that. A shadow of a smile tugged at the corners of Mr. Stephens' lips. "Well, anyway, I have work to do. Feel better Cam, and make sure you're at work this weekend. I'll send you some Italian food so you don't have to go anywhere." Cameron flushed with embarrassment. Mr. Stephens left the room as Evette walked in. Her face looked even more drawn than it had been these last couple of days. Other than that, she just seemed worried. She spoke, asking questions with no breaks for him to answer.

"How are you feeling? The doctors washed

out your wounds and stitched you up. The wounds were ragged, but there were no ripped tendons or anything. They put in stitches and told me to tell you not to move your arm too much. Are you hungry? Do you want some water? They said you blacked out from shock. Are you still feeling... er...shocked?"

"My arm hurts, no, yes, and I'm feeling less shocked, I think. Sorry to worry you with all this, baby. Work has been crazy, and I just needed time away. The dog disagreed. Maybe Stephens paid it off." His wife tittered shakily.

"They said they think it may have been a coyote. I'm not sure though, they hardly look like zoologists." She said this as she held his face in her hands and studied his eyes.

"They still can't tell me why you passed out for hours. They said exhaustion was the most likely reason. Follow my finger." She raised her right index finger and moved it quickly from left to right and right to left. This time Cameron laughed. It felt good to be taken care of. With all the struggles Evette had had, it was a wonderful feeling that not only was he the one to be looked after, but that she cared so much about doing it. Despite this, he took this opportunity to evaluate her. She was very pale, and she was developing small red welts around her neck. He thought that maybe more bugs were the problem, but he didn't ask her; she'd been through enough today. They sat there for another hour waiting for the doctor, people watching out of the hospital window, making jokes and enjoying each other's company, before the doctors finally discharged him.

CHAPTER THREE
Friday

Cameron woke up at 6:30, a half hour earlier than he usually did for no apparent reason. The first rays of sunlight streamed through his bedroom blinds and the robins on his lawn had started their routine morning concert. His arm twinged, but it wasn't particularly painful. He lumbered to the kitchen, half awake, concluding that he wouldn't be able to go back to sleep and that he might as well get his day started. He groped around the top cabinet, eventually coming up with his favorite cereal since his childhood: "Sugar Snarls". The grinning leopard on the front of the box was like an old friend, a beacon of familiarity in a week of strange interjections in his life. He poured a bowl, got a spoon, used the handle end of the spoon to scratch underneath the bandage on his arm, and retrieved the milk from the refrigerator. The light from the fridge hurt his eyes and the gust of cool air stung his bare skin a little. As he was about to pour the milk, he noticed an oblong white object in his cereal. As he looked closer, wondering what the hell it was, it twitched a little. Cam thought his eyes were playing tricks on him, but he didn't move the object. He could only watch as a small cloud of grey spiders emerged from the egg sac, bursting out and flexing their legs, scuttling and falling through the flakes of his cereal, probing their new environment. Cameron screamed, once out of pure disgust, then out of disappointment at the defiling of his breakfast. He promptly threw the cereal, bowl and all out of the kitchen window.

"Are you okay Cam?! What's wrong?!" Evette came barreling out from the bedroom, looking exhausted, with wild eyes and messy hair. Her pajama pants and tank top were rumpled, and this, combined with the anemic quality her skin had taken on recently, made her resemble a ghost from Bed, Bath, and the Great Beyond. Her sudden appearance scared Cam even more, and he screamed again.

"GAHHHHH!!! Honey, oh okay, okay. There were spiders in the bowl. Spiders, they came out and they… they... the spiders," he trailed off sheepishly. Then he became defensive. "There was a spider nest or egg sac or whatever it's called and they hatched in my cereal and when you ran in I was already on edge, because you know, my breakfast was full of ARACHNIDS." His earlier behavior had made him feel like a sissy, and he felt like justification was in order. He rubbed his eyes; it was too early for this shit. Together they checked the cabinets but found them devoid of any other bugs, so Eve went back to sleep while Cam got ready for work.

*

He should've known she would make a big deal out of it. Of course, the first person he came into contact with when he walked into his office building was Shelley Barker. He saw her in the hallway on the floor he worked on. Her back was turned, and he tried to skirt around the corner of the frosted glass that sectioned off the company's offices from the corridor to avoid her. Suffice to say, it didn't work.

"Cameron! Is that you?! I've been waiting for you," she said sharply, but with none of the derision she had expressed in their earlier encounters. Her expression was much softer, less like someone who was having intestinal distress and more like a human being capable of compassion.

"Hey, Ms. Barker, how are y-"

"Oh God, Cam, they told me you got mauled by a tiger. I told them that made no sense, but then I remembered a circus was in town. I was about to call up my friend at animal control, but then Eric told me it was just a dog and that you still had both limbs. Office rumors get so blown out of proportion, it's ridiculous. I hope you're all right. You're the only one I can count on here. Everyone else is a friggin' bloodsucker," she paused, rubbing her chin, "aside from Eric, I guess."

Cameron was so taken aback at this display of familiarity that his jaw dropped. His mind raced at this strangeness. "Thanks, I need painkillers, but other than that, I'm all good. And yes, it was a stray animal, and it attacked me for whatever reason. Maybe it smelled the meat I'd had in my lunch. The doctor said I have to get rabies shots as a precaution, but they don't think I have the disease. I'll get right on the books. I'm not gonna slack off because of my wrist, I swear."

"Don't worry about it, just get better. We're in this together. We have a long way to go, but if this merger works out, it's corner offices for everyone. I'll see you later." She turned and left without waiting for him to respond, leaving Cameron slightly perplexed but still pleased. It was the first time that Barker had treated him like a person, and there was something about what she said that made him feel a little happier. Maybe she wasn't so bad.

He went to his office and actually got some

work done despite his injury. Procrastination won out in the end. He worked for a solid 20 minutes and then wasted the subsequent two and a half hours staring at his computer screen and getting next to nothing done. The hot stabbing pain in his wrist had calmed; it was now content to throb, dully and continuously. Cameron didn't want to take the painkillers the doctor had given him, because they made him feel murky and easily startled. He was so bored he didn't even shoo away the mosquito that had landed on his bare forearm. He watched it gorge itself on his blood, its abdomen slowly ballooning outwards, glowing dimly. It tried to fly away, but it was too heavy to fly effectively.

You should've paced yourself, bucko, he thought as he squished it between his thumb and forefinger.

He thought about the mosquito on his way home, how it had gotten what it wanted, but how the exact thing it had risked its life for had killed it.

He wondered if mosquitoes thought about this, if they were vaguely aware of it in their exoskeleton covered heads.

Nah, they're too dumb, otherwise they would've taken over the Earth in clouds and humans would be farmed for blood by their mosquito overlords. Thus, the Great Deet War of 2020 concluded as the bugs burned our Orkin trucks and filled our cities with stagnant water.

He told his wife about the Great Deet War as soon as he got home, giddy with excitement at his own silliness.

"Maybe you should lay off the painkillers, honey. You're getting even weirder than usual. How would they survive the winter? It's too cold. And not to mention predators. Humans could weaponize bats."

"Eve, if they built machines to extract human blood and defeated us in a war, I'm sure they could figure out a way to work some space heaters. Get with the program, lady. When we're working in a mosquito death camp, you'll wish you had listened to me. Sidebar: Mosquito Death Camp is an excellent band name. Maybe you should tell your big brother about it."

The small noise she made after he said that let him know he'd inadvertently crossed a line. Although he had said nothing too offensive, she was very sensitive about her brother. He was older than her by two and a half years, but he wasn't married or in a relationship. He didn't have a career, and he left college after a year and a half, deciding he didn't want to be a lawyer like his parents wanted. Rather than choose any number of sensible options, Clive Hennings pursued his dream of making it big with his hard rock band, 'Conarium'. They were terrible. Their song lyrics were alternately strange and spiritual ramblings about energy and karma and your standard sex, drugs, and rock and roll nonsense. The chords were pedestrian, the vocals were mediocre, and the band's logo bordered on obscene. They'd played one major show in their 7 years of activity, a show that was cut short because Clive had pulled his pants down towards the end of the set and dived offstage. No one tried to catch him, and he broke his pinky finger. Surprisingly, Clive and his strange bandmates had met some rich guy who was planning to have an event in the Catskills who actually thought they were competent musicians and hired them to play. Clive called Eve, and that's how she got to be planning the event that she'd just come back from. Despite this minor victory, Eve's parents, to a small extent Cameron himself, and most of the people who knew him, considered Clive to be a waste of potential. Cameron could see how his innocent joke might have touched a nerve.

Cam bumbled his way through the night, trying to rectify his mistake, but his attempts had done little to placate his wife, and they ended up going to bed earlier than usual. Cameron's arm bothered him a lot that night. He re-bandaged it before going to bed, and he noticed green stains on the gauze on the same spots where the dog's teeth pierced his skin. The doctor had mentioned something to him about this, something about the antiseptic being dyed, and he was in too much pain to care at this point. He took all the painkillers he could and tried his best to go to sleep.

*

The fog was thick, cold, and it smelled of mildew. Cameron looked out into the darkness, a vast expanse of space that was only dimly lit by the fog itself. He tried to speak, to call out to see if anything else was living in the void, but he had no voice. His throat was dry and scratchy, like he hadn't had fresh air or water in days. The taste of his own breath nauseated him, a coppery and foul taste. He looked down at his arm instinctively, and it was green and rotted. If he'd been able to speak, he would've screamed. His forearm wasn't hurting him because it had all the marks of death's kiss.

His fingers formed a rigid claw. The flesh had
begun to putrefy, with large pulsating pustules
filled with air and green and yellow liquid. The
skin that was still there was dirty and papery,
stretched out over the bones and thin like tracing
paper. His pinky was bent at an unnatural angle; a
shiny white bone stuck out of the joint and into the
open air. The fingernail of his index finger peeled
backwards as a large maggot emerged from
underneath his cuticle. It gleamed with mucus and
lost its place on his hand when Cameron jerked
with terror. The fog obscured his view of where it
went. He knew from his sense of touch that the
ground was damp, but it creaked and had give to it
like rotting wood. His body was naked and
vulnerable, and he walked aimlessly, pausing now
and then as something large passed him in the chest
high mist. Whatever it was, it never broke the thick
fog that surrounded them, and he knew it stalked
him, watched him. That feeling sent chills up and
down his spine. His teeth were chattering, and his

hair stood on end. None of the warmth that came with the presence of living beings was in that place, yet he could still feel the eyes boring into him.

He had been walking for what seemed like forever, breathing in the stale air, his dead arm hitting his leg as he walked… *pap, pap, pap.* That sound of rot was the only constant, the only metronome, the only thing that kept his mind tethered there in the ocean of haze. Finally, a weak gust of wind touched his face. He couldn't see it, but he heard movement, and he turned in the shift's direction. A vaguely feminine noise came from the mist, encouraging him to investigate. Somewhere in his dulled senses, he thought it might be Evette. Then he saw it. In that same direction, in the distance, something large was moving towards him, slowly but surely. The mist curled and covered the enormous figure so that he couldn't see any features, but could vaguely make out its humanoid shape. A limb emerged from the miasma. Cameron spied the same blanched, spidery hand he'd seen in the sewer grate. It was pointing directly at Cameron, seemingly paralyzing him.

"Losssssst little one?" The voice was nothing more than a whisper, but it came from everywhere at once, like a thousand pencils scratching on paper, dry and wispy. He shuddered as he felt something ethereal run over his body, tangible but without weight.

"Haven't lost yet… losing I think." Cameron could not make sense of what was being said, but the voice was no friend. There was a dry wheezing sound that accompanied each strange statement, as if whatever was speaking had lungs but had forgotten how to use them. Each sentence seemed to take great effort, because the breaks between them were protracted and very deliberate.

"We… will... see how you find your way, and what you will take with you, little one." With that, the fog consumed Cameron in a rush and the loud crash that accompanied it woke him up.

He bolted upright, his body glistening

with sweat, and looked at his wife. She returned his look of alarm. Cameron motioned to her to remain silent, reached under the bed and pulled out the metal baseball bat he kept in case of emergencies. He moved slowly and quietly through his bedroom's doorway, and went about checking the house methodically. First, he inspected the closet, then the bathroom, then the guest room. At the end of the hallway, he looked through the living room to find the window smashed. Somewhere beneath the thin veil of fear that had covered his senses, he felt a sharp twinge of anger. He cursed under his breath, inspecting the break, the edges of which were stained with blood. He followed a skinny trail of dark liquid to the kitchen, but it did not lead to its previous owner. The squeaking did, however. Flying in perfect circles around his head was a large brown bat. Cameron lost his composure. Screaming at the top of his lungs, he tried to hit the bat with his bat; the irony lost on him in his hysteria. The bat lazily avoided every blow.

Finally, as if it was tired of this embarrassing display on the human's part, the bat flew directly over Cameron's face and out of the window. As it passed, some of its blood fell on Cameron's face, exacerbating his panic. A rodent had humiliated him in his own house. Evette raced out with a pocket knife.

"Are you all right?! I heard screaming," she said as she turned on the light and looked at him, "oh my God, is that blood?" Her face turned ashen when she looked at the streak on his face.

"It's not mine. There was a bat in here. It scared the shit out of me. Like an honest to goodness rat with wings. I couldn't even hit it, it used that whatchamacallit… Uhhhh…"

"Echolocation?"

"Yes, baby yes, echolocamotions, it was psychic. I don't know I, I, I, I couldn't stop it." The trembling in his voice and hand had infected the rest of him and traveled widespread throughout his body. He had absolutely no idea why he was so disturbed, but he suddenly felt so cold.

"Cam, take some more medicine and go back to sleep. You're probably just not used to the pills. We'll worry about the window tomorrow," and with that she folded up the knife and went back to the bed. Cameron decided to be useful and tape some cardboard over the hole. When he felt stressed, he kept busy; it helped him stay composed, always had, and as far as he was concerned, that wouldn't change. Between the merger, Mother Nature assaulting him at every turn, his wife coming back, and his own mind revolting, he felt helpless. A feeling of futility grew in his heart. He tried to hold the tape still, but his trembling was so bad that he sliced right through his bandage and barely missed his hand. Between his shaking and the clumsiness in his damaged hand, he realized he wouldn't be successful in his task, even though he'd been trying for almost a half hour. He gave up and taped a blanket over the hole. He was beyond exhausted, and was still shivering.

Cameron went to the bathroom and ran some warm water in the sink. Slowly and gently, he washed his face, letting the feeling and blood return to his cheeks. He rubbed his eyes, letting the heavy feeling behind them drift away. Cameron Toker was right there, standing in his bathroom, warming up. The window could wait until the morning. Everything would be fine. He would succeed despite whatever was being thrown at him. The warm water ran over the lids of his eyes and down his face again. Its heat washed the anxiety from his mind. He groped around to his left for a towel to dry his face with. His hand settled where the towel was supposed to be, but he felt something cold, something slimy, something dead. His eyes flew open, but there was nothing but two hand towels in the space. He breathed a sigh of relief, but in the mirror was a white face, a face like death's, skin peeling, grimace frozen in place, behind him in the mirror. And that's how he woke up in his bed the next morning screaming.

CHAPTER FOUR
Saturday

Cam looked at the alarm clock and saw that it was 5 minutes to 9. He was supposed to be at work, looking over accounts by 10. He rushed through his morning routine, foregoing brushing his teeth and using mouthwash instead. His mouth burned as he swished the liquid around in his mouth while he showered, spitting it into the drain when he was finished. He considered peeing down the drain too, but decided against it, it wouldn't save that much time in the grand scheme of things. He rushed into the living room to find his wife curled up in a comforter on the sofa, with classical music playing, Bach or Beethoven or some old composer. Honestly, he hated that kind of music. She was using the same comforter that was previously blocking the hole in the window; meanwhile, the hole was still there.

So the bat wasn't a dream then, he thought in a thrilling combination of terror and satisfaction. Reality had assured that he wasn't losing his mind, and that the medicine that allowed him to get through the day was not the cause for all the baffling things that had transpired recently. On the other hand, what if that meant the face in the bathroom was real? He dismissed the thought, but the image petrified him. What's worse, he couldn't remember all the details of the incident in the bathroom. It was as if the memory had been reflected in a dirty window, or like it was being projected on a screen and then the image was being shown on a phone camera. His mind felt blurry that morning, so much so that he didn't even notice the draft coming from the hole, the classical music creeping from the stereo and pervading his house, the last trace of some long dead Italian's life slinking about.

"Cam, you're going to be late, you should go." His wife muttered this, derailing his train of thought. He was so disoriented that he actually left without telling his wife to cover the hole or call someone to fix it. The syrupy mixture of fear, curiosity, and disbelief enhanced his exhaustion, and he almost hit an SUV on the way to work when that strange face flashed in his brain. He tried to remember it, but the more he tried, the more it seemed to slip from his grasp. No one said anything to him as he walked into the office, partly because he looked like a mess, and partly because it was the weekend and very few people were there in the first place. He managed to get through a solid amount of work when Ms. Barker called.

"Toker, are you at work? It took you forever to answer the phone; you'd better not be at home sleeping! We need you."

"Yeah, I'm at work, making sure all the accounts are in order. I didn't notice how disorganized we were until now. To be honest, I could use some help. If you know someone who's free and wants to help, that'd be super. Plus, my arm still hurts a little." The idea of trying to appeal to Shelley Barker's compassionate side would've seemed absurd to Cameron a couple of days ago, but given her recent behavior and the growing pain in his arm, Cam decided it was worth a try. Surprisingly, it worked. Shelley told him she'd be there in a half an hour.

She showed up precisely on time and Cameron almost didn't recognize her. Clad in a blazer over a flowing yellow sundress, as if she thought it would somehow transform the entire outfit into formal wear. She was 5'9, only a couple of inches shorter than he was, but the way she carried herself made her seem like Kareem Abdul Jabbar. She wore an enormous sun hat over her hair, which she had put in an elegant braid. Cameron had never noticed it through the cloudy lens of dislike, but she was actually pretty in an Amazonian way.

"Ms. Barker?! You own clothes other than pants suits that look like medieval armor?"

"Actually, no, I borrowed this from your mother," she said with a wink. "I was out in the park giving my dog some exercise when you called, but I couldn't let you drown in paperwork.

Well, actually I could, but you know, guilt and everything. And call me Shelley, we're almost the same age. I'm only 28."

Cameron had never considered this. Actually, he'd never connected anything about the two of them. In his mind, they were two opposite poles, oil and water, light and dark, good and evil. It was a little scary to think that they had anything in common. All the revelations about Shelley made him wonder if he had been unfair and even mean in his initial assessment of her. While he was thinking about this, Shelley started clearing everything on the desk and creating neatness almost instantaneously. She was quick, efficient, and focused: everything Cameron found difficult to be.

"Balancing books isn't really my strong suit, but then again, you're the accountant, not me. I can organize everything, though, which is basically half your job here, anyway. You're welcome."

Cameron thanked her sincerely, and by the time the food Mr. Stephens sent came, they were nearly finished. Cameron bought a pie from the deli up the block to thank Shelley for her help. They sat there in the solemn office with food and drinks and had a good time as the dimming afternoon light filtered through the blinds.

"Ugh, I don't want to go home, but I sure don't want to be here at work anymore." Cameron said with his mouth full of apple and flaky crust, "Stephens said I have to stay until 6. I think I'm gonna tear out my hair."

"If you do that, you'll have the same receding hairline as he does. Just leave and come back. We finished most of the work, anyway. You'll probably have to do a bunch of paperwork tomorrow, but for now, you're good. Why don't you want to go home, though? Didn't your wife just come home from somewhere or something like that? Eric mentioned it before."

"I can't tell that guy anything without the entire building knowing about it." Cameron sighed. He took a second before he continued, "Erm, well, my wife isn't really feeling so well and with my arm and work and all that, I kinda need a breather. I just need some time to de-stress. My parents moved all the way out to Washington four years ago, and Eve is really the only person I have. I didn't grow up here and damn near everyone I consider a friend was Eve's friend first. She's incredible, she's the best person anyone could ever meet, but sometimes, I dunno… sometimes I just feel like… like she doesn't even like me, okay?" He blurted the last part out, a little more forcefully than he'd meant to.

"I feel like she only sticks around because she has to, or maybe she feels like she's in too deep at this point. I dunno, it's such a weird relationship. Her twin died in a car wreck two years ago, and we've been dealing with it in our own terrible way." He wondered if he'd veered off into the realm of too much information, but she asked, and with the stress, physical pain, and exhaustion, he didn't really have the energy to care anymore.

"Well, I'm no relationship expert; none of my relationships last over six months, but I am getting one thing from what you're telling me. Your wife seems to be draining your energy, and that's pretty clear from how you've been the past couple of months. I understand you love her and that she's gone through a traumatic experience, but you should try talking to her about it. Maybe the communication will snap her out of it. You're burning the candle at both ends and it's going to burn you out. There are some situations you can't change, and if you can't help her, maybe you should think of something else. It's not her fault that she's having this effect on you, and I think speaking about it will bring you guys closer together. I'm sure she appreciates how much you do for her."

Cameron considered it. He'd never really thought that any kind of action besides therapy and simply being there could help. He loved his wife, but he wasn't entirely sure he could continue down the path that they were going. Had the separation between the two of them become too much? Cameron didn't think space and some conversation would help, but he appreciated Shelley's advice all the same and thanked her. She invited him to go with her and three of her friends to a jazz and comedy club in Brooklyn.

For the first time in what seemed like forever, he'd taken some time out for himself and had fun. As he drove home, slightly buzzed, he felt a little guilty for going out and turning off his phone, but he also felt totally rejuvenated. All the stress from work seemed distant and weak, like when you shine your flashlight on the Bogeyman.

He drove home slowly so that he wouldn't get pulled over, but he'd taken the wrong exit on the highway and ended up getting lost. Then he had to wait for his GPS to update before he could finally navigate back to his normal route. Once he realized how late it was and noted how close to home he was, he raced home. It had rained earlier, but the roads weren't that wet. It was abnormally humid for that time of year, but it was more muggy than actually warm. He whipped around the corner four blocks from his house and got startled out of his brain by the sudden appearance of a tall man running through the road. Cameron barely had the chance to scream. In his panic, he jerked the wheel and barely missed the man, who was wearing dark clothes. He lost control of the car briefly and ended up scratching a parked car when he swerved, but other than that, the car was okay and he was unhurt. The man hadn't even stopped to look.

Cameron stopped his car about five cars down from the crosswalk. His vision blurred a little from the drink and the anxiety, so he had to grope around a little to find the car handle door. *Damn car*, he thought as he finally found the handle. *I really hope that guy was all right. I don't want to see anyone hurt because I was acting like an ass.* He got out of the car and looked around for some sign of the black clad stranger.

"Hey, hello! Anyone out here?! Hello?!"
Cam realized that not only was no one anywhere in sight, but that he was merely yelling for the night to hear. So he did the logical thing and continued. "Sorry if I almost hit you, my bad. I, I, uh, I've been having a rough time and I might've had some uh, liquid refreshments of an alcoholic nature. I do not plan on doing this again, so… please don't be hurt or die or come and kill me with a hook hand. Thanks." Satisfied with his display of remorse, he got back in the car and drove at a much more appropriate speed; hopefully he'd appeased the spirits. He finally arrived at his house and saw that it was 1:37 am. For the second time in the last 10 minutes, he clambered out of the car, cursing and unhooking the pants leg that had gotten caught on his door somehow. He got to the door, straightened his jacket, smoothed the creases out of his clothes, and put on his best "Baby, I'm Sorry" face before going inside. His wife was still on the couch, although this time she had a blanket around her.

The curtains were closed, but the draft told him with a chilly whisper that the window was still open and broken. She turned her head from the TV ever so slightly and spoke.

"Why are you home so late? I didn't know what to do about that window, and it got a little chilly. Don't you get off work around 5:30? I think I tried to call you too."

"Sorry, I went out with Ms. Barker and some of her friends from another department or something. We ended up going to some jazz, stand-up comedy place. It was cool. The jokes were decent, and the liquor was pretty cheap. I turned my phone off so the comedians wouldn't yell at me."

"That sounds fun." She said, her voice sleepy and low. "Can you do something about the window? This place feels like a graveyard."

Cameron wasn't sure what she expected him to say, but in his current state of mind he spoke his mind.

"I get it, but you know, taping the window isn't that difficult. You were here all day. You could have fixed it hours ago."

"Well, excuuuuuuuuse me. So sorry it's my fault that the glass got broken in a situation that was completely out of my control. I should be more like you, Cameron, someone who knows what to do in every situation and knows what's best for everybody."

"Hey, I was just saying that if you had gotten up and did something, you wouldn't be cold right now. It's that simple."

"Oh, another way I can improve by acting like Cameron: make everything simple, because when you're that smart, nothing is ever complicated! This is all my fault because I'm not you. Sorry!"

Cameron's frustrations over the last few days had been simmering, bubbling under the surface of his rational thought. Unfortunately, the eruption was inevitable. "Listen, I don't need this!

The damn window isn't invincible! Quit waiting for me to do everything; if you want something done, get it done! I'm not a lapdog, I'm your husband, Evette. I know this is a hard time for you but-"

"BUT WHAT?! I'm having a hard time because my sister, the person who loved me like no one else, the person who understood me like no one else, is gone! She's dead, and there's nothing I can do about it. I tried to help her, to make things right, but it all went wrong. And I don't know what the consequences will be. It all went wrong and now I feel so scared," she said with her head down, staring at the floor as if the answer were hidden in the floorboards. She shrunk into a ball on the couch, and Cameron was unsure if she was shivering from the cold coming in through the window or the guilt whipping through her heart.

Cameron swallowed hard; he didn't want to fight with her. He didn't even care about the window. Walking over to the couch, he wrapped his arms around her. "I know, baby. It's not something that we can just erase, but it's not your fault. You didn't make anyone get in that car. Let it go. Let her go."

"I can't. I'll never let her go. You don't know what it's like to have someone who's gone, but you can't separate yourself from them. And no matter what you try, it only makes things worse."

"Well, maybe I do… maybe I do." He said his statement with a calm voice, full of pity and sadness. It surprised her, and she looked up at him. Her face contorted with pain, wide eyed, and wild.

"I love you Cameron. Don't forget that. I'm sorry for how I hurt you, but I never stopped loving you." That's all she said. She retreated to the bedroom, leaving Cameron with the draft and his thoughts. He taped the hole, and went to sleep fully dressed on the couch, his arm twinging with pain.

*

Cameron left the house early the next day. Part of it was regret. He felt bad about taking his frustration out on his wife and, although her farewell was almost unnaturally sentimental, it did nothing to soothe his guilty conscience. He thought about what he could do to make it up to her, like dinner or an outing. Perhaps their conversation was just the type of breakthrough they needed. Just the thought of their love enduring made the sunlight a little warmer, the air a little crisper.

He didn't realize it until he was actually in the building that Sunday, but he hadn't done much before Shelley came to help him, and as a result, he still had some of Saturday's work to finish. All that backlog and his current work ended up taking him all day and well into the night. It was almost 1 o'clock in the morning by the time he'd left his job and he was beyond tired. Eve hadn't called all day, but then again, he wasn't sure of that, since his phone had died around 5:30. He wasn't mad at her, not anymore, at least. So much was changing, but the past hadn't released the vice grip it had on his life. Soon things would calm down and he could break everything down. Just like math. There had to be a constant for there to be a solution. The constant that was currently facing him was the bumper to bumper traffic.

Where are these people even coming from? Go to bed!

He kept himself awake and not dwelling on the state of his love life by coming up with different ways to tell other drivers to either go to bed or go to Hell. This was harder than it would seem to be because he wasn't exactly a creative man, and the rhythmic sound of the raindrops peppering the world outside his car, lulled him into a state of drowsiness. It was not a gentle rain; it was harsh, and the wind whipped the water against the windshield with a sort of grim determination. The wind wanted to get in; it wanted him to get wet; it wanted him to be tired and haggard. *Not today*, Cam thought as he turned up the heat in his car. He finally got home after what seemed like forever and six months, and hurried inside to escape the fury of the elements.

The wind whipped and howled around his ears. It almost sounded like a dog whining. He thought he saw blue lights glowing in the bushes, but it must've been a cat's eyes or something. He had more pressing matters to attend to. Cameron took a second to study his house from the sidewalk. All the lights were out, so he assumed Eve had gone to sleep. Still, as he crossed the threshold, he called out for his wife in a half-hearted attempt to see if she was awake, or angry. She hadn't called back, so Cam assumed she was neither. He scrounged around the kitchen a little and found a plate of food with his name and a heart scrawled on the tinfoil covering it. He smiled to himself.

Maybe she does love me. I hope she's sleeping okay.

He put his dinner in the microwave, keeping the lights off so as not to wake his wife. While his food was heating, he thought a bath would be a good idea and went to get his most comfortable robe so he could take a load off. As he turned the corner to go down the long hallway leading to his bedroom, he found his wife. She was on the floor and, much like the house, her eyes had no light. Her jugular veins' previous inhabitants had found a new home on their eggshell walls, their newfound emancipation swift and violent. Her reflection was pale in the crimson mirror that had pooled around her neck and head.

Further down the hallway, he saw a male figure dressed in a black, ragged shroud. This person was enormous, but built with a lithe, wicked looking body. The shroud was draped over the figure's body from its shoulders to its ankles, making its form seem like it was composed of shadow. There were muddy footprints leading up to where he was standing, staining the rug's fibers with inhuman marks. The figure had replaced everything Cameron knew with fear in a fraction of an instant. The figure made Cameron's home a foreign land, something that Cameron knew, but as a concept rather than reality, like a cemetery. He knew nothing about death, but this simple silhouette seemed intent on giving him a crash course. The figure turned halfway, as if he'd just noticed Cameron. Cam could not make out its features, and as if it had known this, faster than the blink of an eye, the creature was face to face with Cameron. The creature lifted Cam by the neck with a powerful and gaunt hand, painfully crushing his windpipe. When the figure lifted him, a beam of streetlight that slashed through the curtains illuminated both of their faces. The creature's lips were drawn back in a startling snarl, or maybe a garish grin. Cameron looked at the intruder's protruding fangs, hard, white, wicked points that had invaded his wife's throat and were now seeking to conquer his own. The monster's face, white like a newly bleached bedsheet, was flecked with red blood. The scarlet and bone white played together nicely. His features were lupine in quality, predatory in nature and intent. He smelled of earth and blood, an intoxicatingly nauseating combination. But the worst part, the part that would never leave Cam's mind, were the eyes. They burned a fiery red in their sockets. Inside those eyes, Cameron could find everything he had ever feared. They held Eve's death, the creaking he heard in his closet at night when he was a child, his anxieties, the cold reality of death. It was over. This was the end of his existence, at the hands of some strange apparition that had risen from the ground and turned his wife's life into a macabre masterpiece on the wall of his former home. Somewhere in the dull part of his mind that was still working, he prayed. It was only one word he could manage, but still he asked God, "please." The creature brought Cameron's neck to his face and Cameron accepted his fate. In a thin but guttural voice, like the purr of a puma, the creature whispered.

"I'm full."

And it was gone. All that it left was a broken window, and a broken life. Any night Cam Toker could forget that face was a blessing.

Blue Heart Blue Trees

CHAPTER FIVE

Two Weeks Before the Portion Control Incident

Moriko Miyazaki looked up at the trail that unfolded in front of her through the windshield of her beat up Toyota with steely determination. She had come all this way, and she'd be damned if she turned back now. There was a sign outside the park entrance which read, "Your life is a precious gift from your parents." She frowned at it. There was a cruel irony in the message.

How could I not think of my parents? My dad committed suicide here, she thought bitterly.

It made no sense. A month ago, her father had driven to this same spot and entered the forest. He never came back. The police didn't even consider it worth investigating:

"He was stressed," they said. "It's not like people come here to sightsee. His car was left in the parking lot and this was the last place he had visited. Simple."

This theory would make sense to the ordinary listener. However, if you'd ever met Eito Miyazaki, you'd know he wasn't the type to kill himself. He wouldn't even kill an insect; he valued life and potential so much. Eito was born and raised in the Kanagawa Prefecture by his grandparents. They were very in touch with their culture, which was something they'd instilled in their grandson from an early age. His grandmother would often go to different people's houses and bless them with protection from evil spirits and other rituals. Both of Moriko's grandparents were *Yamabushi*, monks who guided travelers through the mountains and would help those afflicted by spirits or illness. Eito would often tell his daughter about the different duties of a Yamabushi and all the different Shinto and Buddhist stories, and how their family paid homage to the great gods and goddesses. He stressed the importance of keeping your culture as a part of your life. Even after he started making real money and traveling around the world as an electrical engineer, he always sent money to his grandparents to make sure their shrine was well maintained. He'd visit every year and pay his respects, even though he'd moved to the United States to do business. It was there that he'd met Moriko's mother, Maria Ito, at a conference. She was a translator for some of Eito's associates (Eito spoke fluent English from the time that he was a teenager) and they quickly fell in love. A year later they were married, and two years after that Moriko was born in the same shrine Eito had grown up in. She lived most of her life in the United States, in New York and California, but he made sure she knew she was the product of two worlds. She could name the US presidents and the Japanese emperors of old, tell you about Little Red Riding Hood and Momotaro, and loved the rising sun like she loved stars and stripes.

"You're unique, my darling," he'd often say.

On her 13th birthday, along with toys and games, he gave her a box full of bells, beads, animal bones, and dolls: a gehobako. He also gave her a small tanto, or dagger. "The items in the box are some of the tools of the trade. They were passed down from generation to generation in our family. The knife is a precious treasure. The great sword-smith, Masamune, forged it. It's priceless. I give you these things to show you that no matter what anyone else says, you are the product of two glorious worlds. You are priceless. Please do your best". He'd say things like that to her often, and it always made her feel better about herself. Despite being fully Japanese, her mother was born and raised in America and when their family would spend long periods in Japan, Moriko would often feel isolated. Her Japanese was very good, but not exactly natural. Her upturned mouth, and the tilt at the corners of her kobicha colored eyes, told of her heritage proudly, but kids could be cruel. In middle school she was easy pickings, and she'd get into fights, but she always knew who she was. Her father's speeches echoed in her mind whenever someone called her a name or started bothering her.

She thought about those talks as she sat in the driver's seat with the box in her lap and tears welling up in her eyes. If her father had killed himself after all, she would be the one to confirm it. That's why she'd come to the forest. To find him.

She stood outside her car looking through Aokigahara's canopy. "No turning back now. I'm going to find Dad, bring him back, fix my life. Easy peasy Japanesey." she said, hoisting her bags over her shoulder. The forest opened to accommodate her desires.

CHAPTER SIX
Moriko

Moriko, or "Mori" as most people called her, was not exactly physically imposing. She was short, about 5'1, and she wore her chestnut colored hair cut in a bob, a little higher than shoulder length. Her features were attractive, in a quiet way, high cheekbones on a rounded face, and she took after her mother's petite frame as opposed to her father's thick, sturdy build. She'd dressed for this forest excursion as if it were an ordinary day, wearing her favorite navy capris, ripped above the knee from that one time she fell skating in the summer, dark brown boots and a plain brown t-shirt. The only thing that was unusual about her outfit was a thick, olive green aviator jacket. It was two sizes too big, and wearing it in the sun made her pretty hot, but it had belonged to her father. With the jacket on, she was sure that she'd find him. It was a laughable sight to see this short, 22-year-old trudge through the green gulf of foliage, like a child on a field trip, her brown hair making ripples through the forest pool.

Mori was determined to find some trace of her father's body in the woodland. Her mother had already planned to bring them back to their small house in New York before the week was up, and Mori was dead set on getting some answers about Eito's supposed suicide before their flight on Sunday. That meant that she had 5 days to delve into the woodland and come back with something, anything. Time was not on her side and its passage had inspired and unstoppable determination. Her mother was a wreck. Eito was truly her soulmate, and finding out about his death left her inconsolable. Maria dealt with it with raw emotion, but eventually she started to accept what had happened. She even stayed in Japan so that Eito's grandparents could do his last rites. She tied up the loose ends on the business side and now that it was all wrapped up, she was ready to leave. Maria needed to distance herself from the painful memories of Eito proudly showing his family the place he called home.

For whatever reason, Moriko had an easier time coming to grips with her father's death in the beginning. She'd bought into the idea of his suicide, but she was quiet about it; her mother needed her support and help. They were always close, and the time they spent together was genuine, but Moriko couldn't pretend she was fine forever. So when Moriko started lashing out, breaking small things, or just keeping to herself, Maria understood. Moriko knew her mom was there for her, but she still had things to work out on her own. So when she said that she was going to a friend's house for a few days to spend time and say goodbye, Maria thought nothing of it. Mori knew this, but she also knew that she had a limited amount of time to look through Aokigahara before her mother became suspicious. Convincing her friend to lie for her was easy, and all she'd told said friend was that she needed space from her mother. A 22-year-old wanting time away from a grieving mother is a story anyone would buy.

The forest seemed to swallow her the moment she entered it. The canopy only let rosettes of sunlight reach her, shutting out any trace of the modern world with its immense growth. Wind whistled through the foliage, muting the usual bustle of a large forest. Lines of tape crisscrossed through the main path. They creeped her out to be honest, relics from people who'd seriously considered jumping off sanity's ledge, and some who'd actually taken the plunge. They were morbid, but extremely helpful, at least. She'd read that people who entered the forest and veered off of the path would make trails with the tape leading back to it. That way, if they decided against committing suicide, they would have no problem finding their way out.

Mori went about her search systematically. Assuming that her father was actually serious about committing suicide, he probably wouldn't venture too far into the forest. The actual place wouldn't have mattered. It would've been a matter of practicality more than anything else, logically. There wasn't really a detailed or definitive map to the interior, so she decided she'd make her way through the woods, following the tape as she came across it, then going back to the marked path. She'd come prepared, with her own tape, food, a tent, electric lanterns, a black marker, extra batteries, and some books with Japanese fairy tales that her father had given her long ago. The books weren't necessary. They were actually pretty heavy, but she brought them because she felt like those objects would draw her closer to her father. She'd brought her gehobako for the same reason. She wasn't sure it'd help, but she had nothing to lose. Moriko tried to be as observant as possible as she made her way through the dense underbrush, taking care to tread carefully over the rocky forest floor. It was an especially warm day, the kind that made the bees apathetic in their search for nectar. Bees weren't her only company; the occasional moth fluttered away from her clumsiness. It smelled like leaves and earth, but occasionally the scent of greenery surrendered to rot. It took her two hours before she came across her first remnant of human life. She followed a strand of yellow tape through a tangled mass of branches and at the end she found a small yellowed note. It read:

"The pain is just too much. I can't keep going with this pit in my stomach. I'm missing something, and I feel it every day. I hunger for peace. - Tetsuo."

She took care not to touch the note, not wanting to disturb Tetsuo's last message. Tetsuo's remains lay some five feet away from the note, a vague outline of a body taken over by a tangle of roots. The smell of decay rose to greet Mori where Tetsuo couldn't. Mori refused to get any closer to the body; it clearly wasn't her father, and she had an uneasy feeling. She'd never been around a corpse, and she was fighting to keep her breakfast down. Taking one last glance at the note in the dirt, she followed Tetsuo's tape back to the main path.

There has got to be a faster way of doing this, she thought. *I can't follow everyone's tape. Maybe I can sweep the forest, from one end to another or something like that.* She took out her phone and turned on the GPS. *Okay, so I'll make my way through the center since I've already started that way. I'll be thorough with the tape I come across and once I get to the other side, I'll sweep from one end to the other horizontally. I'll even write on the tape I pass with my marker, so I know what I've passed already.*

Pleased with her own resourcefulness, she put her phone back and trudged off, but stopped when she heard a creaking noise coming from her left. She froze. She was smart enough not to yell "hello". It wasn't the movies, and if someone was there, she didn't know what they might do, especially if they had a weapon. She figured some of the people who came in the forest were armed, and that they certainly wouldn't be in a healthy mental state, so she'd taken the tanto her father had given her along. It was a little silly to her to take this "ancient and holy" knife with her instead of something a little more modern, but she was pressed for time and short on resources. More importantly, it made her feel like she wasn't alone. She stood there for the longest minute of her life and… nothing. She looked around the area one last time, to be sure, but found nothing except Tetsuo in the same place she'd left him. *It was probably just a tree branch or something,* she thought, slightly irritated with herself. She'd wasted time, and there was no reason to be afraid.

She'd been in the forest for about 4 hours when it started getting dark.

Maybe I'll stop here. It'd probably be too dangerous to move on this ground. Plus, this place is supposed to be haunted.

She shuddered when she thought about it. So many people had decided to take their own lives. She wondered if they found peace. She couldn't imagine the pain a person must be experiencing to kill themselves.

Is that what Daddy was going through? Was it me? Was it work?

She couldn't fathom why her father would consider death, knowing what it would do to the people who loved him. At the same time, was it selfish for her to ask him to keep living a life he couldn't bear for her sake? She started putting up her tent to distract herself. When something was bothering her, she tried to convert that energy into productivity. She wanted to be an artist, and in her spare time, she'd often draw whatever she was feeling or practice writing in Japanese. She taught English for work in Japan, and in the month following the death of her father, she immersed herself in art and work. Her friends were impressed at how well she was doing, especially with her art. She'd even sold a few commissioned pieces. But she didn't feel happy, she just felt numb. The work was good as a distraction, but when she finished, her feelings came crashing down all at once. It was classic Moriko. Build levees against the flood of emotions until the strength of the tide became too much.

And so she found herself brushing aside tears as she finished pitching her tent and opened up the instant meal she'd brought. The process of her cooking seemed to go by in a blur, and soon she was finished eating and curling up in her sleeping bag. The food wasn't really satisfying, but she didn't feel very hungry anyway. She smoothed out the blankets that she lined out over the tent's floor, stopping to take the big brown spider that was scurrying around and throw it out of the tent's front flap. It wasn't a memory foam mattress, but it didn't matter. She was exhausted, and she drifted off almost immediately.

CHAPTER SEVEN
The Sky Was Red

The sky was red. Not a natural red, like when the sun sets, but a strange crimson. The shading of the color felt almost radioactive, and it hurt her eyes to look at. The forest itself seemed much greener, as if it were openly defying the red that surrounded it. She squinted up at the sky, seeing no sun or any kind of celestial body in it. She found herself lying on her back, with no sign of her camp anywhere. Her surroundings were totally unfamiliar to her. There was moss covering everything, and the previously rocky, treacherous ground was carpeted in a wet, spongy padding.

What the hell?! I don't even remember waking up. Everything looks so different now. What the hell is going on?

She glanced at her phone, which told her it was 4:44. There was no AM or PM reading. *Dammit, how is it in the afternoon already? I don't know what's happened, and the day is almost over. It's going to be dark soon, and I'm not any closer to finding Dad.* She stood up, deciding to continue moving forward in an attempt to accomplish something, but she couldn't even sit up. She struggled to prop herself up on her elbows as waves of nausea washed over her.

I just ate! There's no way I should be this weak... I... have... to keep... moving.

But she found herself on her back once again, feeling like someone had filled her body with lead. The sky blazed above her, burning her eyes with its violent sheen. She couldn't stop looking at that hellish hue and with each moment that she stared, her gut and chest felt more empty. Her breaths came in painful rattles, and Mori could feel something moving inside her chest. She started hearing noises, a groaning, like an enormous stomach growling. Suddenly she retched, but the only thing that came out of her mouth was a single bee, which fluttered weakly and then died. She looked at the bee in horror, its freedom found only in death.

The earth shook fiercely and opened up,

enormous fissures yawning at her. She looked
around and saw green, mossy hands pulling her
into the soft earth, their dirty fingernails caked with
blood and soil, crushing her body as they pulled her
down into the bowels of whatever Hell she'd
entered. Through the ground she saw tongues,
mouths, and eyes, not arranged into faces, but fused
together by roots and mud on misshapen heads.
Eyes that were milky with cataracts, but that moved
restlessly as if they were dreaming. Sharp teeth
sliced the very tongues that inhabited their mouths,
and the actual mouths sprayed blood, bile, and spit
as they opened and screamed. It was a scream of
pain, coming out in unison from hundreds of
malformed beings, tongues lolling about, inviting
Mori to join them. That primal, horrifying noise
was their version of begging. They were asking her
to join them in their madness and pain, to enter the
purgatory they'd created, and be at peace once she
became a part of chaos. She tried to fight their grip,
but the hands were too strong. She came to just as

they were about to drown her in the dirt.

CHAPTER EIGHT
She Woke UP

She woke up staring into the dark eye sockets of a human skull about six inches away from her face. Mori took pride in her nerves of steel; when most of her friends would shudder at the thought of a bug or some blood or something nasty, she would be unfazed. But the dream combined with morbid reality was too much, even for her. After a solid minute and a half of pointing and screaming, she regained some semblance of composure. The sky was blue again, and her camp was unchanged aside from her visitor. Her phone told her it was only 10:23 in the morning, so she still had most of the day at her disposal.

It was just a dream. Nothing's changed. All the legends of this place were making her imagination act up. That's all, she thought.

Before doing anything else, Mori forced herself to take a good, hard look at the skull and study it. She refused to be shaken, and now that her surprise had faded, she felt more comfortable inspecting the skull from a reasonable distance. It was an umber color, mottled with green from being in the shrubbery for so long. It was missing its lower mandible and most of its teeth. Other than that, it was intact and seemed to be relatively untouched by decay. Next to the skull was a boot and some miscellaneous bones and clothes. Above it all was a broken rope. Against her better judgement, Mori used a wet wipe to cover her hand and picked up the skull. It gazed back at her with its blank sockets, flashing her a gap-toothed smile, like it knew what she was in for. Mori was always the type of person to face her fears rather than run from them. That's the reason she'd entered a forest that's supposedly haunted and evil, the reason she rarely told other people about her problems, the reason she was not the type to be rescued. Considering all this, she wrapped the skull in some plastic bags she'd brought, and decided to take it with her. She decided the skull was male, and that he would be called "Yorick" or "Rick" for short. He would be her guide. Since he was already dead, he had nothing better to do.

"Hey Rick, would you mind helping me find my father? He's probably dead, just like you. I don't mean to be a bother, but you're dead too, so you're probably not busy. Come with me. I'm an excellent conversationalist. What do you say, buddy?" She made the skull nod in agreement, feeling that Rick was satisfied with her substantial offer. Although she couldn't remember if it was a Shinto practice, Moriko remembered that many cultures offer the dead food. So after packing up her camp, she made a little portion of oatmeal for her deceased buddy, ate her breakfast with him, and then trekked on with him resting in her backpack. She continued with her tape following method, this time choosing a deep blue line. Her father's favorite color was that same shade of blue, so she thought it might be a good bet.

"You think it's a good idea, Rick? Beats the hell out of following every stripe of tape we come across. I'm gonna go for it." She was sure Rick approved of her idea and followed along with the tape. "You're so supportive, it's refreshing."

She had followed the tape for about two miles when she saw something that chilled her blood. In one of the taller trees, about two stories up, was a wind chime of flesh and blood. She couldn't make out any discerning features, but it was definitely a man of a solid build hanging from the tree. The pleasant breeze that caressed her cheek rocked the corpse back and forth. Maybe it was that lifeless sway, but this felt different from Tetsuo. Moriko felt no fear looking at him, but this hanging body felt ominous. There was something electric about it that made the hair on the back of her neck stand up. Nailed to the same tree was a piece of paper with writing on it, but she wouldn't read it. It wasn't her business. A cloud covered the sun, and suddenly it was dim in the forest.

Damn, the weather didn't say it'd be overcast today. I hope it won't rain. I only have a poncho for the rain, she thought grimly.

Mori tried to turn her phone on and saw how her breath had formed frost on its screen. A chill ran up her spine and she hurried away from the tree, but could only get a few steps before she froze. It was as if someone had driven stakes into her feet. Despite the cold snap, her ankles felt warm, as if huge hands had wrapped themselves around them.

There was a loud thud behind her. Then she heard shaking, like something barreling through the brush. She was ready to scare off a fox, but when she turned around, there was a sight that was much, much worse. Directly in front of her, flickering like the picture on a TV with a weak signal, was a man. He floated about a foot off of the ground, with his torn and muddied clothing covered with twigs and brush. His shirt was open, revealing a swollen and distended belly. Wild hair covered his head and his body was as pale as the moon except for his face; his face was blue, like he couldn't breathe. That blue face sat atop a neck that was longer than any person's neck should be. It was bent at an unnatural angle while his tongue lolled out of his mouth. It was the color of asphalt. His expression was twisted and scrunched up, like he was still in pain, but his eyes were wide and had a hungry look in them. His arms stretched out, spasming, and a hissing noise came from his flickering form. The phantom charged her, his body twitching and gliding her way. His presence chilled the surrounding forest. Mori ran at full speed, clutching the tape in her hands so hard her nails drew blood. She could feel her feet getting tangled up in the underbrush and the great, brown roots, which curled like the tentacles of some arboreal demon. There was a clearing ahead, maybe thirty feet away? It was hard to judge, but thirty was a number that was concrete. She could take thirty steps. But what could she do even if she made it that far? The clearing drew closer and closer, tall grass carpeting a circular spot the trees had abandoned. She looked over her shoulder to see where her pursuer was, but the forest behind her was uninhabited. Then the world turned upside down.

She hadn't noticed the root sticking up out of the dirt directly in front of her, and it sent her tumbling to the ground. Her arms and side ached from where they crashed into the hard earth, but that was the least of her troubles. Moriko had rolled over to find the ghost appearing over her, almost as if it was pouncing on her. Its twisted body had no weight, but pinned her down with sheer malice. Its long neck twitched as that black tongue appeared before her face, smelling foul. No matter how hard she struggled, she couldn't break the force of the weight atop her. Just as the phantom's hand was about to touch her face, the clouds moved in the sky, bathing the clearing in sunlight. As the clearing became fully illuminated, the phantom disappeared.

The spot on her arm where it'd grabbed her was freezing even through her coat, leaving a spider web of frost. Mori had never been so afraid in her life. She halfway expected to wake up again, like after the nightmare she'd had yesterday, but this seemed very real. Her heart was beating like a percussion section. A cold sweat covered her forehead, but she tried to keep her composure. She checked the tape, but the starting end must've ripped when she was running, because it was limp. She definitely could not go back the way she'd come. The only solution was to move forward. Her phone had no signal, and the GPS showed a route that could only be the product of a malfunction. Her hands were shaking so hard, she wasn't sure she would've been able to read it, anyway.

Damn, I must've run into a dead zone trying to escape that...that thing. It couldn't have been real! But it definitely wasn't a hallucination. I'm healthy, I'm not starving or on drugs. It had to be real and I have to get the hell away from whatever it was. It stopped when the cloud moved and the sun came out. So I'll follow the tape and stick to the lit areas.

"Hey Rick, I think I was just attacked by some kind of spirit, and I'm freaking out. He grabbed me and it really hurt. I'm pretty afraid now and don't know what will happen during the night. Do you think there are anymore spirits like that? I can't call anyone anymore. My phone has no signal. I...I hope I can make it out of this. This can't be happening. It may seem weird, but talking to you makes me feel better, and I'm not so good at talking to people when I have a problem. I go through the motions, but I'm a bottler. I bottle emotions and make sure no one can see me as weak. Thanks for listening. I think I've said too much." The next few hours passed by in slow motion, and it felt like her attack had happened years ago. It was strange. The fear had melted away from her chest, leaving a clean hole and a strange, empty feeling. She noticed she was tired shortly thereafter.

"Ugh Rick, what is the point of this? I'm frickin' shuffling through all these STUPID

PLANTS! I'm not even sure what this is accomplishing."

Yorick said nothing, as usual. He was a skull in a backpack, after all.

"I wonder if I'll be able to get out of here. I had such an efficient system, I just hope it works. You think anyone would miss me if I died here? It's a creepy question, right? Might just be a reality once the sun goes down."

Thankfully, that night was calm. Mori set up her camp again, ate, fed Yorick, and got ready for bed. She put his skull over the tape so that it wouldn't slip out or anything while she was asleep. She was sure Yorick wouldn't mind being a paperweight for a few hours. Her mind drifted as she slept, but thankfully her night was dreamless.

CHAPTER NINE
The Third Day

Mori had prepared for the third day. She woke up early and since she'd packed most of her belongings up the day before; she didn't have to waste much time putting things away. Her phone was charged, and she felt a little better. It was a quiet and pleasant morning, with birds chirping in the distance, the sun filtering through the trees, and a new sense of direction growing in her chest. The tape was intact, right where she'd left it. Strangely enough, the beginning of the tape was gone. It now started from where she'd put Yorick over it. Now she couldn't even trace her path back to a familiar area. She wondered how all that length just…disappeared. She also wondered how the tape had gotten cut yesterday, and how long it had continued for. What if the tape had nothing to do with her father and it was just some random person's tape? She didn't believe any of it. There's no way this tape could be as long as it seemed to be. She looked at Rick, who stared back as if to say, "You saw a ghost yesterday and you're letting some tape throw you off?!"

"You're right. As weird as it sounds, I know this is the right way. I'm going to find my dad. I may talk to skulls in the woods, but I'm not crazy." Unfortunately, she couldn't shake how she felt lately, even with that small, humorous reprieve. She just couldn't focus. It wasn't exactly a physical thing. Actually, although she was a little hungry, she felt full of energy. But mentally, she felt drained. She'd been following the blue tape for a day and a half now, and she felt like she was taking the same steps over and over again. The tedium never led to any meaningful discoveries. She came across a few crows and took their inquisitive glances as signs to move on. The remains of camps left by those who'd met their makers and gnarled trees that curled in sharp bends were littered throughout her path. Eventually, even the camps started looking familiar.

Her buzzing phone startled her out of her stupor.

YES! I finally have service. Now we can finally get a sense of direction here. This is just one step closer to the end. Finally, I'll get some answers. She took the phone out. The screen read 4:04 pm, and there was a text notification.

Hm... I wonder who texted me. The text was from her mother, and it was much lengthier than your ordinary, 'just checking on you', text. It read:

Mori,

I thought things were going well. I know your father's death was traumatizing, and in the beginning, you seemed to take it well. You were doing wonderfully with the paintings, expressing your feelings, even just us talking. But recently you've changed. Sometimes I feel you don't care about anything. You've been acting out. I noticed that hole in your wall. Sometimes, I find things you've broken all over your floor. We've been drifting apart; you get consumed in your own little world and it's hard for me. And now you go off on your own to God knows where. No

call, no contact, and I'm alone again. I've lost so much and you pull this stunt now? Well, I'm not taking it anymore. I bought another plane ticket and I'm going back to the States today. Alone. You're not dealing with this like you should be, Moriko. I expected you to be doing better, socializing more. You're all cooped up in the house when you're not working. Figure out what you want or you'll go crazy. Listen, you can make it on your own. You're doing well enough with your work, and we still have a lot of money left from Eito. At this moment, I think we should figure out how to live life and it'll be easier if we're living separately. The apartment in Tokyo is all paid off and you can stay there. Come back to the States when you're ready.

Love, Mom

The tiny words hit Mori like a truck. The message became blurry from the tears that filled her eyes, tears of rage, hurt, and sadness. This came out of nowhere. Mori thought her relationship with her mother was stronger in the aftermath of her father passing away and that they'd spent more time together. Her mother's comment about her being apathetic infuriated her. If anything, the loss of her father made her more passionate. What made her the most angry was the fact that her mother was so quick to abandon her. It was hypocritical. Her mother felt alone, so she's going to leave someone else? How would splitting up help anyone cope with the loss of a family member? It made little sense. It seemed almost spiteful; if Mori seemed withdrawn, why would her mother withdraw? Mori threw her backpack across the small clearing where she'd set up camp.

"I can't catch her even if I leave now. And I can't leave now because of Dad. I'm stuck. This stupid forest! I can't be with either of my parents because of you!" She screamed at the sky, scooping up handfuls of dirt and throwing them around the clearing. She kicked and trampled the greenery, screaming, "It's your fault! You're ruining my life!" After a while, she just sat there crying until her eyes were red and puffy. Finally, Mori got up and continued following the tape.

I might as well finish this. There's no way to stop her. My phone delivered the message but I can't call back or text. I'm gonna find Dad, then fly back to New York and figure out what the hell is going on. I won't lose both of my parents.

Her journey had taken on an extra weight. Mori felt her mother's message on her shoulder, like a second backpack with a tombstone in it. She could barely digest what her mother had said; it was like a personal attack on her. It gnawed and tore at her worst moments of grief, targeted the dark times and overlooked the progress. Her stomach growled and growled on and on, and she had to stop a few times, the salty taste of vomit creeping up in the back of her throat. It got dark really early that day, or maybe she'd lost track of time. Her phone was acting up. It showed 4:44 pm and am. She was sure that wasn't at all accurate.

Exhausted mentally and physically, she tried to set up camp. It couldn't have been long, but it felt like years in her head. She started feeling lightheaded, so she drank water to regain her composure. It didn't work.

Okay, here's what I'll do. I'll focus on something else by writing something down. Yes, I'll just write something on this little piece of paper and it'll clear my head. Did I bring this paper? That's definitely my pen. Did I buy paper? It doesn't even matter, I'm just going to write.

My name is Moriko Miyazaki, but my mom calls me Mori. I'm 22 years old, and was born in Kamakura, Japan. I love my mom and dad so much. My favorite color is green. My hobbies are baseball, skateboarding, animals, and card games. I hate hiking, so this trip has been really irritating. Drawing and painting are some of my passions, and I want to design clothes, even if they're just for me. I don't want to be alive.

Moriko rubbed her eyes. She didn't write

that. No way she wrote that. She re-read the paragraph.

My name is Moriko Miyazaki but my mom calls me Mori. I'm 23 years old, and was born in Kamakura, Japan. I will die in Aokigahara, Japan. Baseball won't matter then.

"Oh no, oh no, oh no, what the hell?" Moriko scratched out the paragraph, but one sentence remained.

My name is Moriko Miyazaki, and I want to die.

She looked away from the paper, tears blurring her vision. She wiped them away with her right hand, barely noticing the object she held within it. When she did, she saw that instead of the pen, she had her tanto pressed to her wrist, hard enough to leave a red line.

That's when she heard the voices.

They started off softly, just a little more than a murmur. She thought it was the wind and continued pitching her tent as the shi shi shi shi shi

shi shi sound carried through the trees, a fearful, frantic whispering noise permeating the forest. It chilled her bones. Sometimes, she'd see dark figures looming around the camp, then they'd disappear as quickly as they'd come. She grabbed the box her father had given her and took out an omamori, or a portable talisman that gives a person protection. It was a small piece of wood in a cloth bag, with the name of a guardian spirit carved on it. She hung it around her neck by the bag's strap and curled up in her sleeping bag without dinner. All she wanted was for the noise to stop.

Dad always said these protect against evil spirits. Hopefully, it can keep me alive for the night. I don't know what to do. I, I, I, I can't. I can't stay here another night. Every moment is torture. I'm not any closer, and I don't even know if this will help me. Maybe Dad really committed suicide. Maybe he was just tired of life. And can you blame him? There's so much pain and suffering, and THERE'S THAT DAMN NOISE!!!

She bolted upright, having drifted off slightly. To her left, she saw the omamori on the tent floor beside her; the talisman had been removed from the bag, and the tanto she kept by her pillow lay unsheathed. Behind her, she heard a noise that was distinct from rest, a raspy sucking noise, like air flowing through a backed up pipe. She turned slowly, and as the light from her lantern faded, an apparition flickered into view. This time, it was a woman. She was wearing a short white dress that looked almost like a pillowcase. It was yellowed and crusted in many places, and she reeked of stagnant water. From two long slashes in her wrists, black liquid flowed. Stringy hair that was plastered to her head by some kind of muck, obscured her face. She sat there for a moment, her neck jerking unnaturally as the sucking sound she was making became louder and more intense. With her twitching, sticky fingers, she grabbed ahold of Mori's face and sharply shoved her face into the inky mire that had flooded the tent. It was acrid and thick, stinging Mori's face and neck as she struggled against the shadow's firm grip. The woman whispered in different voices, sometimes sounding like Mori's mother, and sometimes her friends. It sounded like radio static, boring into her brain, endlessly distracting and annoying.

I have to break this thing's grip or I'm gonna drown! I need to get to the talisman.

Moriko groped around the floor of the tent, which had filled more than halfway with the spirit's venom. Mori found that the ghost's grip was not invincible; she fought her way to the surface more than once, but she was starting to tire out. Soon she'd be out of energy. It seemed like an endless struggle, first a refreshing gulp of air, clawed hands smashing her head into the murk, victory with life giving breath, then defeat as the paws of death pushed her closer to its jaws. Her time was running out. The spirit had laughed at her, mocking her struggle for life. Finally, her hand found the tanto. Using the last of her strength,

Moriko slashed at the revenant, cutting through it and the tent as well. The tent burst open like a corpse's belly. The spirit vanished, along with the liquid and the entire tent. In the cold air of the night, Mori saw bright eyes had surrounded her. They edged closer, clearly kept at bay by the small sword, but daring still to come closer. Clawed arms groped the ground surrounding her. The foul light coming from the ghosts made Mori dizzy.

To Mori's amazement, it wasn't just the tanto keeping the evil spirits away. Yorick's skull was glowing in the center of her camp. The image around his skull was that of an old man, smiling with his wrinkled face and wearing old-fashioned clothes. He pointed north of the camp to one last strand of blue tape leading deep into the forest. Then he disappeared, skull and all. The twisted figures around the camp charged.

Mori took off running after the blue tape, slashing in every direction to keep the dark spirits at bay. The entire forest erupted in a scream.

Sounds of pain ebbed and flowed, reaching peaks and then quieting right when Mori had had enough. Then it started again with renewed vigor and rage. The cacophony hit what seemed like its highest point as she got closer to the tape, the anger and pain became resolve, the confusion became an answer, and life became death. Images flashed through Mori's mind as she raced through the forest. They showed her art being thrown away, her mother boarding a plane to a far off destination, her father hanging himself, her own broken form crying alone, swallowed by the dark. The thought made her trip as roots grasped her legs. The entire forest was coming alive around her. She saw leaves with eyes, and teeth through the dirt.

Face to misshapen face with the same beings she had dreamt about, she stifled a scream. Hot, stale breath filled the air as the tower-like heads of the forest's prisoners sprouted around her. She held onto the blue tape in one hand and tried to pry off the thorny roots, which had formed deformed hands. The tanto was gone; she must've dropped it when she fell. The mangled things grinned at her, beckoning her close. They had bruised appendages, some twisted the wrong way around, ending in impossibly large and spindly hands, if you could call them that. Through the screaming, she could make out words. The beings were speaking to her with broken whispers, fear, alone, left, easy, comfort, let go, go ahead, tears, end, end, end, end, END, END, END, END, END IT!!!

"ENOUGH," Mori screamed.

The tape felt warm in her hand, and she saw her father standing above her. He had a loving expression on his rounded face, and he looked just like she remembered him. He reached out to her, his hand just out of her reach, but with an expression on his face, one of encouragement, one that told Mori she could do it. With tears in her eyes, she looked up at the shining figure of Eito Miyazaki, nothing but love and light filling her heart. Her fingertips brushed his as she reached out, but as she lunged, the forest-born pulled her back. Her shoulder ached as she stretched to escape, to get away, to get to her father. They refused to let her go. Mori looked back down at her feet, the rotted hands reaching so close, so easy, so quick. Why struggle? Why follow rules given by those who didn't understand? Mori looked into their pained grins, reflecting the madness that had possessed them, their broken forms, testaments to their own means of escape, the wretched creatures that were tricked into choosing a path, but she chose her own. Moriko Miyazaki chose to fight. With one final surge, she reached out and grabbed her father's hand, and the vengeful spirits dissipated.

"Dad...Daddy...Oh my God Dad! I was looking for you! I never stopped looking for you. No matter what they said, I always knew that I'd sort this out. I'm so glad I found you. I, I knew you weren't dead, that you wouldn't do anything to hurt yourself..." but as she said it, she realized he was gone. The warm feeling had faded from her hand, and Eito's grip became intangible. He was leaving now. "You know, I thought that maybe by finding you, I could've pieced everything back together. That maybe by proving you hadn't killed yourself, I'd save us from some shame or something. Now I feel different. Now…I think I needed this to move on. You're not here anymore. Somewhere along the line, we lost you. I have to live with that. But that's just it, isn't it? I have to live. I love you." With that, he was gone, his body slumped against a tree marked by blue tape. The forest opened up in front of her, flooding the clearing in light. Cool, sweet air washed away the heavy stench of rotted vegetation. She'd won, or so she thought, as she slipped into unconsciousness.

CHAPTER TEN
The Hospital

Moriko woke up in a hospital bed to bright lights. Her vision cleared slowly, and her eyes stung. She could hear, but it was muffled, like she had a head cold. With great difficulty, she moved her legs. Her mother and a strange visitor were in the room conversing over her. He was a tall black man with a kind face. He had strong features underneath a well-groomed beard and wore a cream-colored suit, a straw hat, and round dark tinted sunglasses. The suit fit his stocky build well, which was like that of a retired wrestler; strong, but some of the muscle was giving way to fat. He noticed Moriko's stirring and took that opportunity to place a cup of water by her right arm on a small table. Pointed rings of gold and silver adorned most of his fingers. He spoke slowly:

"Good afternoon, Moriko. I know you've been through a lot recently, and I think you're owed an explanation for some of the stranger occurrences in your life." His voice was raspy, with an accent Moriko couldn't quite place. The way he pronounced the letter r sounded like a w sometimes. He spoke with a soothing and collected air, as if he were in complete control of the situation at hand.

Mori cleared her throat and sat up. Her strength was returning to her. She cocked an eyebrow. "You think you can explain everything that just happened to me?"

"I have no doubt that I will make it all very clear to you. Allow me to introduce myself. My name is Dominique Augustin, and I was a friend of your father. Would you mind answering some questions for me so that I can make sense of what happened to you?"

Mori frowned. "I have no problem answering your questions, but only if you answer mine. Where am I? How did I get here, and how do I know you two are even real?"

Dominique smiled slightly, which made Mori even more defiant. *This guy appears out of thin air and says he's dad's friend and that he has all the answers? I don't trust it*. Mori looked at her mother for backup.

"Moriko, I called him. I called you to see how you were doing and you weren't picking up. Your friend didn't know where you were. That's when I called Dominique. I knew you could only have gone to one place. Strangely enough, they found you right by the entrance. Then we brought you here to recover. You've been asleep for a day and a half." Moriko noticed her mother's voice was trembling as she spoke, and blotches of color kissed her cheeks. She instantly felt bad for putting her mother through this entire ordeal.

Dominique spoke next, "It's a good thing we'd found you when we did; if anymore time had passed, we might've been too late. You're only being treated for exhaustion and dehydration. You'll be fine in no time. As for all of this being real? I'll leave you to decide that."

"Thank you." She murmured, her head bent down. It was embarrassing that someone she'd never met had come and helped her like this, especially because her mother had called him in. She felt like a little kid.

"No need to thank me. You saved yourself. If you hadn't had such a strong will, you would've died. But I have to speak to you about the situation now. Would you be comfortable with that?"

"I don't know about comfort, but I'll speak to you about it." Mori braced herself.

Dominique gave her a reassuring look. "You entered the Aokigahara forest for some clue of what happened to your father, correct?"

"Yes, I saw him. I know what happened now. He's dead, he must've killed himself, or those things killed him. All that torment, and it didn't even make a difference. He's gone."

"I'm very sorry for your loss. Eito was a good friend of mine. I will sorely miss him. There's a deeper explanation of what happened to him and why, if you'd like to hear it. I understand this is hard for you, but I think you deserve to know and that it might bring you a little clarity. Is that what you want?"

"Yes, I think you should start with how you know my father, what happened and how you know about it."

"Your father and I have been friends for a good 10 years. We met in Japan. I was doing a job. I think it was the Onryo case near Hakone. Excuse me, let me back up. I am a member of a consortium that has existed in one way or another for centuries."

"Big word."

"It's a good one, isn't it? We are known in very small circles as BRAHMASTRA. In the ancient Vedas, the Brahmastra was a weapon given to humans by higher beings. Its purpose was to give humanity a means to protect themselves from creatures that come from places of misery and darkness, from spirits, from the unexplainable, and the supernatural. It's a dramatic name, but we study those literatures carefully to do just that. Protect humanity. We make sure those things that lurk in the dark stay there."

"I think I know where this is going, but what does this have to do with my dad?"

"Your father, Eito, was a member of our society, and he was looking into a case involving a troubling group of inexperienced mystics. We're not sure of the circumstances, but they managed to trap your father in the forest. Now, the forest is a very unusual place. From the information we've gathered, that place has been soured. We can't tell if it was always like that or if all the death has changed the very land. The forest itself seems to feed on the negative emotions of those who enter it, but it can't do anything on its own. There are wrathful spirits, yes, but they really only seek to spread the misery they're condemned to. They cannot leave the forest, and it has mutilated their spirits. They're trapped there, damned to feed the forest and to starve."

"If all that's true, then why aren't I dead? If

this forest is cursed or evil or whatever you say, it should be more powerful than a 22-year-old. And people go in and out all the time. How do you explain that?"

"From studies that we've done, we're guessing the forest can really only feed if a person willingly commits suicide. That's why it keeps you alive for so long. It uses the spirits it has consumed and your own fears, flaws, and emotional turmoil to torture you into killing yourself. The forest probably stopped trying once it realized you wouldn't kill yourself, and that's why you survived. I'm sorry about your father. He really was a dear friend of mine."

"So Dad really did it. He wasn't strong enough…" Tears streamed down her face as she gripped the sheets of the hospital bed. In the end, he was gone. Her mother came over to the bed and wrapped Mori up in her arms. Mori didn't want Dominique to see her cry, but she couldn't control it. At the very least, Moriko knew the circumstances. "So how can we find the people who did this to him?"

"Well, I've been working on getting to the bottom of that. Things are changing. Paranormal activity is getting worse and worse. It's more noticeable now than ever before. On top of that, there's been a resurgence of a group of dangerous individuals and they were probably involved in what Eito was investigating. Your father asked me to bring you two back to New York if anything happened to him. That's why your mother was booking the tickets. I only came here because you'd been missing for so long. If you really want to know what happened with Eito, I'll set you up with a contact back in the States. That sound good?"

"Can you leave me and my mother alone for a minute? I want to talk to her about this."

Dominique nodded solemnly and left the room, closing the door gently behind him. Moriko paused and turned to her mother, her jaw set in anger. "So you were going to leave me and go back to New York?"

Maria gave Moriko a confused look. "Didn't you see my text messages? I was trying to make sure you were ok. I gave you some details, but you weren't responding."

Relief flowed through Moriko's body. It was just the forest playing with her mind. Her mother seemed as normal as normal could be, and there was nothing but love in her voice. "It was horrible in there. That place threw every fear or doubt I'd ever had in my face."

Moriko's mother sat on the bed next to her, and Moriko could see the toll her time in the forest had taken. Maria's face was drawn, and lines of worry had sprouted on her forehead. Maria hugged her daughter and kissed her forehead, wetting both of their cheeks with her tears. "It's OK. It's all over Moriko, now you're safe."

"Are we really safe? It's just us now, and who knows if the people that went after dad will come after us? I just want to protect you?"

"You don't have to worry about that, Moriko! I'm the one who's supposed to be protecting you, and I need you to let me do that."

"But I want to protect you! I have to. We're all we have, you and me! It's not fair what they took from us!" Mori shouted, slamming down on the hospital bed with her fist. She felt like crying, but no tears fell from her eyes. She'd cried enough over the past few days. "They're people we've never met, people we can't find."

"It isn't fair. That's why I called Dominique. Darling, I made a choice when I married your father. I knew the kinds of things he was involved in. Now I think it's time you're allowed to make your own choice. Either way, we will be ok. Either way, I'll be there for you." Maria ran her fingers through her daughter's hair soothingly. At that moment, Moriko felt like a little kid again.

"Dad died for what?"

"Moriko, what do you mean?!"

"He's gone, and what did he accomplish? Was he saving something? Was he protecting someone, us, the world? Was it worth it?"

"There's no way to know, darling. You can't blame the people you love for their choices. You don't know what they're dealing with. I know you're angry, and hurt, and I have my own…feelings about the situation myself. But I don't blame your father; he wouldn't have thrown his life away. Everything he did came back to us eventually, because he loved us."

Moriko slumped back on the bed, letting her body melt into the mattress. "I guess we'll never really get any answers then."

Maria sighed impatiently. "Well, what are you going to do about it, young lady?"

"Make my own answers, I guess."

Bellyaching

CHAPTER ELEVEN
Clear Mind

His mind had finally started to clear. It was a chilly night; the wind whipped furiously on the rooftop of the office building he'd finally perched on. He'd had his fill, the clawing and gnawing in his brain lessening as the blood coursed through him. His body was returning to a more humanlike shape as he brushed the dirt and salt off of his black robes. Now that he could think, he was angry. For the first time in over 70 years, he was awake. He smashed the air vent on the roof into pieces and didn't stop until the red hot glare that had taken over faded away. All he really wanted to do was go back to sleep. The fact that he was awake scared him a little, along with guilt and frustration which bubbled up from within the pit of his stomach and settled into his chest. He remained a creature of destruction, a predator, a consumer that could never fill his belly or quench his thirst. The vampire, a parasitic artifact that was born from a decades-old perversion. He shouldn't be awake.

He covered his tracks on the rooftop,

making the damage seem coincidental. His outburst had surely drawn attention and, as a man who had no current identification and blood on his anachronistic clothes, he was not eager to meet the authorities. It was shameful what he did. He remembered the woman's broken form, remembered watching her fingers twitch like the legs of a crushed moth. She'd had to die, though. He had an unsavory job ahead of him, and that woman was only the first of three. Her husband was lucky; his bloodlust had cleared long enough for him to spare that man. Killing was never pleasant to him, but a wolf does not attend a rabbit's funeral. At least, that's what his father had always told him. It was a statement that justified barbarism and selfish greed, but who cares as long as you say it in a pretty way? He'd always respected and hated his family for their sense of entitlement to whatever they pleased and their shrewd way of making it sound almost noble. On the other hand, they'd instilled a strong sense of duty, and this is what prevailed at the moment. He knew his duty. But he was so damned tired. He stopped flying over the Manhattan skyline and searched for more derelict surroundings. Eventually, he happened upon a string of abandoned buildings. Scaling the surfaces of the urban jungle like a reptile, he took the broken windows as an invitation and nestled himself in on the top floor of a particularly rundown building. Rubble covered the floor, but the roof was intact, and there were areas where the window would not let the sunlight in. Perfect for his purposes. Hiding himself beneath the wooden floorboards, he closed his eyes and drifted off, his dreams nothing more than memories surfacing from the mire of his consciousness.

CHAPTER TWELVE
Vincenzo Abbandonato II

His name was Vincenzo Abbandonato II, born April 15th, 1919, and named after his grandfather. He was the youngest of six children born in the ultimate generation of the Abbandonato family, the sole surviving boy preceded by four graceful ladies and one late brother. The Abbandonato family was one of great status, always enjoying respect and admiration in the hilly Montagna region of Italy. Vincenzo's father had told him wild stories of how their ancestors had descended from Romulus himself and fought great monsters before moving north.

"We've got the blood of the wolf inside of us *cucciolo*, never forget that. We've always been warriors and royalty, and in the jungle, the strong need meat." He was skinning a rabbit in the snow when he'd told Vincenzo that. The rabbit had been Vincenzo's pet for 4 years. That night, the rabbit was their dinner. His father Aldo was obsessed with keeping their family in powerful positions. As a family, they'd had money for generations, maintaining their palatial stone castle by owning and running one of the largest and most productive coal mines in Italy. Unfortunately, famine and other unforeseen circumstances had put the family in danger. For years, Aldo had worked to forge political connections to ensure that his family's survival. The Abbandonato family was one of the biggest supporters of Fascism, the Axis, and the Nazis, to the point where their greed had led to them being erased from the public's mind. The people saw to it that the stain of the Abbandonatos was bleached out of history forever.

It was all so much easier before Vincenzo had been born. The lack of an heir had torn Aldo apart, but it was still one less mouth to feed. He hadn't worked so hard and done so many unsavory things before his son's birth. Vincenzo was born pale, sickly, and withdrawn. The only way Aldo could have been more disappointed in him was if he were a female, and Vincenzo often thought that he would've been kinder if that were the case.

"God is quite the prankster, giving me a son like you."

"What do you mean, Papa?" The boy could think of nothing more serious than the Creator.

"We run as wolves and He's given me a sniveling jackal, leaving my wife even worse off. It's a great joke," he'd said, skinning the rabbit as Vincenzo's silent tears froze on his cheeks.

The process of giving birth had taken its toll on his mother Lia. Complications had left her bleeding profusely, and while she'd recovered eventually, it left her pale, anemic, and weak. Somehow, little Vincenzo suspected his father was almost as disappointed in her for being frail as he was in his son for being the same. Vincenzo was a slight boy, with sandy brown hair and olive skin. He'd never been athletically inclined. On the contrary, he was quick to become fatigued. He wasn't particularly good at school, either. He took to English and German quickly and with ease, but that was the extent of his academic skill. His tutors always made sure to let his parents know he was learning well, but Enzo's general mediocrity never escaped his father's notice.

"Don't worry, we'll make an Abbandonato of you yet, boy." His father would often say with a pat on the shoulder and a grimace on his face. Despite this, Vincenzo found worry decorating his father's brow, a diadem darkening the glances sent towards his son. On that particular day, as they stood ankle deep in slush, Vincenzo noticed that his father was almost compulsively looking at him with each stroke of the knife into the former pet. Aldo had strange periods of behavior like this; though he was seldom physically affectionate, when he embraced Vincenzo it was as if he expected his son would evaporate in his arms. As much as Aldo seemed almost disgusted by Vincenzo's precarious hold on life, he also seemed fearful and fiercely protective.

"Boy, are you still bawling?"

Vincenzo took a deep sniffle, which did

nothing about the mucus already on his face, and answered. "No, Papa."

Aldo sighed. "Let me ask you a question, *cucciolo*. Do you know the average lifespan of the European rabbit?"

"No Papa, I do not."

"Nine years. One year older than you are right now. I tell you this because the fact of the matter is, only the strong can endure the passage of time. No matter who or what you're thinking of, all that matters is that you last."

"But Papa, everyone dies."

Aldo looked at his son with a grave look in his eyes. "Yes, son, death is an enemy with quite the résumé." For a moment, he was quiet and lost in thought. Then he snapped out of it and patted his son on his bony shoulder. "We'll make an Abbandonato out of you yet, boy."

Then he took his son to a family staple, their kennel. The Abbandanato family had their own unique breed of hunting dog, part Doberman, part

Pharaoh hound, part Sardinian shepherd. The family had been perfecting this mix for decades, buying hounds from far-away lands like Egypt and Germany, and now their own hound was a wonder of Italy. Fiercely loyal and protective, they were as much Abbandanato as the rest of the family.

"First lesson we learn is how to discern things, how to differentiate. That rabbit was not a pet, that was food. These are pets." That was the beginning of Vincenzo's work in the kennels. Years later, he gave Vincenzo two puppies to look after, a rusty brown male, Vergil, and a blue female named Bice. Vincenzo came to find that Vergil took more after Vincenzo's father. The dog loved him almost as reluctantly as the man who had bred him. Bice was more timid and kind. They were some of the more notable gifts Aldo Abbandanto would give to his son, but unfortunately for Vincenzo, they did not have the honor of being called the last.

CHAPTER THIRTEEN
Aldo And His Wife Lia

For all that Aldo was, his wife Lia was different. She cared for her son as much as she was able. Mostly confined to her bed, she would read Enzo history books, books of myths, books that had kings and queens and serpents, stories of the dead exacting their vengeance and angels calling from the light. He loved seeing the words transform from marks on a page to lurid pictures and scenes in his mind when his mother read to him. They'd often have the same look in their eyes of visiting a faraway place. Every day, after his afternoon lessons, Enzo would knock on his mother's door four times and wait for her weak voice to say, '*Entri.*' Lia rarely mentioned studies or anything that so concerned her husband, Aldo.

"What I really want is to expand my only son's mind. I'm limited to this castle, but my intellect is a seasoned traveler. My little Enzo shall be free." She'd say this to the servants, the tutors, her husband, and anyone who'd listen.

"My first son sings with the angels now. My

girls have left me. Either they've been married off or they're studying elsewhere. The only child I have left is this clever little boy!" When she felt up to it, she'd take Enzo around the castle, to the observatory to watch the stars at night, and through the drafty halls of the spacious home in the daytime. He never went exploring by himself, and wouldn't go with anyone but his mother. It didn't last.

Enzo took after his mother, with a mop of tawny hair much lighter than Aldo's. Lia herself wore her hair in a loose bun most days, wispy strands defying her will and crawling onto her sculpted features. Despite a marked thinness, she had maintained a striking and attractive appearance. She would sit by the window, the sunlight illuminating blue veins on her face and arms, reading and directing the servants when they needed it. She came from a simple but wealthy family, bankers that were integral to the funding of Mussolini's war effort. Her marriage to Aldo

Abbandonato was a profitable venture for both parties. And even though Aldo was neither a violent nor rude man, she found he was colder than the mountain winds which whipped around the castle he'd grown up in. He was always involved in the children's lives, but it seemed like his pride was the motivation behind his actions. He'd made sure that his daughters were well taught in the expected academic subject, that they were fluent in multiple languages, so that they'd be able to marry men born in families of power. Vincenzo never spent much time with his sisters. They were all either away studying or married, living outside of the castle. Vincenzo's whole life was behind the gray walls of the Abbandonato castle, but Aldo would rectify that.

It was October 1940, an especially cold year. Snow hadn't started falling, but the soil was still brick-hard and unforgiving. The clang of a pickaxe on dirt and rock was even more pronounced. Metal crashed on earth, a grim song that Vincenzo had memorized even though he never sought its performance. With the British blocking the supply of coal to Italy, the Abbandonatos were valuable as political allies. Aldo had begun holding meetings that week with war generals in a richly decorated room on the west side of the castle. It was in one of the observatory towers, just below the stargazing room. He'd proudly dubbed this place "The War Room."

"He's so creative. Who could have come up with such an inventive name to describe a room where silly fighting is discussed? I suppose 'Hell' was already taken. It's certainly where most of these men will go when it's all said and done." Lia would mutter to her son while rolling her eyes. Vincenzo was supposed to be present and attentive during all the meetings. He'd often doze off looking at the velvet draped, warm room. He remembered how the heavily perfumed carpet, red like the petals of a rose, the oppressive warmth of the room and the burned oak table, seemed especially comfortable, like a pillow in those instances. Looking at the embossed spines of the books on their shelves, the gold astrolabe on his father's desk, and the inkwell whose pen bore a red falcon's feather, he'd try to keep his eyes open. He also remembered the sharp crack of his father's hand on the back of his head.

Vittorio was an ever present attendee to these meetings. He was a tall man, a head taller than Aldo, who was a man of impressive stature. Vittorio had grown up working in the Abbandonato mines, but his physical strength, wicked aim, and love of money quickly took him into military and mercenary work. Aldo had used his influence to turn Vittorio's unit into his own personal combat force, even though they had officially been drafted into the war effort and had been deployed a number of times. Vittorio was a kind man, seemingly, and was fond of Vincenzo.

The faces of the other men were blurs; there was a revolving door of unscrupulous men entering and leaving the room. Except one. The man was obviously from Italy. Anyone could tell that from the way he spoke the language, compared to the bumbling tongues of the mercenaries that guarded the castle. On the other hand, Enzo had never seen anyone like him. He always wore a long purple robe, and a long, thick beard. His face was heavily wrinkled, and he was tanned like a sailor, with his skin peeling in many places as if he were still standing in the sun. He would come to every meeting accompanied by a small girl who spoke with a strange accent. The man performed strange tricks for what Enzo assumed was for his amusement. Mostly, the tricks were terrifying. The first time they'd met, he asked Enzo about his rabbit. When Enzo told the man that it had died, the man said, "If you'd saved the bones, I could've fixed your problem." The man did other strange things around Enzo. He'd make his shadow move in strange ways, would make animals sing songs in voices like a human's, and he'd make the room

darker than the blackest pitch. Enzo didn't like
him. The man always smelled like spices. His
laugh was a little too loud, and he did something to
the animals; Vergil always growled at him, and
Bice always slunk away when he was around. The
girl, however, intrigued Vincenzo. She looked
roughly around his age, but her frame was so petite
he had no way of knowing. She dressed plainly
except for a necklace of lapis lazuli and never
seemed happy to be there, never seemed astounded
by the ghoulish man's tricks, and never seemed to
listen unless the man was giving her orders. One
boring afternoon, Vincenzo made a point of
speaking to her during the intermission.

"Pardon me, but you've come to a good 4 or
5 of these meetings, and no one has introduced you.
My name is Vincenzo, and I welcome you to my
home. May I ask where you're from? I've never
met anyone who looked like you."

The girl's dark eyes narrowed. Her hair was
tightly curled and her complexion was much darker

than anyone Vincenzo had seen, sun kissed or otherwise. "Why do you ask?"

Vincenzo smiled sheepishly. "Well, all the attendees are men old enough to be my father, and you seem to be closer to my age. I'm 21. My birthday was earlier this year."

"I'm a bit younger than you, sir," the girl said, her eyes darting towards the old mystic.

"That's fine. I really just wanted to talk about something other than the war." Vincenzo's eyes followed her to the old man. "Why do you serve him?"

"He is a cruel man, and I don't serve him by choice, but I don't think you could understand that. You have the world at your fingertips." She could not hide the disdain in her voice, and Vincenzo could not hide the hurt on his face.

He spoke in hushed tones, "I want nothing to do with what is being discussed in this room. I'm only here because of my father."

"And you think that makes us the same?"

"No, no, please don't misunderstand. I really would only like to be your friend. The things that go on in this room are frankly a little beyond me. The circumstances of these meetings require more life experience than I have. But please, let me help you if I can."

Her expression softened slightly. "You might need to worry more about helping yourself, sir. But my name is Akila."

"It is my pleasure to meet you Akila."

She smiled slightly but gave no other reply and moved to an unobtrusive corner of the room. Vincenzo himself shadowed his father, who, along with Vittorio, was already in a very animated conversation with the old man.

"As I'm sure you know, I represent the Partito Nazionale Fascista. I have been handpicked to help the Italians stay one step ahead of the other world powers. Mussolini himself believes in what we can do. Do you know what the future of this war will be fought with?"

"Hopefully insatiable women wearing red lipstick." Vittorio said with a wink in Vincenzo's direction.

"If only, dear soldier. The war might have ended already if that was the case. The occult, Mr. Abbandonato. Whomsoever masters the occult arts will control the world. The Nazis are already making progress, Aldo. They had been planning something codenamed Ragnarok or something like that. From what we understand, the Abbandonatos have something that could very well give our great country an advantage over the entire world. Aldo, I know that you, more than anyone else, know the value of the blood that courses through one's veins. I also know about the treasure hidden in the basement of this castle. Perhaps you would allow the war effort to explore this asset?"

"Well dear sir, I am honored that Mussolini has chosen my family for this great service. Now it is time for the world to truly see our family's strength! Give me some time and I can prepare the

Abbandonato treasure for you to see. You won't be disappointed. I think you'll find this is just what Italy needs to come out of this war as the greatest force in human history." Aldo's promise satisfied the man, and the old mystic and Akila retreated to their quarters. Aldo used this opportunity to dismiss all the other men in the room. Vincenzo moved closer to speak to Vittorio. He hadn't seen Vittorio in a few months, although very little had changed about his friend. He still had the same rough, rusty-colored stubble on his face. His skin had tanned considerably though, and it made the two white scars that criss-crossed his right cheek stand out even more. Even at this age, Vincenzo admired him: big, strong, intimidating, and capable, Vittorio was a man anyone could respect. Anyone ignorant of his actions, that is.

"And how are you, *bimbo*? Have you been good while I was gone?"

"I'm not a child anymore, Vittorio. You don't have to call me that."

Vittorio smiled. "You certainly aren't a child anymore. So I suppose I shouldn't give you these Swiss chocolates then? That's more for children, eh?"

"No, no, Vittorio, that's our tradition. It doesn't count. You bring me back chocolate every time you go away."

"You know, *bimbo*, I wonder what I get out of our little arrangement?"

"The best friend anyone could have!"

"Oh? Is that all?"

Vincenzo pulled his friend close and whispered in his ear. "I also clean up the ash you leave when you smoke in the library, seeing as Father has told you not to, and you keep doing it."

Vittorio flushed. "Ah well, I always knew our arrangement was worthwhile."

Aldo had cleared the room out while the two younger men were bantering. He sat at his desk, poured himself a spritz, and motioned for his son and his employee to take a seat.

"My dear Vittorio, How are you? I've been trying to let you rest these last couple of days, but now we need to discuss your travels. I'd like a full status report."

"I'm good, Signor Abandonatto. Thank you very much for asking. We can get right into my report. I feel like we are close enough to dispense with pleasantries and you are eager to continue." Vittorio paused and waited for Aldo to give his permission, which came in the form of a nod. "As you might know, we returned on Sunday night after a 32 day expedition. We were mixed in with the Maletti Group, who I frankly believe are a bunch of moronic bastards." This elicited a giggle from Vincenzo and an indulgent smile from Aldo. "Our group was part of the flanking maneuver that allowed Italy to occupy Sidi Barrani. At this point, it had already been made clear that we would never make it to the Suez Canal. The British retreat made it relatively simple to slip through the cracks, as territory lines were being redefined. I took 20 of our men, the best suited for espionage, and we took 2 British soldiers and 3 locals and forced them to smuggle us inland. We came up with the perfect ruse: we traveled as a water truck."

Aldo raised an eyebrow. "A water truck?"

Vittorio seemed pleased with himself. "We had to pilfer supplies from the army, but that wasn't too difficult. It was just a matter of greasing the right pockets and getting tired foot soldiers drunk as fish. Then we had two trucks, one that was repurposed from the British and one of our own. The hostages alerted us to where there were British checkpoints and then we led with the British truck. When there were none, we led with our own."

"Those guys sure were helpful?" Vincenzo said with a wholesome smile.

"*Bimbo,* people are quite cooperative when you torture them."

The smile melted off of Vincenzo's face.

"Anyway, we got further inland, but we

ended up losing a quarter of our men to the elements alone. Nature is a woman you love and leave. You see, when we ran into checkpoints, we would actually have to give the hostages water. We had accounted for this, but eventually we were cutting into our own rations to give to idiots. And what's worse is, we only had to go through two British checkpoints, and although the first one was easy enough, the second one turned into a full on fire fight. We lost another 4 men, and both hostages died too. The worst part was, when we got to the Canal and followed our intel to the mouth of the Red Sea, there were Italians there already. They must've been with the Facistas."

"Did you make contact?" Asked Aldo, unable to conceal his concern.

"Signore, the ones who made contact aren't around to talk about it. We had the advantage. Even though the Facistas had gotten there first, they didn't know the actual story of our little package. The exhuming process was anything but simple;

thankfully the currents there are weak, so using the cover story, our own ingenuity, and some manpower, we were able to get our little treasure. But there was a small snafu."

"What's the problem?" Aldo's tone should have been wary, but instead was giddy with the undertone of a child waiting for permission to open a Christmas gift.

"That girl the old bastard is toting around might be important. The necklace she's wearing is the same kind of necklace I saw the people wearing in the village at the Suez Canal. She might know the legend."

Aldo considered this. "What do you think, Vincenzo?"

Vincenzo's heart dropped. "Um, Father, I don't really have any background information about this situation. I'm not really sure I can be of any help here."

"Listen, boy, here's what was just laid out in front of you: we have procured something of great worth that the old man was interested in. Well, either him or his employer, it doesn't matter. Someone was looking for something we now have. And that girl you were chatting with might be of use. Think on your feet."

Vincenzo swallowed hard. "Well, uh, she is not fond of that man. If it is within our means, we could free her of his control. And if she has information we don't, then she can help us."

"Ah, my son, the merciful saint of the Abbandonato family," Aldo said with a smile that could have easily been a sneer. "Vittorio, I thank you for everything. As usual, you are indispensable. Son, over the next few days, make sure you endear yourself to that girl. For now, I want you to put the dogs to sleep and then come back here. It's time I take you to the basement."

"Father, why are we going to the basement?" For as long as he could remember, the main room in the castle basement had been chained shut. Vincenzo seldom went down there, partially because of the awful smell, and also because his sisters had told him stories. In a dark room by the firelight, the girls would frighten their brother with tales of the apparitions in the dungeon, the torture that took place there, and all the crazy characters their little minds could imagine. A man who'd been impaled and would shake the spear at little boys, then tie them up and use them for target practice. A woman who'd been boiled alive and flopped around like a tortellini who would eat children just like pasta. An old man who'd been stuffed in a coffin and would scream at night that he was hungry. As Enzo got older, he found the stories were just that, although sometimes he was sure he heard something. Once, when he was 14, Enzo remembered being caught outside the castle in a blizzard. He had been out on the castle's grounds and had gotten lost. He found his way back, but many of the doors had been frozen shut and no one inside had noticed that he was gone. The castle was a big place. Because of this, he had to take a different entrance to get back in. Secret entrances and exits had existed in the castle since its construction, and these passages had only multiplied over the years. The children had been taught about them from a young age. It was a good way to prepare them if the castle was attacked.

Enzo knew that at the castle base there was a small tunnel that fed into the basement. He trudged through the thick snow, his boots getting sucked in with each step. Finally, he reached the spot. Digging into the frost with the determination of a miner looking for gold, he reached stone. Removing the loose rocks from the aperture, he quickly scooted himself inside the hole, which was big enough to accommodate two people side to side if they were crawling on all fours. It was about three feet high, so he fit comfortably inside. It wasn't his first time in the hole. He'd played hide-and-seek in it with the castle servants frequently. It was comfortable and familiar, so he felt no fear as he closed the entrance once again and the tunnel

filled with darkness. It was much warmer in the
tunnel, and he was glad to be rid of the shrill
howling of the wind in his ears. Now the only
sounds he'd heard were the crunching of old leaves
underneath him and the squeak of the occasional
mouse he'd startled. He started moving once his
eyes had adjusted to the dark. The exit was a large
circle of warm light. He knew to keep his eyes on
it; he didn't want to look at the bones. The
basement of the castle doubled as a crypt for dead
Abbandonatos. Before Enzo was born, there was a
flood, and it washed the entire basement out. Most
of the sarcophagi had opened, and the corpses were
strewn about. A servant had been killed in the
accident, but whenever the story was told, they
never mentioned the boy drowning. Enzo shrugged
off the thought as he kept his eyes off of the bones
that were on his left. In less than five minutes, he
was out of the tunnel and standing inside the vast
basement level of the castle. Cold air filled his
lungs as he breathed deeply. He cursed his frail

nature as he surveyed his surroundings. A thick layer of dust coated every surface except the rusty steel door that led to the upper levels. In the dim light that glowed from the naked bulb in the ceiling, he could see the layout of the floor. It had a circular organization and featured a bunch of small rooms that looked like cells around the perimeter, with a large room that took up most of the space on the floor in the center. At regular intervals around the great circle were lightbulbs that kept it from being too creepy. Enzo had never been in this area before, and he was a firm believer that curiosity killed the cat. He also believed that was why cats had 9 lives. He tried the largest door against his better judgment.

What am I doing? Mother forbade us from ever coming down here and although we play in the tunnel, we never actually came in here. I've never even seen Father come down here, either. I should go upstairs, before Father gets angry. This is foolish and I'm going to leave. I'm going to leave now. Just let me leave, please.

He'd never been curious about what was down there before, but now it was like he couldn't stop himself. Nothing was down there. But what if something was? Vincenzo felt uneasy, but something from beyond the door was calling to him. In the back of his skull, someone was whispering from inside the room and he couldn't tell what the person was saying, but he just knew the person was talking to him. It scared him, but he also wanted to open the door more than anything. The knot in his stomach was the same mix of fear and excitement he felt when he first rode a horse, or when his father took him out hunting and he pulled the trigger of their Carcano rifle. He gripped the handle of the center door and steeled his nerves. Sweat dripped down his nose despite the biting cold he'd just been in. He could hear the tiny splatter of his perspiration hitting the stone floor. Finally, he found he could no longer resist. He turned the knob to find... the door was locked.

Enzo let out a sigh of relief. The voice had dismissed him. He walked to the door opposite the main entrance. The door reminded him of a prison door, metal, with a sliding tray slot for passing food and looking in and out. He slid the metal partition to the side and peered through it. It was dark in the room, but from the lighting in the corridor, he could make out something. He strained his eyes to see into the room and finally made out a figure. It was barely more than a silhouette.

"… Hello?" He tried in vain to convince himself that his eyes were playing tricks on him. He spoke, hoping the sound would bring him back to reality. Somehow, at the very core of his being, he knew that the vibration of his voice could save him. With all the electricity of disobedience and horror, a mind numbingly simple question would ground him and dispel the charge. He looked around, as if he expected the rest of the room to become less frightening, the lights to become warmer, the cold steel and stones to soften. It was all quite ridiculous. He turned back towards the dark slot to feel a ragged breath on his cheek. Someone or something was face to face with him at the door.

"VINCENZO!!!" He leapt back from the door, scared out of his wits, to see his father standing by the exit, looking furious.

"What are you doing down here, boy?! We're in the middle of a blizzard and you decide to disappear? Is being difficult a personal goal for you, or are you just prodigiously incompetent?" His tone was angry, but his face was anxious.

"Father, I was just... there's someone in there and I was just coming in from the snow, but I wasn't going to stay down here. I promise! Father, you have to beli..."

"Boy," he said with a sternness far beyond what he usually employed. "Come upstairs and stop snooping around alone down here. Your mother is worried sick about you and I've reached the limit of my patience."

His father had tried to persuade him it was his imagination, but the smell of stale breath stuck with Vincenzo. Now, when he thought about the dungeon, he couldn't help but remember that smell.

"Vincenzo, look sharp! I'm about to show you something very important." His father's voice snapped Vincenzo back to the present. He was following his father back down those same steps, with the fear of his younger self growing as he took every step. They arrived at the main door, and as his father fiddled with the tangle of chains, Enzo couldn't help but stare at the other door from his past. It was a little tarnished, but otherwise, it was unremarkable. A childhood imagination had embellished its features, but it was just a door. The tray slot was closed.

His father took him through a set of metal double doors, which led to another spacious, circular room. This part of the castle was unfamiliar to Vincenzo. The room was ringed with rolling stretchers and medical instruments. IVs were set up around the room, with some of them full of what was surely blood. Oddly, it seemed the room was prepped for an operation. Every instrument was clean, every station meticulously organized. Workers dressed in blue scrubs and aprons scrutinized every station. In the center of the room, was an ornate silver sarcophagus with gold accents on its edges. It was an oval shape, with rounded sculpting around the edges, formed in the shape of a man. A humanoid image distorted into a beautifully grotesque creature in what must've been artistic liberty adorned the top. The wide eyes were made of some kind of red metal, faded with dirt, but still blazing in the sarcophagus. The mouth was filled with sharp teeth that seemed to be made of some sort of crystal, crystal chipped and damaged after centuries of wear and decay. Pointed nails adorned the hands, and the body of the image was naked except for an ornate loincloth and gold bracelets and anklets.

"This is our secret treasure, my son. When

Italy invaded Egypt this year, our family retrieved something more valuable than mere baubles. The story I was told goes something like this. Centuries ago, a greedy man lived in a remote part of Northern Africa. He was a powerful man, a shrewd fighter, and a warrior. He controlled a vast territory that stretched throughout the Northern and Western parts of the continent. After one of his conquests, he was stricken by great hunger and thirst, but the village he found himself in had little food and drink. The people of that village revered the cow as sacred, such that the blood of a cow should only be spilt in an offering to their god. This man had every cow in the village killed and had the blood of those cows mixed with what small amount of liquor the village had. Drunk on wine and slaughter, he fell asleep. Taking this advantage as a sign of their God, the villagers bashed his skull in with a rock and killed him. But that was not the end of his suffering. No, he was stricken with a great curse."

Vincenzo, a young man of 21, could not

believe his father was telling him a scary story. He would've laughed if not for the grave look on his father's face. He listened attentively, and with each word, a lump of uncertainty hardened in his throat.

"This man's blood became fire, and he couldn't bear the light of the sun. He became a parasite and could only steal the life of others. They said he was two men high, with teeth like daggers and his skin had turned the color of chalk. He led a band of barbarians that would only attack in the night, following the light of his red eyes, eyes belonging to a man who could have only been a demon, who would bathe in the blood of his enemies, whose followers would dance in frenzies on the corpses of their victims as if bitten by the tarantula." Aldo picked up a large knife, scrutinizing it as he continued. "People would find their villages burnt to the ground, littered only with gore that was once their loved ones. The Egyptians combatted the beast. Gathering a party of their strongest men, equipped with some of the finest weapons at their disposal, they attacked this magnificent beast at dusk, before the sun had set fully and caught the barbarians by surprise. They burst into the camp and found the monster resting in this sarcophagus. Using holy herbs and garlic, they felled this great monster but found that although weakened, he would not die. So, packing this beast in the same coffin they found him in, these brave men weighed it down and dropped him into the Red Sea. They'd hoped that the salt of the sea would keep the beast dormant. That was then. This is now. I'm on the brink of unlocking the secret this coffin holds. I tried to experiment with servants, to give them the powers these legends promised." With that, he gestured to one scientist, who took this as his cue to speak.

"Our first subject was a boy named Raniero. He was sick and we, we were trying to help him. We thought leaving him in the room with the inert creature would get the desired result. With no food or water, eventually we'd hoped he'd ingest the blood of the creature. We'd set up our cameras and started recording the events as they occurred. Unfortunately, the boy tried to eat a rat, and instead the rat bit him. Raniero went over to the tables to get a bandage and his bloody hand touched the coffin. The blood woke the monster from its slumber and attacked Raniero. At that point, we lost time and some hope. We couldn't just test this on anyone, and we'd lost our first subject. In the meantime, we've subdued the beast with special UV lights. They're not like sunlight but they do a good job of stunning him. Considering our situation after moving Raniero to his cell, we received a blessing. At the next sunset, Raniero came back to life… changed. He was almost mindless, and bloodlust was the only thing that interested him. We've kept him around, weakened of course, just for further studying." Aldo kept a tight face while the man described what had happened to Raniero, and beneath his usual steely glint was something Vincenzo could not quite recognize. However, that was of minor concern compared to everything he'd just heard.

The same feeling that he'd had felt years ago looking through the food tray slot had resurfaced with a vengeance. His lips became dry, but he was with his father, so he could not show how shaken he was. Was that what was in that cell all those years ago?

My father sentenced this boy to death and for what? What did anyone gain from this? And now I have to be involved in this? I can't do this. I can't harm innocent people.

"Father, why are we doing all of this?"

"We've observed a marked increase in strength and ferocity, with no need for conventional sustenance. The only weakness we can detect is an intense aversion to sunlight. One of his fingers turned to ash from direct exposure to sunshine. His strength is superhuman, but because of his ferocity, we haven't been able to conduct measured tests. An army of these soldiers might be the key to our family becoming world leaders. The entire globe would recognize Italy as the great country it is. But the mixing of blood has not occurred. I believe that is the key to the true power housed within this magnificent monster. So we will show the mystic the prototype and convince him that Raniero is our monster. The blood of this one," he said with a flourish of the knife he was holding, "belongs to the Abbandonatos."

Vincenzo knew nothing about politics; he was a sheltered boy who spent most of his time with family members. He rarely left the castle, and what he knew of the outside world was limited to what he'd read in books and newspapers or seen on the television. You would not call him a hero, soldier, a scholar, a man of the world, a lover, or a villain. He wasn't sure what he was, but he knew that no matter what his father had done to him, family should protect one another. This had been instilled in him since childhood. He couldn't bring himself to argue the situation with his father.

"Whatever you say, Father. Thank you for making your intentions clear. I'm just trying to make sure I haven't misunderstood anything," Enzo said with his eyes glued to the floor. His father, fortunately, had misinterpreted his timid expression as one of awe and respect. In reality, it was more a look of shame and bewilderment. Enzo wasn't sure if what they were doing was wrong on several levels, but he knew the guilty feeling in his chest meant it probably was. His father was not a nice man; even through his rose-tinted glasses, Vincenzo knew it. Still, against his better judgment, and in keeping with the only thing he knew, he chose blood over justice.

Aldo beamed at his son. "Yes, my boy, it makes me happy and proud to see you becoming a man worthy of your name. Now, I think you can prove yourself. Here is what we'll do. I think this coming Wednesday will be a good time to show our little friend to the mystic. You will take him down here. He will observe little Raniero, then we can show him some footage of his capabilities. Don't worry, we have precautions in place in case something goes wrong. Hopefully, the fool will find Raniero satisfactory and then we can look into making the family as powerful as we know we can be. This is what I entrust you with, my boy. I know you will not disappoint me." With that, Aldo handed Enzo a simple two toothed key, patted him on the shoulder, and then whisked him back upstairs. Aldo wore a smile the likes of which Enzo had never seen, a fully satisfied and victorious look. Meanwhile, Vincenzo wore a mask of happiness that clung limply to the fractured face of his integrity.

CHAPTER FOURTEEN
Dungeon

Vincenzo had never dreaded something like he dreaded the day he'd faced the fruits of his father's labor. He thought about Raniero in that Godforsaken dungeon, with gnawing hunger and gnawing rats as his company. Down in the dungeon with the lifeless body of a monster, just trying to fill his belly until he became the prey. Vincenzo could see the creature's eyes fly open with blood in the atmosphere, wild and red, treating Raniero like a rag-doll and holding his limp, broken form in his arms. He shuddered at the thought. That grotesque face etched into the sarcophagus had wormed its image into his mind.

The mystic came around occasionally, making pleasantries and inspecting things with an air of unconvincing innocence. The Abbandonatos and their staff watched him with a similarly transparent vigilance. Vincenzo considered telling his mother about everything: the basement, the plans to get involved in the war effort, the ghastly task his father had issued him. Ever since he'd become a teenager, his father had taken an increased interest in his son's life. Although neither of them seemed to enjoy the time they spent together, Aldo seemed determined to mold his son. Vincenzo had less and less time with his mother, and their time spent together was brief and relatively superficial. His mother had sensed something amiss in her son, but could not unearth what was bothering him.

One night, she sent a servant to rouse him from his sleep. It was late, after 3 am, and she held his sleepy face in her hands. He felt almost uncomfortable, like he'd betrayed her by going along with his father's plan. She looked strange in the moonlight, with her anemic face dry from the night. "So it takes dangled cheese to rouse a mouse from his hole?"

"Mother, why are you speaking to me in riddles?" he said, rubbing his eye with the palm of his hand. There was irritation in his voice, and it wasn't just from his being awakened. It was the irritation of a child who had been caught red-handed.

She examined him carefully. "Son, a man uses his free will and makes his own choices. What people don't tell you is that being a man is a constant endeavor. It's never too late to make progress on that path. We must reap what we sow."

"Suddenly you're religious, Mother? "

"No, but I will preach to you if I have to."

Vincenzo didn't think the midnight sermon was necessary, and for the first time in his life, he openly contested his mother. "What is the point of this? Do you doubt me? Is this some kind of fit of jealousy because I'm spending more time with Father? He's not always the warmest person, but he's still my father and I love him! I can make my own choices."

"Vincenzo!" her voice sliced through his rant and echoed on the stone walls. "Son, do not let blood turn you into something you're not." She said with an eerie calmness. There was an urgency in her voice. She'd always lived in the world of fantasy, and recently the fevers had left her incoherent, sweating at night and hollering about black clothes. Nightmares weren't anything new; his mother had had them for as long as he could remember. He could recall her telling him the castle made them worse, and that she'd fall asleep with no warning and see things. Usually, he could tell when she was caught in the fog of her ailments, but when she uttered that sentence, she was perfectly lucid.

"You know, I thought I could always count on you to fight for me, but it seems I can't please anyone. No one has any faith in me. So, if that's the case, I'll make all of you believe in me." With that, he walked away and left his mother in the dark. His mother's last remark haunted Enzo just as much as did his undertaking. Two monkeys were on his back, weighing him down. He barely slept, alabaster teeth gnawing at the edges of his psyche. He laid awake at night thinking of who he was, Vincenzo or the soon to be Lord Abbandonato?

Was he a sheep in a wolf's dress? Did his blood make him a monster or a god? Or was it simply a name, a cobbling together of letters that would persist in people's minds only as long as fools and weaklings shout it in town squares? These were questions that had always hounded him and his situation gave them newfound strength.

He tried to keep busy. Bice sensed his melancholy and was always weaving around his legs. He rubbed her face and behind her ears. Her blue eyes seemed to pity him. "Aw, Bice, if only I had a life like yours. All that's expected of you is to follow your instincts. At least until you poop on the rug." The thought made him laugh, and the noise roused Vergil. The rusty dog started jumping on him; he was ready to go outside and play. Enzo always obliged; taking care of the dogs was something he could do at any time without reproach. Vergil and Bice were exclusively Enzo's, but all the dogs belonged to the family and Enzo took care of them regularly, taking them out for exercise, feeding them, and training them. They were hunting dogs, originally used for hunting bigger game, but birds were the usual fare nowadays. Today the servants were cleaning the cages, and most of the dogs were running around the grand lawn, a stretch of land of about 150 feet, roughly half of the castle grounds. Enzo was used to keeping track of the 23 dogs. They all responded dutifully to his orders, and the servants usually kept them out of any unattended brush. Vergil was impatient and nipped at his fingers playfully. Vincenzo threw Vergil's rubber ball as far as he could and watched it sail through the air. Vergil tore across the lawn so quickly he reached the ball before it landed. Bice ran a little behind Vergil, but never really went for the ball; she left that for her brother. Most days she got bored with playing catch fairly quickly and would sit at Enzo's side. But today something was different. After she decided she was done running, Bice started sniffing around the passage Enzo had used long ago. Ever since that day in the basement Enzo had called it "The Wolf's Mouth."

"V*ieni qui!* Stop! Get away from there," Enzo said. He rarely had to raise his voice at Bice, but she wouldn't listen to him. She'd completely disappeared into the bushes, which was saying something, considering her size. Enzo dropped the ball and ran over to Bice to make sure she was all right. She was whining, and he didn't know what to make of it. He knelt down, pushing aside the growth, and looking into the dark hole of The Wolf's Mouth, and found a dead dove.

"Bad dog! Why did you kill it?" Bice growled a little, which was unlike her. At a glance, the bird had been dead for some time, so there was no way Bice had killed it, but he was not about to look again to confirm that. The sight of the bird made him sick.

"Sad isn't it?"

Startled at the voice, Enzo turned to find Akila standing there. "I don't know how to feel about it."

"About the bird, or about you?"

"Why would I be thinking about me? I'm perfectly fine." He brushed the dirt off of his lap and tried to make himself seem busy with calming Bice.

"I know there's nothing but trouble in that basement. Your people took something from my home that should have been forgotten."

"I suppose you're here to convince me to stop this all somehow?"

"No. You all deserve what you get. I just want you to know. These dogs and these soldiers can't save you. You don't seem so bad. You should save yourself."

"How do you know I'm not bad?"

"If you were bad, you wouldn't be so conflicted. Like I said, save yourself."

"I can take care of myself, thank you very much."

"It's your choice, I suppose. Can I play with

your dog?"

Before he could answer, she was rubbing Bice around her neck. Vergil had wandered back, wondering what had interrupted his game. He let out a low growl, but when Akila patted her lap he came over and let her pet him too.

"Vergil doesn't like anyone. That's very unusual for him."

"Most people make the mistake of assuming that an animal wants to interact with them. Like the animal owes them something."

"Hmmmm. Can I ask you something? Something serious."

"Go ahead."

"Can we run away?"

Akila laughed, a pleasant, twinkling sound. "What? You can't run away from who you are?"

"Who are you to tell me what I can and can't do? I'm so sick of everyone thinking they know better than me. Everyone knows what's best for me except me! I can't stand it! I won't stand it!" Vergil and the guards reacted to Enzo's outburst, the dog's fur standing up and the guards inching forward.

"And what will you do about it?! You're throwing a tantrum, and who will act? The dogs? Those guards? You whine and cry and do nothing! And your only solution is running away!"

"How could you understand? My life is being decided for me!"

Akila looked at him with hard eyes. "You don't belong here and neither do I. We are the same, except I don't cry about it all day." There was pity in her eyes, but it was the disgust that hurt Vincenzo more. He had disappointed someone he'd just met; it was pathetic.

"Do you hate me?" he said, his lip trembling.

She bit her bottom lip for a moment and collected her thoughts. "I don't hate you. I couldn't hate someone who's done nothing to me and who I barely know. But when I look at you, I see a child, and that makes me sad."

The words stung, but they weren't wrong. Vincenzo fought back tears with gritted teeth.

She continued. "I don't mean to be rude, but you can't help anyone else if you can't make your own decisions. And if you make deals with devils, you have to live with that. There's the comfort of that castle or your soul."

"It's a lot easier to say that when you aren't in the situation," Vincenzo said defiantly.

"That's fair. I don't know what you're going through. But that isn't an excuse, and it doesn't justify what you're doing. We all have choices to make. It's not hard thinking for yourself. Try it."

"And what would you do in my shoes? What suggestions do you have?"

Akila gave him a hard look. "I don't have an answer for you. I don't have an answer for myself."

Vincenzo plopped down on the lawn next to her. "In that case, do me a favor?"

"And what would that favor be?"

"Be my witness right now; I don't have the

answer, but I promise I will figure it out."

Akila nodded gravely. "I will do the same. I hope you find it soon."

CHAPTER FIFTEEN
He Had Slept Little

He had slept little the night before, tossing and turning before falling into a deep and dreamless sleep. The next day, he woke up with the sun and looked out at the dark green land that had been in his family for generations, slowly being set aglow by the orange sunbeams. He watched the shadows dissolve, looked at the river glitter like the fuse on a firecracker, observed the birds' restlessness and hunger. He could feel the air begin to warm up, the dew evaporate, and in the peace of the morning he had time to think. No more fear. It was his turn to face the monster at twilight, like those heroes of Egypt he'd heard about. He would earn his name. He bathed and dressed himself meticulously in his nicest clothes. He sat in his father's meetings and contributed meaningfully. He tailored his whole schedule to fit his father's desire, attached to Aldo's hip like a conjoined twin. Aldo noticed the marked change in his son's behavior and was genuinely happy. He paraded around the castle with a smug air of victory, as if someone had created his son as a challenge. Finally, as the sun set, and the light greens and dark blues of the sky muddied to black, Vincenzo made his way to the west wing of the castle. He was aware of every step he took on the velvet covered steps leading up to the west tower. He stood outside the mystic's door for a minute, inhaling, then exhaling. Then he raised his hand to knock on the door, then lowered his hand again. Inhaled. Exhaled. Wiped his brow. Coughed a little. The door flew open.

"Ahhhhhh, the boy. How are you dear friend? Are we ready for our little show?" He said, smiling, showing his crooked dark teeth. He smelled of incense and wore his signature purple robe slung around his wire thin frame. He had strewn a number of knick knacks over the desk, an array of hats scattered over the bed, and had books piled high on an armchair. It was clear that he had made himself at home in his relatively short stay. Akila sat cross-legged on a mat, with a few measly possessions spread at the foot of it. The sight of how she was forced to live lit the fire of anger inside of Vincenzo.

"Yes, tonight is the night. We've prepared everything and now I will show you the prize jewel of my family." Enzo tried to adopt his father's confident and commanding tone, hoping the old man could pick up on it and that somehow it would impress him, despite his contempt for the old mystic. Meanwhile, the man's giddiness had overridden his false humility. He ushered Enzo on with an almost frightening urgency, dismissively mumbling something about returning to Akila. Vincenzo waved farewell to her over his shoulder, and then it was just the old man and him. He led the mystic through the labyrinthine halls of the castle, the winding staircases, all the while trying to engage the man in some feeble conversation.

"When did you decide to practice the mystic arts, sir?" Enzo asked.

"... Hm, did you say something, lad?"

"Um, it was nothing. I don't mean to pry."

"Then don't. Do what you mean to do."

Enzo let some time pass before he tried again. "So, sir, would you mind telling me about some of your travels or experiences? You must see a lot of interesting things as a mendicant."

"I have seen many wondrous things and I shall share none of the experiences with you. There are secrets that we cannot understand, boxes that were shut for a reason."

Enzo tried at the most basic level of interaction. "Uh, my name is Vincenzo. I'm sorry we've never been introduced."

"Are you sorry about that? What a thing to be sorry about. Nice to know."

"Yes... what can I call you sir?"

"You shouldn't call me. Names are powerful."

Enzo sighed deeply, relieved at having reached their destination. To call this man rude would be an understatement. He was unnerving, something about the way he carried himself, the little rock and lurch in his step, like a praying mantis before it strikes. He took out his key and unlocked the basement door, which took the strength of himself and the mystic to drag open. Following Aldo's instructions, they went down to the 17th cell. The mystic rushed in right as Enzo unlocked the door, but Enzo paused, looking around the main room. If this was to be the place where his old life ended, he'd take his sweet time. Once he stepped through that threshold, he would be a new man. Next to the cell, he spotted several long black lights.

Hmmm, there's really no reason to be afraid, but maybe taking one of these could benefit me. He grabbed a light off of the rack and studied it. It was about as long as his arm, and heavy because of the metal that housed the bulb. After steeling his nerves, he entered the cell, which was dimly lit by a naked bulb. He saw a human figure scribbling and scratching at the floor, and his mouth went dry for a moment until he realized the figure was just the mystic. The room seemed empty otherwise. The scratching was immediately annoying, a small sound magnified by the vacancy in the cell, and accented by irregular dripping. Wet stone walls surrounded them, a dampness that never went away or seemed to have a source. Because of this, the cell reflected the faint light of the bulb, and gave everything a dreamlike sheen. It wasn't very big, with only enough size to accommodate a trio and the dingy bed attached to the left wall by some rusty chains. There also seemed to be a chain or two on the wall he was facing, but the light didn't quite reach it. After briefly surveying the room, Enzo remembered why he was there. He registered the man's strange actions in his mind and decided he'd take charge of the situation.

"What are you doi... HLT," the rest of his sentence was cut off by the bony but surprisingly strong grip that had tightened across his windpipe. The mystic had risen up faster than the flash of a rifle and was choking the life out of Enzo.

"You should've just minded your business. You must've had the wonderful idea cross your mind that I might be acting for my own benefit here. Now, although you're a bumbling fool, you're also loyal, which means I have to kill you before I can make this beast mine." The mystic said in a menacing whisper. Enzo smiled defiantly and pointed at the camera in the lit corner of the room. The mystic laughed at him.

"Do you think I'm some sort of fool? I know your jackass of a father is watching us! What does it matter? He can't come down here to save you, and once I've finished my spell, I'll have full control of that creature. Anything left to tell me before you go to Hell?"

Enzo let the black light speak for him and smashed it over the mystic's face. The mystic let out a howl of pain; glass shards lodged themselves into his arm as he tried to block a second blow. Enzo sensed his advantage and let adrenaline take over, striking the old man over the head again. The man retreated to the far wall, blood streaming from his wounds. Enzo moved closer, afraid, but prepared to attack again, when he noticed extra sets of arms and legs. It confused him until he realized the mystic had crumpled onto another person. Blood covered both bodies, but they were hard to tell apart in the dark. The man was still groaning, the sound of pain slowly turning croaky and sharp. That harsh sound mixed with a cry of fear.

"Help me, boy, help me!"

The body's eyes opened, wicked red coals burning in the dark. Enzo could not make out any other feature on the body, but he could feel the shifting of air as the creature that was once a boy named Raniero grabbed the mystic in a bear hug and squeezed. His bones groaned. Enzo ran to the door as his screams grew louder and more desperate. The last words the mystic could form through his agony were "help me." Enzo only barely heard them through the slamming of the heavy cell door. He fumbled with the keys and finally managed to lock the cell door. The screams continued for what seemed like an eternity behind him, while Enzo ran to the basement's exit. The world seemed to move in slow motion. As he reached the door, he heard a loud crack, and the screams stopped. A faint gurgle echoed down the hallway, and then a tremendous sound, like that of a grenade exploding followed. The noise startled Enzo, and he slipped and fell on the wet stones. He turned over, going from lying on his belly to sitting up and clutching his right ankle. He looked down the hallway to see Raniero walking slowly towards him. In the cold light Raniero shuffled towards Enzo, with a dead, gray tint to his skin, blood covering the rotted scraps of clothing on his body and dead glassy eyes glinting with malice. As those eyes trained on Enzo's helpless body, the corners of that papery face pulled back, conveying twisted joy, even though the rest of the face remained stationary. Raniero's mouth was crowded with jagged fangs like that of a shark, fangs that dripped with the mystic's blood. Enzo tried to move away from that cruel perversion of humanity, painfully crawling like an insect that had been stepped on. Then he heard a horrid noise, like paper getting shredded. Enzo looked back to see Raniero laughing at him and then pouncing on him. He landed with his full strength on Enzo's good leg, cracking it open and busting the bone out of Enzo's thigh. More laughter mixed with Enzo's cries of pain. Enzo pleaded, looking at the cameras for help. Raniero responded by plunging his face into Enzo's midsection and biting down, ripping sinew away from Enzo's body with his fangs. Bolts of pain rippled through Enzo's body, paralyzing him. Enzo's vision started to blur with tears of pain. Raniero seemed to be deliberately avoiding his vital areas as he bent limbs at unnatural angles, laughing as he continued to tear into Enzo's body. Finally, Raniero got to his neck, and opened his jaws.

BANG.

The door to the basement complex flew open, and armed soldiers flooded in with Aldo Abbandonato at their head. A shot rang out and hit Raniero on the shoulder, blasting him back a few feet. The bullet left a smoking hole. Aldo and a pair of soldiers knelt down to tend to Enzo, while the other soldiers used black lights to corral Raniero into a cell and then opened fire. Aldo cradled his son in his arms.

"Son! SON! Listen to me. All you have to do is hold on. I will save you, don't worry." Then he barked at the soldiers. "Prepare the lab. We're going to have to conduct the experiment sooner than we expected. Don't worry Enzo, you will be the greatest Abbandanato in history."

CHAPTER SIXTEEN
Death's Kiss

What followed was a blur. Vincenzo remembered lights, an immense man with skin like a statue's, tubes and snakes, flames in the dark, Akila's face, the sound of blood pounding around the inside of his head, Death's kiss cruelly snatched from him. He woke up the next morning in the main room of the basement on the table that had previously held the sarcophagus. He was only wearing a hospital gown, but the metal of the table was not cold on his body. His head throbbed dully. As he held his face in his hands, and he realized how impossible that action should be for him. Raniero had broken both of Enzo's arms, exposed bones, torn out viscera, maimed and tortured. He looked at his body in astonishment; he was alive, more than that he was whole.

He scanned the room as the light stung his eyes. Aside from his father, who was slumped over in a chair across from the table, the room was empty. To his left, there was a sink with surgical instruments and IV tubes, all covered in gore. His shifting woke Aldo Abbandonato from his sleep. With large bags under his bloodshot eyes, he looked exhausted. His clothes were disheveled, and his hair unkempt. He woke with a start and his eyes flew to Enzo's position on the table.

"Excellent!!! You're awake. Thank God! We've been working all night. That spineless bastard got a real demonstration from Raniero. Not only did we have to destroy Raniero, but we also had to sacrifice the creature to save you."

"I could feel my bones snapping. I was bleeding to death. How am I here right now?"

"Don't be foolish, boy. I wouldn't allow you to die. We knew Raniero wasn't a vampire. He wasn't nearly as powerful as the being in the sarcophagus; he was little more than a hungry corpse. That's why we could kill him. The silver in the bullets and the UV lights were enough to put him down. After carefully researching ancient texts and old scrolls, we found our issue. If a true vampire like the one in that coffin kills a person by drinking their blood, they return at sundown as a monster like Raniero. According to an old tome I'd collected, the only way to become a true vampire is to mix one's blood with that of a vampire. So, as a last ditch effort, I drained the monster from the coffin and gave you as a transfusion. It was an arduous process; as weak as he was, that creature still resisted. But, after hours, we healed you using the blood. We've disposed of the creature by putting him in the sunlight, which is a universal way to destroy them. It's better this way. The only vampire left is loyal to the family. So, my son, how do you feel?"

Enzo's head swam. He had no way to process all the information his father had given him, and his throat felt like sandpaper. He opened his mouth to speak, and then retched, spewing a black, foul substance into the trash can placed beside his bed. Enzo's father waited patiently until he was done and then continued speaking.

"I think we should strengthen ourselves.

Who knows when that old fool's allies will come for us once they realize he's dead? I will collect you tonight. Rest my son." Then Aldo left the room. Enzo got off of the table and put on the fresh set of clothes that had been left for him. His legs quaked as he stood, and he'd barely managed putting on his pants before he collapsed. He looked around the room from the floor, staring at the domed ceiling as everything became dark again.

CHAPTER SEVENTEEN
Parched

Enzo woke up with his head swimming. His headache was gone, but he'd never felt parched like this in his entire life. Thirst scorched his throat, his tongue felt swollen and his breathing was labored. Still, his limbs had regained their full strength, and he got up, scanning the room. His eyes found a small sink a few feet away, and before he knew it, he was drinking from it. The water was cool, with the slightest hint of earth in its taste, and he drank for several minutes. After slaking his thirst, he tried the door of the chamber and found that it was open. He looked around the chamber, which had, much like him, seen better days. The heavy metal door that was once attached to Raniero's cell lay crumpled at the end of the hallway. Rubble and shell casings blanketed the floor, and his footsteps kicked up thick clouds of dust. Bloody scraps of cloth lay by the door and Enzo recognized them as the clothes he was wearing. He looked at the leather, the cotton, the pieces that had been stripped away from him. He crouched to pick a particularly soaked shred of cloth when he heard the unmistakable sound of a gun cocking. A soldier was pointing a large handgun at him. From his rusty colored hair, Enzo recognized the soldier to be Vittorio. The light right above him flickered slightly as Enzo spoke.

"Buona sera, Signore Vittorio. How are you? I've only just gotten up and about. I feel quite good. Strange how a brush with death can do that, eh?" Enzo said, smiling.

All the color in Vittorio's face drained as he looked at Enzo's grinning face. Enzo's smile flickered in confusion, but he had other things to worry about. He needed to see his mother, who he knew had been worried about him.

"Vittorio, please take me to my parents. Father is probably expecting me and Mother is probably losing her mind if she knows what's happened." Vittorio stood aside to let Enzo squeeze through the doorway and walked side by side with him through the winding staircase that led to the upper levels of the castle. The stairway was narrow enough that their shoulders brushed with every step; they looked ridiculous, with Enzo's slight frame right by Vittorio's broad torso. Enzo's throat burned again, and he wondered if maybe he was coming down with something. Vittorio never looked at him, keeping his head straight ahead and unwavering. He hesitated, and then spoke.

"I've always been a strong man, little Vincenzo. Always a soldier, I've been fighting since I was young. I've seen scary things, but whatever came out of that prison cell is the most horrifying thing I've ever seen. I don't know which shook me more: seeing you all torn up or gunning down that demon. It... It looked like a child Enzo." He spoke with tears in his eyes and stopped on the steps. "He was the same age as my daughter."

Before Enzo could say anything, more soldiers came to escort Enzo up the stairs to see his parents. Enzo thought about Vittorio's daughter as he made his way upstairs, oblivious to the looks he was getting from every observer. All the soldiers were sweating in the heat of the castle, which was sweltering to combat the cruel frost outside. Of course, the entire castle was in a hectic state. The story of a crazed cook, which was the least fantastical version of the events, carving the lord's son up, had spread like a plague.

The atmosphere had changed in more ways than that. The smells were more vivid, the colors sensual. Every sound penetrated Enzo's ears. He'd just noticed it at that moment - the sweet music of life that was always playing, the humming of circulation while heartbeats kept time. It was so intoxicating; his world was like getting drunk on some well-aged wine. Unfortunately, this new awareness only heightened his burning thirst. He was so distracted, he hadn't realized that he was outside of his mother's room. The door was slightly ajar, and he could hear the heated argument taking place inside.

"... Aldo, how can you expect me to tolerate

this?! This is unnatural! Or did you forget what happened before? You'd think there was no clearer reminder, and yet here we are!"

"Don't you dare Lia!"

"No, I think you dare, fool! What are you-"

"Lia, I had to save him. I couldn't let another son die. We are survivors, and they were both sickly. In both situations, I did all that I could to save them. You have to understand."

"I understand that your own pride has turned our son into something foul. I can feel him in the castle's belly, Aldo. Did you think I wouldn't find out what you were doing? That I would never notice? I may be unwell, but I'm not a fool. I will not let you twist our family, Aldo."

"Lia please. I've done the research and I know how this works. We could be invincible; we could fix you. Just wait until you see Vincenzo."

Enzo decided he should intervene. "I'm sorry to enter unannounced, but I'm here and feeling much better, Mother. Father has healed me!

Neither of us expected that old man to betray us, or attack me-"

"Will you be quiet!" Aldo snapped. "Do you want everyone in the castle to know what happened? If that man was willing to try to kill you, there may be more people like him."

Lia just stared at her son with a look of sorrow and pity. She spoke in a shaky voice. "My little boy. The only one I had left. I've lost both of them."

"Mother, I'm better than ever now! I walked all the way up the steps and I didn't even feel tired. Maybe we could make your body strong, just like mine. Your mind has always been strong, now you can have a body that is the same." He smiled at her, but she flinched.

"My poor boy, they've turned you into a monster." Shots rang out before she could continue. The soldiers stormed in from the narrow spiral staircase and flooded the chamber. Vittorio led the change, but he wasn't the one who fired the shot. A skinny soldier with blotchy patches on his cheeks gasped.

"Hold your fire, you dumb bastard!" Vittorio roared. "Don't shoot!"

Aldo rushed to his wife's side. The bullet had grazed her arm, but she was still on the floor. Every muscle in Enzo's body tensed, and in response, the soldiers raised their rifles.

"WHAT ARE YOU DOING?! What is the meaning of this?" Aldo snarled.

"Aldo, I've kept your dirty secrets. I've lied for you and killed for you. I've done my duty as a soldier and as a friend... but what I saw in that basement, what you did to that boy, I cannot tolerate. I can kill a man, a man can make his choices and can defend himself, but you turned Raniero into a beast! You denied him his peace, just because you couldn't admit defeat! Well, now you have to pay for your crimes."

"Vittorio, you don't know all the details of that situation. Put the damned gun down and I'll explain everything to you," Aldo said in a controlled voice. His eyes betrayed him, however, and panic played behind them like a movie. The soldiers' eyes were blank, though, as if made of stone.

Vittorio spoke again. "It's too late for any explanation. There are too many kids getting hurt, Vittorio. On all sides. Deranged magicians taking girls from where they belong, boys getting turned into monsters-"

Vittorio didn't get to finish his statement, because at that moment Enzo fell to the floor gasping. The sudden spasm spooked the soldiers surrounding them, and despite Vittorio's cries of protest, they followed their instincts. Every soldier in the room opened fire until their clips ran dry, spraying the walls and soaking the Abbandonatos with blood. Enzo's body was still, but Lia was barely hurt as her husband shielded her. He had absorbed most of the first round of firing. After the salvo, Vittorio hefted Aldo off of Lia, who began crying.

"Clean this up and burn the bodies. We don't know what other devilry that evil man has tried," Vittorio barked and put Lia over his shoulder. "It's all right Madam. We'll make sure you're safe."

"How could you?! How could you, you monster?! You killed my son. Oh God, you killed my son! Put me down. They didn't deserve to die. Enzo shouldn't have died..." Her sobs echoed through the castle hallways, bouncing off the walls. They seemed to go on forever, long after Vittorio had whisked her away from the chamber. Her sorrow was like a stormy sea, ebbing and flowing, swelling in its fury and then breaking but never ending. Vittorio carried her all the way to the infirmary three floors down, on the other side of the castle. The doctors there were in on the coup the soldiers had planned and were prepared for the worst. The head doctor Umberto had been around for the entire ordeal of little Raniero nearly 3 decades ago. After Enzo's operation, he decided he'd had enough and took part in the betrayal.

"Mio Dio! I was getting worried, it's been a while. You must be getting old, Vittorio."

"I must be, because you're getting less amusing every day, Umberto. Lia had no part in this; she can live, but poor Enzo had to go down. We've finished the job, dirty as it was. She only needs a few stitches, I think."

"Who's the doctor here? You or me? What if she needed some alcohol, too? Hell, I need some to deal with what I saw last night. All these monsters were so much more appealing in the stories we told around campfires. To be honest, I don't think a vampire can survive in Italy with all the garlic in our food."

"*Stai zitto*? I'm trying to think and remembering last night is not helpful to Umberto." Umberto examined Lia closely and found a gash where a bullet had grazed her. He sewed the wound, which was on her left thigh, while Vittorio chain-smoked. He inhaled deeply and watched the ash fall like the sleet outside because of his trembling hand. "You're really lucky you know, signora, all those bullets and barely a scratch. Some would say it's magic. I sure hope you have a better heart than your husband."

"What he was doing definitely wasn't magic, and you know damn well I had nothing to do with it, Vittorio. But what's wrong with you? Feeling guilty, perhaps? Maybe you can't quite justify murdering a boy you had a hand in raising? Or a man who, despite his faults, gave you a home and honor when you were a seedy mercenary? Is the betrayal shaking you?" Lia's eye burned into Vittorio from across the room as she threw her words at him like knives. Vittorio had done things he wasn't proud of in his life. Killing wasn't something he was ashamed of. This was different; Being around a grieving mother, seeing someone he'd loved like a brother and watched grow up get gunned down, watching defenseless people die. It shook him. It was like an icy hand squeezing his spine.

Hours passed until Vittorio decided he needed a distraction. He pulled out his radio so he could check on the other soldiers. The plan was that Aldo's personal army would join the war effort so as not to be arrested for his murder and the mission in Egypt. Lia would gain control of the Abbandonato's estate, which wouldn't be met with much resistance; Aldo was a mean bastard.

We should leave soon. Who knows what Lia might try? Why are they wasting time? I don't know if I can take another minute in this castle.

"This is Vittorio. There has been no communication in the past 3 hours. Report! What's going on? Over." He paused for a moment, waiting for a response. No answer. He tried three more times, to no avail. He was getting nervous. They were running out of time. The mystic's death might go unnoticed, but the end of the Abbandonato family would be a huge topic of discussion. His battalion needed to vanish as quickly as possible.

Finally, he decided he'd investigate.

"You all stay her*e*? I'm going to make sure everything is all right." Umberto must've sensed Vittorio's unease, because he nodded quietly. It was almost as if speaking would bring misfortune to them, like disturbing the silence in a graveyard. Lia stared at the floor, eyes glazed over. The doctor, his assistant Horatio, and one of the maintenance men named Luigi were playing cards, oblivious to the eerie cloud that had descended upon the castle. They didn't even bother looking up when Vittorio left the room and the sliding door was locked, dead bolted, and barred again.

Vittorio had noticed this, and it put him in another mood. Adrenaline raced through his veins as he made his way unsteadily up the steps. He wandered the stone spiral staircases that lead to the ground floor, checking rooms in the gloom. All the torches had gone out, which was incredibly strange to him. It was still warm in the castle, but there was only moonlight from the equally placed windows to illuminate his surroundings. The moon was out early tonight. The other strange thing was the lack of activity. If he hadn't known any better, this castle would appear to be deserted. Not only that, but he didn't see any evidence of a human's presence until he got to the second floor, which contained the living quarters of the family and Aldo's study. Everything was torn apart and searched, but almost aimlessly it seemed. It was too sloppy to have been his men. Even if it was them, they would've had some idea of what they wanted to find and the search would've been over. He knew the soldiers would come down through this area; it was the easiest way to slip out of the castle undetected. They'd stored supplies on the fourth floor and in the towers, and they'd be coming through this part of the second floor to get to the basement. The plan was simple. So the question remained: where in the devil were they? Had an opposing party been in the castle after the coup? Or was it a simpler explanation that his men deserted him? Occasionally he'd hear sounds, strange sounds, groaning and sucking, something like suffocating.

Slow down Vittorio. You're a soldier who's fought and killed. Your mind is playing tricks on you. Just find the rest of your men and get the Hell out of this godforsaken place. And where is that girl? We definitely have to take charge of her. She's witnessed everything that happened here.

Vittorio wasn't always the hardened man who ordered the execution of his mentors. His first kill was unforgettable, even traumatic to an extent. He'd cried about it for weeks. As a child, he'd been afraid of a clown doll that had belonged to his sister. He'd always imagined the doll growing, long and haunting, strands of scraggly red hair hanging over its sinister features, features that were familiar but inhuman, the eyes too small and close together, the nose pulling the entire face forward, the mouth too high and toothy. He'd imagine this image slithering across his floor, climbing the foot of his bed, creeping over the foot of his bed and dragging him by his toes to some dark and unknown place. Those nightmares ceased when he was 13. After killing for the first time, he would dream of his victim, a villager that was opposed to the Axis, coming back for him. Vittorio wasn't even trying to fight; the villager had ambushed him and his reflexes were better. The man was riddled with bullets, but Vittorio never forgot the look the villager gave him before he died. It was a sorrowful look. The man mouthed the word 'aiutami' before he died. It was a pity to watch a man realize he was about to die and see the fear in his eyes, the helplessness. He would see the vengeful spirit of that man in his dreams, with that same look in his eyes. The spirit would claw at his throat, would seek to do him harm, but achieve nothing more than chills and horror. After a few weeks, Vittorio had stopped being afraid. If that was all that death could do, then why should he be afraid? This man is just as helpless as the day he died, nothing but a dream in another person's head. That night, he'd decided he would always have a choice. He would never be helpless, pathetic, incapable of choosing his own fate. He wanted to feel like it was up to him. But in this moment, in the darkened and cursed walls of the castle, the clown doll, the dead villager, every moment of weakness in Vittorio's life hunted him with hunger in their bellies and bloodlust in their eyes. An emotion he hadn't truly felt in years had returned to him: fear. It had come back when he saw Raniero and ever since then, it was present in one form or another. Actually, he'd wondered if he was even human anymore, if the fighting had damaged him. Every shadow mocked him, every creak laughed at him, every chill prodded his skin.

A sharp crack penetrated the thick haze of fear covering Vittorio. Placing his faith in his rifle, he investigated. He looked just like how they'd taught him to in his military days, sweeping and leaving nothing uncovered, pivoting around doorways, maximizing his field of vision whilst minimizing his uncovered body. He shined his light through the darkness, hoping that dawn would come. Finally, the cracking became louder and more pronounced. It was coming from the entrance to the staircase on the fifth floor, a wide bolted door that was wide open. The landing was clear, but from just around the corner seemed to be the source of the sounds. He switched off his flashlight quickly. If there was someone or something dangerous around that corner, he was going to need the element of surprise. He looked out at the square of space, which was slightly illuminated, no doubt by the twilight. Vittorio controlled his breathing and tried to make himself calm again. He was exhausted, and he'd spent all the adrenaline that had fueled him for the last day and a half.

You can do this. Just focus. You're in control.

He let the rifle butt dig into his shoulder. Smelled the gunpowder, ready to fire. He felt ready. With all the strength he could muster, he turned the corner, rifle raised, and wits about him. He looked at the foot of the landing and saw Enzo standing there, soaked in blood. There were bullet holes in his clothes and a smile carved into his porcelain face. He was clutching a broken soldier by the uniform, and behind him, bodies were piled all the way up the staircase. Enzo threw the soldier at Vittorio like a javelin, much harder and faster than any human could throw such a heavy thing. Vittorio dove to the floor to avoid it, but he wasn't fast enough. The body crushed Vittorio's legs with a sickening thud. He tried to turn over and fire at Enzo, but he could only turn halfway and when he did, he saw Enzo was already upon him. Vittorio twisted the rifle onto himself, muzzle to chin. He would die of his own volition. Unfortunately for him, Enzo tore the rifle and one of Vittorio's hands away and tossed them both into the gloom. He grabbed Vittorio's shoulders in a vice-like grip and bit down on Vittorio's jugular vein. All Vittorio could wonder was whether he had that pathetic look of fear and powerlessness on his own face when he died.

He did.

CHAPTER EIGHTEEN

45 Minutes Later

It had been 45 minutes since Vittorio had gone to find the rest of their brigade, and Umberto was done waiting. He was a patient man for the most part, easily appeased and forgiving, but this applied to situations in which he was not an accomplice to murder. Doctors were in high demand and he had a family to look after. He told Horatio and Luigi to grab Lia so they could go. Lia didn't even protest.

"Listen you two, this is of the utmost importance. We have to make sure-" a knock at the infirmary door cut off the rest of Umberto's thought. The sharp rap, rap, rap spoke to them through the heavy iron. Umberto pulled his Beretta from the holster on his hip; he was by no means a fighter, but he also wasn't a coward. He motioned for silence amongst his comrades and moved to the door so his eye was level with the keyhole. He gulped and looked through it to find... nothing.

"Who...who's there?" He'd tried to bark the question with authority; it came out timid.

"It's me, it's me Akila," a female voice answered frantically. "Let me in, please. I don't know where he is."

"Don't let her in. Vampires can't come into someone's house unless you invite them!" Luigi hissed.

"Idiota! She's already in the castle. It doesn't work if she's already inside. She doesn't have to ask to get in every room!"

"Can you please let me in? He's killing everyone!"

Umberto tightened his grip on the gun, unlocked the sliding door, and opened it a crack. All he saw was a frightened-looking girl of about 17. She slipped through the space with little difficulty and suddenly there were 5 of them. Umberto spoke clearly and methodically. "We need to know where he was last. Did you see him?"

"I did, but only in the beginning. The shooting of Vincenzo and his father happened on the same floor where I was staying. I'm guessing you guys killed the old man too, because I was stuck in that room for at least a day."

Luigi piped up again. "Actually, that monster in the basement killed him."

Akila spat on the floor. "Good riddance. When I checked earlier, there was no guard outside of my room. I wandered outside to see what was going on and I saw all these soldiers firing into a room. I ran away, because why would I stay if people are firing guns?! But I heard them calling Vincenzo's name."

Umberto wiped his glasses on the front of his medical apron. "Vincenzo is, well was, supposed to be dead. We gave him a blood transfusion from a corpse. How were we to know what would happen? We didn't believe all of that nonsense."

Akila's response dripped with derision, "Oh, you didn't? The genius doctors didn't notice how noxious that creature in the sarcophagus' blood was? None of you saw that ghoul in the basement that you say killed two people? You all didn't believe in anything?"

The old men lowered their heads in embarrassment as Lia's scornful laughter echoed throughout the infirmary. Horatio, the eldest of the three, however, was not so humble as to endure any mockery, whether he deserved it or not.

"All this talk of monsters and devils is driving me mad! We are men of science! Do you really believe in all of his nonsense?" He gave his fellow doctor a look of reproach and pulled his own Beretta from his hip. "Cold steel. This is something to be afraid of! Not ghouls and goblins and creatures of myth that peasants whisper about to keep their kids in line. We are educated men."

"You're educated in the wrong things, doctor. I'm the only one that can help us get out of here. I'm the only one who can save you. Not science, not reason, and definitely not your fucking pea shooter." Akila's words shocked the room into silence.

Umberto looked dubious, but hopeful. "Can you actually help us? I fear all of our men are hiding out, or worse."

"If they aren't dead yet, they will be soon. And we will be too if we don't get out of here," she replied.

Luigi piped up again, "Can't we just wait here until sunrise? If what you say is true, then we can let the sun do its job."

Akila cocked an eyebrow. "You think he can't break in here? That door isn't even stronger than the cell doors in the basement. And we can't fight him. He survived all that gunfire without even feeding. By now, he'll be drunk off of the blood of your friends."

"But what if he leaves the castle? He might not stay to attack us?" Luigi's optimism was misplaced.

"Let's say he leaves the castle and goes to the village. He may very well slaughter the entire village. And then by the next sundown we will have a village full of ghouls, like Raniero. Does that sound appealing to you?"

Luigi shook his head like a scolded child.

"We need to get out of here, get to the village and destroy this place before sunset tomorrow. Otherwise, all your friends will be back and they won't be friendly anymore."

"Excuse me, but what makes you qualified to lead us?" Horatio sneered.

"My people kept the creature you idiots drained into Enzo sealed away for centuries. The only reason that godforsaken mystic brought me here was because I know all about the 'vampire' or whatever you all call it."

Umberto snapped his fingers softly, commanding attention. "She's right."

Luigi offered his opinion again, but this time it was relevant. "I have a few suggestions on how we should escape. I know this castle like the back of my hand."

"Do you have the blueprints?"

"No, I'll try to draw the castle; pass me that pencil, Lady Lia?" Luigi pulled a large sheet of paper from one of the doctor's notebooks and deftly sketched the castle from a top-down view. On the one side he drew the first floor, which showed from West to East the garage, the infirmary, the main and secondary halls, and the kitchen. He then flipped the sheet over and sketched the basement level, which was less complex. He then went back to the first sketch, drew a large X and pointed. "This is us. The infirmary doesn't have any direct routes to get to the outside, unfortunately. The logic was that there are secret passages, little levers and pulleys used to get back to the garage if really necessary, but injured people probably won't need too much movement, anyway. It wasn't like there was much need for a full medical set up around here anyway, so the infirmary doubles as a safe room. That's why it was fitted with reinforced doors. We could use the passages, but we would have to split up at some point as they would only accommodate three people maximum."

"I don't think we should split up." Umberto said in a small voice.

Everyone else in the room nodded in agreement.

Luigi continued, "I also think the passages are a bad idea, because they would funnel us like rats. The best way to go about this is to move through the basement. Then we can go through the front gate?"

Horatio scoffed. "The front gate is locked. And we never finished our card game."

"We have guns. We can figure it out. The main entrance is the closest." Luigi challenged.

Akila's eyes narrowed. "Your friends tried to figure it out with bigger guns and now they're playing cards in Hell."

Umberto winced and put his hands up in a placating way. He didn't know Luigi too well and wasn't sure how to gauge his temper, but the girl wasn't one to mince words. Lia had become apathetic to their situation, and Horatio was an ass. Umberto had to keep them together. "If the young lady says something, we go with it. The only thing I ask is that she sometimes softens the blow and gives us her good name."

"My name is Akila."

"Umberto." He pointed to himself. "This is Luigi. I'm sure you've seen the Lady of this house, Lia Abbandonato, and the malcontent is Horatio. I wish we could've met under better circumstances."

Akila nodded in acknowledgement. "Is there a way out through the kitchens, Luigi?"

"There are service doors and all of that. Mostly used for stocking and throwing out garbage. The kitchens are all the way on the opposite side of the castle, though. It's like, 2 and a half kilometers from here to there. The crew was also doing construction in that area."

"Yes, but the kitchens might give us some advantages. Vampires hunt using their sense of smell first and foremost. Any garlic in the kitchen might be enough to make the kitchens seem unpalatable."

"That's a big assumption," said Horacio.

"It's all we have," Akila said with a shrug. Just then, all the lights went out. A stifled yelp was heard on the right of the room. The shuffling of feet followed, and fear permeated the darkness. Then, total silence. Total stillness.

As if the tension had charged the walls of the infirmary, the lights came back on. Everything was exactly as it had been, except for a rough mechanical humming.

Umberto's eyes were still wide. "Where did that scream come from?" He scanned the room warily, looking from face to face to face, but seeing Horatio's face turn beet red let him know they weren't in any immediate danger.

"I scratched my arm on the table," Horatio said apologetically.

Luigi wiped the cold sweat off of his brow

as he spoke. "That noise is the backup generator. He cut the power."

"How long will we have power for?" Umberto asked.

"I'm not sure, but all the black lights and the equipment that might actually keep us safe need power to run."

"And our route?"

"We'll move down to the basement, move through that to the dungeons, come out into the corridors, and from there, it's a straight shot to the kitchen."

Umberto took a deep breath and exhaled slowly through his mouth. "And where might we meet him?"

"Well, the entire drainage system runs through and under where we'll be, so I can't tell. He could be anywhere. We would have to keep our eyes peeled. It's about a 20-minute walk, like 2,500 steps. I remember, I counted once when I was bored on while on security detail."

They had no other options. The only way to their freedom had been clearly outlined.

Lia spoke, startling everyone in the room. "Well, that settles it. We need to go now."

CHAPTER NINETEEN
These Were Not Normal Circumstances

Vincenzo Abbandonato was a gentle person. Under normal circumstances, he wouldn't hurt a fly. These were not normal circumstances. Cruel animal instinct fueled his movements. The need to feed drove his body to wicked machinations, the closing of vents, cutting power, and worse. It was his first feeding, after all. The new blood coursing through his veins had whipped his mind into a frenzy, which only worsened his mental state. From the moment he'd awakened from his brush with death, memories flashed and flicked across his vision. Deserts and warriors, and flaming villages weaved themselves into reality. Sometimes he was present in the castle, but he was fighting men of a far-flung time. Sometimes he looked down at his blood-soaked body and saw gold and jewels, vestments of a hellish religion of carnage. He moved silently, from the floor to the wall, sometimes on all fours, like the shadow of some unknown predator, sometimes upright. With the blood came understanding. The fear of the sun was felt, understood, not told. He slaughtered every soldier he came across, but he was learning which ones to drink. The acrid taste of disease swelled in the back of his throat after a while, from the bodies of men given over to vice. His nose would guide him to sweeter pastures, and all those who could not slake his thirst were thrashed for their insolence. In all senses, Enzo was the wolf now, perhaps even more so than his father could've ever hoped. He stalked the halls of the first floor, irritated. All those flashes of memory hurt his head. He tried to wave them away with his hand, like one would wave away a mosquito. He remembered he was holding the leg of some poor soul in his hand and looked down to find a man still attached to it. The man's hands grasped Enzo's clothes with desperation, clothes Enzo himself didn't remember putting on, robes with all kinds of jewelry. The man was shouting in a language that was unrecognizable. Enzo brought the man's broken form closer to his nose, ignoring the yelps of pain his rough action caused his captive. The man's blood was streaming out, but it smelled sour, like fumes. It wasn't fit to drink. He'd fed on dozens of soldiers by now, and his thirst remained unsatisfied. It was just maddening. The joy was gone from the act. He dashed the man against the wall in frustration. At least that had reduced his hollering to nothing but a wet gurgle.

Enzo needed more. The thirst was burning at him now, and he had to at least try to stop it. He sat down and stayed completely motionless, listening to the wind howl at the castle walls, to the crackle of fires in the hearths, cut through the sounds of agony he'd left on the second and third floors of the labyrinthine castle and the hum of the backup generators. And then he heard it. The dull scrape of heavy metal and the pitter patter of footsteps. It was faint, tantalizing, and their pulses were like the whispering of a lover to his hunger. His feet danced to the beat of their hearts.

CHAPTER TWENTY
Five hundred thirty-five

Five hundred thirty-five, five hundred thirty-six, five hundred thirty-seven.

They had only been walking for maybe 5 minutes. Akila knew not to put too much stock in that estimate of 2,500. It wasn't even like that number was actual feet. They were the half remembered log of a grown man's gait, and who knew what his pace was? All that said, Akila liked numbers. The counting did two things for her. For one, it reminded her that there was a goal, that there was an end in sight to this nightmare. And second, it took her mind off of the fact that each one of these steps could be her last. There wasn't much going on to take away from that realization, either. Luigi had taken the lead, as he was most familiar with the castle layout. Umberto was next, then Akila, then Lia, then Horatio. Horatio had said it was just in case Lia had any health problems, but everyone knew the truth; he was a coward. They couldn't blame him, they were just as fearful as he was. Even so, they trudged through the dimly lit corridor until they found their gate to hell.

One could see no affixed light on the threshold, and the door led to a staircase that could only accommodate one person at a time. This was their road to either salvation or damnation. They looked at each other and nodded; this was it.

One thousand-one, one thousand-two, one thousand-three.

The temperature dropped the moment they crossed over. They had all traversed similar passages in the castle made of the same granite, with the same contours and details. This passage felt like another world now. Slick with condensation, or perhaps their own perspiration as they brushed past, the walls sweated profusely. The chill brought their breaths out in ghastly clouds, and their footsteps sounded like the galloping of some multi legged beast.

One thousand seventy-five, one thousand seventy-six.

The steps ended. Akila kept looking back in

vain; it was too dark to see anything except the faces of her companions. The dark blurred their pale faces into ghostly figures, but everything came into focus in the basement. Flickering fluorescent light bathed the vast dungeon. It was circular and funneled into narrow lines of cells through a huge steel door. They stood still for a moment, letting their eyes adjust to the dim lighting and surveying the newfound space. It was just as dank in the basement, and the light made the stone glisten like a fresh wound. It was quiet as a grave, but that wouldn't last. The group could hear commotion beyond the cell blocks, somewhere deep in the innards of the great beast of the castle.

"Through here. We have to go through the cell blocks to get to the kitchens. It was a good way to keep prisoners fed," Luigi explained, urging the party forward. "We have to act fast. I think I hear him."

And into the corridor they went, one, two, three. Akila, Umberto, Lia.

Then the door slammed behind them.

"Luigi, what is the meaning behind this?" Umberto cried.

Luigi didn't look at any of them; he just bolted the door frantically.

"You should've come through the front gate."

Akila pressed her face against the small window set in the center of the door and hurled a barrage of insults at him.

"Don't blame him for picking better odds. We didn't sign up for any of this," Horatio said with a sick smile on his face. "You should thank us. Splitting up might actually increase our chances of survival. I hope to see you all outside. Let's get out of here Luigi."

"Luigi, please. You can't do this. You can't leave us, we're friends. We have a sick person among us," Umberto pleaded. He was a proud man of good stock, but now was not the time for pride. "Help them at least, take the girl and the Lady. You can't sacrifice them."

Luigi opened his mouth to respond, but a loud crash cut him off. It sounded close, right outside the cell block. Luigi muttered an apology and ran. All Umberto could do was stare after him.

"It's getting louder," Lia said almost absentmindedly. She wasn't lying. The ruckus coming from the cell blocks beyond their own was increasing in volume. Or perhaps, just maybe, it was getting closer.

Akila was fiddling with the door, but it was futile. That hulking slab of metal was meant to withstand much worse than a teenager's fists.

"We have to hide. There's nothing but terror on the other side of this block." Umberto said in a voice much too high to be his own.

Akila had no time to protest, as she could hear the scream of metal rending. She saw Umberto and Lia throw themselves into the cell opposite and pull the door shut between the two of them. She followed suit, leaping into her own cell, and pulling the door with all her might, but to her horror, the uneven floor of the cell kept the door halfway open. The noises were no longer far away; in fact, they were right outside the cell block now. Akila could actually see the dents forming on the door that separated their block from the next. It was the only thing between them and certain death. The steel was fighting a losing battle.

Umberto and Lia frantically motioned for Akila to hide through their cell's bean slot. Akila squeezed herself into the space between the door and the cell wall. The cell wall was as cold as the sweat running down her back.

The noise stopped.

Akila covered her mouth and closed her eyes. She could feel a presence standing in the doorway of her cell. The air felt heavy as she inhaled as quietly as she could. She opened her eyes to find a vicious profile inches away from her own face. The bean slot's few inches of space showed her Death in all its harsh splendor. The smell of carnage wafted out of the vampire's open mouth, which was stained with butchery. Worse still, beneath all the blood, beneath the dry, pale, cracked skin, beneath the predatory fangs, was Enzo. Even through the bean slot's narrow point of view, she could see someone who, despite everything, was a friend to her.

The vampire's face turned towards hers. Blood dribbled down his chin. In a voice like the creaking of a long shut coffin door, he spoke. "Now where did they go?" Chills ran down Akila's spine with every syllable. She shut her eyes again. She didn't want that devilish mouth to be the last thing she saw, but she couldn't bring herself to watch whatever happened to her.

"There you are."

Metal screamed like an animal being slaughtered, but the sound was gone almost as quickly as it had started. The vampire had entered. What felt like an eternity passed.

"Just kill me, please, don't make me wait."

Small, clammy hands grasped her shoulders, as if to answer her plea! Akila wasn't one to die without a fight. She threw a punch with all her strength and even though her eyes were still half closed; she connected with an anemic jawline that did not belong to any vampire.

"It's just me Akila, it's Lia!"

Akila's eyes flew open. "What? Where's the vampire?"

Lia rubbed her jaw ruefully. "I don't know where my son is now, and with the way you hit me, I almost wish he was here to defend my honor."

Umberto and Akila both laughed out of nervous energy and embarrassment, respectively.

"I'm sorry, I thought you were… you know," Akila said.

Umberto grimaced. "It appears our friend went that way," he said, pointing at the door they had entered and been subsequently locked out of by their former companions. The door had been folded like a futon and left hanging from its lower hinge in the doorway.

"Why didn't he kill us?" Akila wondered aloud.

"Maybe he didn't want to hurt us?"

"I don't understand this," said Akila in a faraway voice.

"What's troubling you?" Umberto asked.

"Why would Enzo stay in the castle? Why wouldn't he flee into the night? Vampires are usually at their most vulnerable after feeding. They expend so much energy hunting that once they feed, they need rest. Enzo has been feeding for hours now. He should be exhausted."

"Well, that's a good thing, no? It means the odds of our escape will be better? Right? Right?"

Akila just looked at him with uncertainty etched across her face like glyphs on a stone. The three of them clambered through the ruined door of the cell block into the next, which was identical to the block they'd just exited, down to the wreckage left by the vampire's entrance. The party passed through block after block, passing cells that blended into infinity. Akila had lost track of their steps. It had to be around two thousand. She couldn't even remember how long they'd been walking. She would guess that maybe they had five or ten minutes left. They heard what they prayed were mice scurrying in corners and behind doors, but other than that there were no signs of life. Eventually, the cell blocks reluctantly let out into a large pantry. The ceiling was low, to the point where a man of average height like Umberto could touch it without stretching too much. Creaky floorboards announced their arrival, groaning with every step. A steady drip drop resounded throughout the cellar, landing flat on the floorboards, but echoing off the stone walls. Stacks of dry goods and barrels of wine created a uniform maze with clearly defined paths for carting these items to the kitchen which, even in the dimness of the pantry, was visible through a small barred window in the door. This was the home stretch.

Akila went first, with Umberto following and Lia last. The kitchen was warm, the first warm room they'd encountered the entire night. A hanging rack was on the wall opposite the way they'd come in, showing off vegetables and roots used for spicing. Underneath that rack was a massive brick oven, and underneath that was a hearth. With no flame to give it life, the hearth gaped like the maw of some great, long dead animal. The room was divided into quarters lengthwise by two long rectangular kitchen islands, and another two counters attached to the walls. It was dim; the moon generously provided light through the wide windows. The shutters were wide open, but bars prevented an easy escape.

"There's a door in the corner, but do you know where it leads?"

Umberto shook his head. "I've only really been in the infirmary. I do my work and go home."

"I haven't been down here recently; my illness keeps me in my chambers these days," Lia replied grimly.

"Maybe we should cut these bars. It might be quicker than actually using the exit." Akila pulled on the bars hopefully; they didn't budge.

Lia snorted and spat blood on the floor. "We don't have anything to cut with. Plus, it'd take too long."

"Do you think one of us could fit?" It wasn't an unreasonable question; Akila or Lia were both petite, but the space inspired doubt.

"It isn't too hard. Give it a try." The voice was a chilling, sloshing, bloated sound like a drunken person in between sips. It wasn't loud. On the contrary it was like the whispering of the wind, and came from above them or perhaps, all around them. That one sentence drowned them in dread, but what dragged itself from a dark corner of the ceiling was worse.

In lurching movements, streaking blood down the wall, a tangle of limbs dragged itself down the wall. The mass was mangled into a broken, rail thin form, dyed crimson, and breathing in a haggard way. Bones cracked back into place to form legs and arms that could support a humanoid form, and the skin of the creature ballooned as blood rushed to each part of its body. In a few moments, the pulped mass had reconstituted itself into the shadow of their dear Vincenzo, wearing the ornate funerary robes of that devil from Egypt.

Lia drew a sharp breath, "L'amato figlio!"

A low growl was Enzo's only response. The air was charged. Enzo the vampire bared his fangs. It was now or never. Akila threw herself across the kitchen island in a scramble to get to the oven. From the corner of her eye, she saw Umberto halt the vampire's chase with a kitchen knife in his hand.

She knew what she had to do. As fast as her legs would take her, she skated twenty feet to the oven, and clambered up to the hanging rack. She tossed heaps of meat and vegetables to the floor, working as quickly as she possibly could. Her reward was a large clove of garlic. Placing the bulbs on the counter, she crushed them with her palms.

The scene she'd turned around to was dire. Umberto was using the kitchen knife to make space between the vampire and himself, swinging it in large arcs, but to no avail. Even in his sluggish state, Enzo was still much faster than Umberto's feeble resistance. With every slash dodged was a light blow, like a cat toying with prey. Umberto's face was red with exertion.

Akila had to act fast. Gathering the garlic in her hands, she crossed the counter and shouted at the top of her lungs. Enzo turned to her and for a second she was frozen. His cruel fangs were bared, bloodshot eyes burning in his skull, face scrunched into a snarl even the fiercest animal could not match. Thankfully, it was only a second. She launched the garlic directly into Enzo's face.

Enzo howled and lashed out blindly. In the splash of moonlight, our heroes could see boils erupt on his face. His eyes were cloudy, and drool and mucus were streaming down his face.

"We need to go!" Umberto urged. He had collected himself, but the adrenaline wouldn't last long. The three of them ran through the door in the corner, throwing it open and rushing down a set of shallow stairs. A moonbeam illuminated the staircase, and the newly finished wall it led to.

"What? Oh, no. No. No, no, no, no, no, no," Akila said as she slammed her fists against the wall until they turned red. It was solid all the way through. Then she remembered. "The construction." As soon as it dawned on her, something eclipsed the moonlight. She turned around to see the vampire blocking their light.

Enzo barreled down the steps with unnatural speed, but stopped at the landing. He shook his head wildly, with his chin tilted up in the air.

"We blinded him," Akila whispered. Enzo stopped moving at the faint sound of her voice. She flattened herself against the wall. She looked around the room. Umberto was low to the ground, wincing, but he seemed fine. Lia was wiping her nose. There were red spots on her wrist when she pulled it away.

Enzo struck faster than either of them could react.

"Run!" Lia shouted right before her son's jaws crushed her windpipe. Akila watched through the mirror of moonlight as Enzo's body changed. The skin on his face cleared, the cloudiness in his eyes lifted, and the tension left his body. Lia went limp in her son's grip without a word. Akila watched as minutes passed. Enzo's head drew away from his victim's neck, but other than that, he was motionless.

"Akila, don't," Umberto said breathlessly as she inched towards the vampire.

"I think he's done. If he wanted to kill us now, he could. I think he's done." Akila put her hand gently on Enzo's shoulder, which was trembling. He looked up at her with tears of blood streaming down his face.

"She's gone," was all he could say.

CHAPTER TWENTY-ONE
A Murky Jumble

What followed was a murky jumble, possibly because of the quality and quantity of the blood he'd ingested. Enzo remembered Akila and that doctor coming back in the daylight with the entire village in tow. They'd wrapped him in cloth and put him in the same sarcophagus that once held the ancient vampire. The same vestments he'd seen in the operating room: the charms, the symbols, the pageantry, were all being used on him under Akila's direction. Now he was the evil of a far-flung era. After that process, they'd weighed the sarcophagus down and thrown him in the river that slashed through the castle grounds. They used explosives to demolish the castle careful so as not to block the flow of the river, and burned everything inside. They left no stone unturned. Sunlight would reach every cranny of that estate. It was a matter of life and death.

He remembered smelling the smoke. He didn't resist. In all actuality, he wanted them to kill him, but maybe he'd made enough of an impression on them for pity to stay their hands. He didn't deserve his father's meddling. Vincenzo Abbandonato had been a gentle boy. Unfortunately for the world, Vincenzo Abbandonato was now dead.

He remembered the sound of the river washing over his prison, day and night, his dreams swirling like the eddies of the river that kept him from the rest of the world. Scenes of the creature that used to sleep in that same coffin would play in his mind's eye, and sometimes there were memories of a soldier, and other times he would see himself and his mother. These were the fragments of the lives of others jaggedly piecing themselves into his consciousness every time the sun came up, and when night fell he was dimly aware of his own loneliness. Decades flew by in this way.

Now in the attic of some derelict building halfway across the world, a lifetime later, Vincenzo Abbandonato's eyes flew open. Bice had curled up next to him at some time during the day. If he looked closely, he could see her veins spiderweb over her body, crisscrossing, carrying his own cursed blood through her body. Vergil entered the room silently. It was almost nightfall. His time for dreaming was over. He could live the lives of others no longer. He clenched his fists so hard he drew stigmata on his palms. It was time to finish what he started. It was time to hunt.

Blood Feud

CHAPTER TWENTY-TWO
The Saturday of Portion Control

The reflections of neon signs shone in the large puddles forming on Malcolm X Boulevard. It was a rainy Saturday night in Harlem, just cold enough to be annoying, and just warm enough that you wouldn't want to wear a bubble coat. Jahari Jones trudged along, fresh off a flight from Mexico City, pushing along his bags and trying not to drop any luggage. He crossed the street. He had the right of way, but a taxi sped up to catch the light, an impossible task. Jahari didn't speed up. He just frowned and crossed the street as the taxi sprayed him with water. The driver rolled down his window and barked a common New York term of affection, "asshole!" and sped off.

"Takes one to know one!" He yelled after the car. He sighed; the night was getting worse with every second, and the rain was following suit. Struggling with all of his bags and cursing under his breath, Jahari passed Marcus Garvey Park, which was his North Star. If the park was nearby, then so was home. Squat, square, apartment buildings loomed over him like broad chested guards, and the gargoyles that sat on the older ones jeered at him. "Only a real jackass would be out in weather like this," they seemed to say in their frozen grins and grimaces. Skeletons of buildings, long since abandoned by the living, stood like headstones, marking Jahari's path. One side boasted the life of the park, the greenery, even the homeless trying to find easy shelter. On the other side of him stood the carcasses of development, and those who never made it out in their lifetime. Sometimes he would see them in the windows. They sent a chill up his spine.

Cold moonlight filtered through the thick smoke that blanketed the city, and its shine made the fetishes in the windows of the neighborhood visible. It was all right below the surface, everywhere in the world, not just in Harlem. Jahari knew all it took was one step to be in a world much darker than most could imagine. After what seemed like forever, Jahari arrived at the weathered 5 story apartment building he lived in. As he stepped into the lobby, the radiators blanketed him with warmth. The building gave him that sense of peace that could only come from familiar territory. What it didn't give him, however, was an elevator, and he had to lug his belongings up five flights of stairs before he could finally rest. He unlocked the door, going through an elaborate sequence of steps to disarm the traps that allowed him a safe entrance to his apartment. With that done, he plopped his luggage on the long coffee-colored sofa he'd fallen in love with.

The organization hadn't set him up in the Ritz Carlton, but as one of their star agents, he had more than most. He sighed heavily and looked around the safe space that he'd been away from for what seemed like an eternity.

It's gonna be a while before I take another case abroad, he thought as he stretched. His home was in its usual state of organized chaos; tomes, old scrolls, and comic books were organized in messy piles on a two tiered workbench facing the north wall of the apartment. The workbench was next to one of the expansive windows he'd installed, but there was a large lamp that sat on the desk for when it was dark outside. The bench was littered with small artifacts he was learning to use, trinkets he was sending to BRAHMASTRA for containment or destruction, and other objects he was researching and studying.

The powder blue walls were bare aside from the bookcases that rested on them. He hated mirrors; the only one was in the bathroom upstairs. He looked at his luggage for almost a minute and then decided that unpacking was beyond his capabilities at the moment. After procrastinating awhile, he got into his pajamas, warm flannel pants and an undershirt, and went into the bathroom. It was time. If only it got easier. Jahari stood just outside the mirror's plane of reflection, fear welling up in him for a moment like tears in the eyes of someone who's lost a relative. He'd seen things in mirrors, horrible things, and he wasn't a fan. But tonight when he finally looked he was alone in the mirror. He took the time to study himself. Standing at 6'2, he had a wiry build, and large, brown eyes that were so dark they were almost black. His skin was the color of raw umber. The pitiful amount of peach fuzz on his face reinforced its boyishness. There was almost a shadow above and under his full lips, and he thought to himself that he should shave. He ran his fingers through his curly hair and stared at himself, searching for something, anything, new. He had to do this after these long trips. You never knew what you might bring back with you. Bone tired, he got into bed hoping the exhaustion might keep the dream away. It didn't.

CHAPTER TWENTY-THREE
The Memory

It always started the same way. He saw it in a third person view; it was the only time he remembered seeing his parents. His only memory of what they looked like was in a dream. It was kind of pathetic, considering the circumstances. They were holding a newborn version of himself, chanting in an enormous courtyard somewhere unidentifiable. Uncle Dominique had always said Jahari was identical to his father, and other than a certain heaviness under his father's eyes, Jahari could confirm that. His mother had pretty features, sharp and authoritative. Her demeanor was calmer and steadier than his father's. Where she was stone faced and motionless, his eyes scurried about, from her to the rest of the yard, to the huge fire that raged in the center, to his fellow heretics. The fire pit was about 10 feet deep and the same width. Figures surrounded the pit, chanting with babies in their arms, draped in bright red cloaks, yellow eyes blazing on the hoods. Jahari couldn't hear what they were chanting, but he could see them throwing their babies into the fire. One by one, these people raised screaming infants above their heads and fed them to the inferno, which would flash different colors as the flesh hit the flames. He used to look away, to shield his eyes at this part, but he'd been having this dream for years. It was almost like an old horror movie now; it was still terrible, but he was no longer afraid of it. His mother and father never stopped chanting, but they seemed to have a conversation with their eyes. Jahari's mother restrained his father; as if being too hasty would ruin something huge. His father seemed pressured. Eventually, his parents took their turn. He wasn't sure what incantation they were attempting, but there were symbols that appeared all over. The pressure built to where he could feel it in the air. He could feel the energy heavy on his skin like thick smog. Right as the energy reached its apex, there was an explosion, and the dream would end right as he got thrown into the fire.

CHAPTER TWENTY-FOUR
Feelings of Fear and Anger

Jahari woke up with a jolt. It was that horrible feeling that had become so familiar to him; the hair on the back of his neck stood on end, and he could sense something in the air, a stinging energy, like a static shock. He looked over at the closet, and he knew that was the source of what he was feeling. There was an intense feeling of fear and anger.

"Who's there? Show yourself!!" It sounded stupid, but there's a reason people are always yelling at the ghost in the movies. Jahari had dealt with other beings before, and he knew confidence and focus could save his life. The closet door opened slightly, as if responding to him. Small ruby points glowed from around the corner of the door. Jahari knew what he was dealing with. He tried to relax a little and reached out with his mind. He exerted his will on the closet and placed pressure on the specific area where he saw the eyes. The closet pushed back, creating a tug of war, Jahari's own determination crashing against a swell of desperation. The two currents washed over one another, roiling until Jahari made his move. He switched on all the lights in his bedroom with his mind and pushed the being with all of his power in one deft motion. He could feel the force retreat into the closet as soon as the light came on. Just as Jahari started to release his hold on the closet, the creature struck. It was small, about 3 feet tall, and covered in an old shredded sheet, with only sharp teeth and fangs visible. Using his psychokinesis, Jahari threw the sheet off of the creature. It writhed in pain as its leathery skin smoked slightly in the lamp's light. Jahari stared at it with determination. It was a horrible sight. It clawed the air, trying to scrape and scratch deep in his skull and nest in his fear and pain. Jahari rotated its gnarled head until it was looking directly at him. Despite the horror that grew in his chest, he did not stop looking at the creature. It stopped thrashing and grew still until its aura of negativity subsided. All its deformed skin seemed to disappear until all that was left was a little boy no older than nine. Jahari understood him. They both knew what it was like to be feared, to repulse people, to be out of place. The boy disappeared, but his eyes still said, 'thank you.' It took Jahari an hour to get back to sleep.

CHAPTER TWENTY-FIVE
New Case

Jahari's alarm went off at 10:00 am the next morning, much to his chagrin. Even though it was late in the morning, his jet lag along with his little visitor last night had ruined his sleep. His phone buzzed with a reminder: Aisha Visit, New Case. He groaned. It had already been a long week; now his Sunday was about to be hijacked. He had about half an hour before Aisha came. He needed to be at least somewhat coherent by the time she arrived. Jahari thought about last night as he got up and brushed his teeth. That thing was definitely a cucuy. He'd just been in Mexico helping a friend shut down a group of mystics hellbent on sending the Yucatán Peninsula to another plane of existence. The cucuy must've latched onto him while he was there. He'd memorized some notes on them from a while back and recalled them: Cucuy are children who die from abuse and neglect and, because of their grief and anger, turn into something… else. They're still afraid, so they hide in the same places they'd escape to in life: closets,

under beds, in attics and basements. They realize
people are afraid of them, so they wrap themselves
in scraps of cloth and hide in the dark. Their
presence involuntarily causes terror, but if you
truly acknowledge them, you can help them. Jahari
had heard it was easier in the light, and he'd
followed the protocol, but he remembered thinking
it might've only been easier for him.

The sacrifice had changed Jahari. He could
move things with his mind, he could see spirits and
all manner of beings from darker planes, his
memory was nearly photographic, and astral
projection was extremely easy for him. Most
people could feel the difference in him. He thought
about the poor cucuy and wondered if it'd reached
a better place. There was a small part of Jahari that
envied its freedom, even in without the knowledge
of the situation it had moved on to.

He never quite understood the purpose of
the sacrifice his parents had taken part in. He'd
investigated it with his Uncle Dominique, but the

ritual itself was unprecedented. Apparently, after they'd completed the sacrifice, BRAHMASTRA agents had raided the sacrificial altar and found Jahari as the only survivor.

Despite the constant warmth of his apartment, Jahari showered, shaved, and put on a thick hoodie and some sweatpants. Thinking he might go out later in the day, he put on his silver chains. He had three of them, which he put on with care. All were for his protection, and ended in charms, a Nrsimha Kavacha, a scarab of onyx, and the palm fronds of Ayizan.

He went to the kitchen, poured himself some cereal, and mentally prepared for the tedium of finishing the paperwork for the Mexico case. He stared at the folder for several seconds, opened it, closed it, opened it again, and then got his laptop. It powered on, displaying his last open page, something about bush masks and a Sekhmet cult in another tab. He spent 15 minutes putting together a playlist, 5 minutes answering an email, and lastly another 5 minutes changing the playlist. Right when he'd finally gotten around to doing some work, his doorbell rang. Aisha was right on time, of course. Jahari lazily strolled over to the door, disarmed the traps, and let in his cousin and the familiar scent of rosewater.

It'd been two weeks since he'd seen Aisha, who was more like a sister than a cousin to him. She wasn't particularly tall or imposing, about 5'5 with a slight build, but she carried herself with a much larger and more dignified air. They didn't look much alike; his face was more angular and hers more round, her eyes were a lighter brown, and she looked more like her mother's side of the family. Her hair was in fulani braids, which was new, but other than that, she looked about the same as always. She wore a long black peacoat, and knee-high boots over her jeans. She had a messenger bag on her shoulder, no doubt containing the details of his next case. Dominique had raised them both in the world of

BRAHMASTRA, but they'd taken different paths when it came to what they did in that world. Jahari was an advisor, a field expert, and a last resort. He was no stranger to combating some of the darker things that dwelled in our world. Aisha was more involved with the more mundane organizations in the earthly realm. Interpol had a division that worked closely with BRAHMASTRA and investigated paranormal cases, and she was one of the liaisons in North America.

"Hey Ja, pay attention!"

"I was paying attention. Thank you very much!" Jahari lied as he pulled her in for a hug. She was a head shorter than him, but she resisted with surprising strength. They'd probably already exchanged pleasantries, but he didn't remember them.

"What was I saying then?" Her lips pursed and her eyes narrowed with disbelief. She started chewing the inside of her cheek, and the whole thing completed the classic "irritated Aisha" look.

"You were saying how I looked like Hell, but it was good to see me," Jahari answered with a smug confidence, even though it was a wild guess. Her eyes narrowed even more to where they were nothing but slits.

"Mmm... lucky guess. How are you? You didn't call or anything after you left, and Dad's been in Japan. Y'all are so annoying. He's just as bad at keeping in touch as you are."

Jahari let out a guilty laugh. "I meant to reach out. It was chaos over there. I was with Mike, and things got hectic. The mission wasn't exactly straightforward, and there were decisions we both had to make with little time to think about it. He... didn't make it." Jahari didn't need to elaborate. She got the point.

"How're you taking it?"

"Huh?"

"I said, 'how are you taking it?'" Aisha had that look she gave sometimes, the look of concern sprinkled with bits of pity. He hated that look. Part of it was the fact that he knew she really cared, but the pity was irritating. It wasn't intentional, but it was a look he saw a lot. He went to the refrigerator and poured himself some orange juice, then gestured to the appliance with the bottle.

"I'll have some water, and not the tap water. I'm not a peasant." She said it to make him laugh. It didn't work.

"It feels like it was my fault."

Aisha opened her arms as if to give him a hug. "But why would it be your fault?" Instead of responding to the embrace, he turned away.

"It's just like, how am I this powerful but also this helpless?"

Aisha put both her hands on Jahari's shoulders. "Aw, Ja, you're only human. It isn't your fault. You can't expect to save everyone from everything."

"If I can't save everyone, then what's the point? I'm in all this pain and I can't even justify it. There's no blessing with the curse." Jahari said, balling his fists. All the books on the shelves rattled. He closed his eyes and took a deep breath. "I'm good, really. It's just that none of this shit is getting any easier."

"It will get easier, though! And it has! You've got much more control compared to when you were younger, right?" A noncommittal grunt was Jahari's only response. Aisha decided not to press further. "Did you speak to Dad?"

"Nah, I didn't even realize he'd left; I was in Mexico. He sent me a letter when I was at the outpost telling me something about sacrifices. An actual letter like he was the 1800s; he's buggin'."

Aisha's eyes widened. "Sacrifices, like in your dream?"

Jahari's face darkened. "Seems like it. He said something about someone coming to meet me with information. You know how Pops gets. Mad cryptic for no reason." There was a pregnant pause, Jahari trying not to think of the last few weeks, and Aisha trying to figure out what to say next.

"Hmm, well listen," she said as she pulled out a manila envelope from the messenger bag on her shoulder, "this case should be light, but Dad told me to put you on it because it might have something to do with your sacrifices. There's been a pretty messy murder on Long Island. They drained the victim of her blood. Her husband might've had a psychotic break. He says he saw the Devil, dressed in all black, and that this devil killed his wife and drank her blood. Now usually we wouldn't call in the paranormals; he sounds crazy as hell. However, we found traces of salt and grave dirt on the floor by the victim and witnesses can confirm that the husband had been out of the house for most of the weekend. It all seems a little strange. Think you're up for it?"

Jahari scratched his head and sighed.

CHAPTER TWENTY-SIX
The Crime Scene

Aisha dropped him off at the crime scene, which was still active. Jahari got out of the car into the warm fall sunlight, wearing a heavy purple windbreaker more suited for the winter than the current weather. He squinted up at the chunky seafoam green colonial house, which only partially eclipsed the late morning sun. Uniformed men and women swarmed the place like ants on a picnic blanket, controlling the small crowd that had formed. He passed through, showing the agents his clearance, and entered the home. There was a small foyer, with an open kitchen on the left and the living room on the right. The bloodstained hallway was straight ahead. There was a chalk outline of a woman's body in the center of the hallway.

"Can't even be normal on the Lord's day, eh?" It was Mario, Aisha's partner. He was a swarthy Mexican man, middle-aged, with a patchy beard covering his chubby face. He was scratching his goateed chin, which Jahari had noticed was a nervous tick. On the back of his right hand was a white scar about an inch long. Mario always told the story of how he got that scar and exaggerated it into something impressive, but Jahari was there when it happened. To most women, he'd gotten it while bravely slaying a monster in the tundra; in reality, he had tripped and fell on a tree branch while they were searching for a Skudakumooch. "You look like something the cat dragged in, ate and then shitted out."

"Thanks man, you like my shoes?"

Mario made a perfunctory glance at Jahari's feet. "I guess. They're the same boots you usually wear. Why'd you ask?"

"Cuz I'm gonna break my foot off in your ass. Now, why the hell did you guys call me in today? This doesn't really seem like it would warrant me being here. This is a job for Donovan."

Mario grinned evilly and winked. "Normally I'd use any excuse not ta talk ta you, but we're having a hard time figuring out the 'why' here. Also, we found this in an open drawer in the bedroom. We think she might've been trying ta get ta it before our vampire entered through there." He said, gesturing to the broken window that was barely visible from their vantage point. It was far too small for any adult sized person to get through. Mario held in his hand a silver amulet attached to a chain, with a charm about the length of a thumb and the width of a quarter. The charm was of a silver eye turned vertical, with an iris painted violet. Although the color was different, it was an unmistakable symbol. The same design was on those heretics' cloaks, the same eye he'd seen on and off in his dreams for 23 years. "As soon as we found it, Aisha and Dominique told me ta get you on the case. Dunno what's inside. I don't enjoy messing with this monster shit. My wife's Roman Catholic and this is your job, anyway."

"Thanks Mario. This actually helps a lot. We gotta be careful with the vampire talk too. A lot of different beings could be behind this blood drinking thing."

"Whatever you say. Does this amulet mean anything ta you, though? I'm not going ta interfere with your process. Just let me know what the deal is once you unravel stuff, Okay?"

"Of course. I'm just gonna look around some more. See if I can find anything else."

Mario frowned, but he didn't push further; Jahari obviously wasn't going to answer the question. "Hey, in a half an hour we're going ta speak ta the husband. We took his initial statement, but with all this talk of ghosts and devils, it might be more helpful for you ta do your thing with him."

"Cool. I won't be long." Jahari turned away and tried not to let Mario see the excitement on his face. He'd been searching for information on the cult his parents had joined for years now. The eye was their insignia, and after all this time searching, it wasn't a coincidence that Dominique had put Jahari on the case. It was showtime. Jahari swept the house briefly, but found nothing else of note. He returned to Mario, who was arguing with a man on the front lawn.

"Look, this is an active crime scene. We're not going ta answer your questions. Please keep it moving, sir." Mario looked like he was just about done dealing with the man. The man didn't look suspicious or even noteworthy, although his cap concealed a fair bit of his face. He had light brown hair, with tinges of red, and wore a tracksuit, like he'd been jogging.

"I just want to make sure everything is safe in the neighborhood. That's all, that's…that's all." The man looked shaken, and he kept sniffling as he spoke.

"It will be. That's our job," Mario said, shooing the man away, but the man didn't quite get it.

"Do you guys have any suspects or anything? Can't you tell us anything?"

"No comment, bucko. Now I'm not going ta tell you again. Get out of here."

"Who the hell was that?" Jahari asked as the

man walked off, out of earshot.

"Apparently, he's the neighborhood watch. He was asking about a dog that had gone missing. Big mixed breed dog, he said. Then he decided ta get nosy, and that's where I pulled the plug. He was strange, that's for sure."

"Hmm, yeah, well, that's New York, right?" They made their way to an all black car and waited as Mario leisurely found his keys. "How's the victim's husband doing?" Jahari asked as he climbed in and closed the AC vent on his side.

"Well, he's doing better than most of the bystanders we've seen. He's not like Frank Shelley."

"Frank Shelley's mind was destroyed because he tried to make contact with another realm of existence in his basement. Also, he wasn't a bystander, he was trying to kill his dentist for sleeping with his wife." Jahari replied.

"So definitely better, right? Cameron Toker is pretty coherent depending on what you believe in. He called the police after he found his wife and didn't move until they got there. They found him in shock, with her in his arms. Poor bastard. He's already told us he'd seen the... murderer for lack of a better word, twice between the attack on his wife. Something about a sewer and a mirror. Here, we have his statement and his accounts of seeing the creature. There are photos in there. Let me know if you need to see the body in person, because if not, we have to destroy it. Once he started spouting that stuff and we ruled out drugs, we got your sister on the phone."

Jahari carefully read Cameron Toker's accounts, making notes with a blue ink pen and post-it notes from his coat pocket. After about 10 minutes, he knew enough. "Well Mario, at least we know your hunch was right. This is probably a vampire."

"That'll be five dollars, please and thank you."

"C'mon, that was the obvious choice. It

could've been a chupacabra, or a jiang-shi, but you don't know about those, do you?"

"All I know is that I was right, as usual."

Jahari made a big deal out of patting Mario on the back and continued, "There's something bothering me about this entire story, though."

"Yeah? And what's that?"

"Freshly awoken vampires aren't really the stalking type. Being untraceable is a vampire's style. Stalking this guy for days without killing him and then killing his wife? That's odd." Jahari trailed off and fidgeted with the radio dials. Mario had gone off on some tangent that was more distracting than helpful. Jahari's mind was elsewhere. He thought about the house and what he felt there. Death had a certain… energy. It was like the tingle after you get shocked by static, sparks of energy that linger in the air, in the bloodstains on the carpet. It was never pleasant. Jahari didn't even need Mario to bring him to where Cameron Toker was being held. He followed the energy, feeling the tingle intensify as he got closer. He tracked it down the stairs of the building and straight to the interrogation room; Mario would deal with all the agents, who were puzzled by his sudden appearance. Jahari entered the gloomy room as gingerly as possible, but his entrance still startled Cameron. Jahari saw a thin and ragged man with a drawn face and swollen, red, glassy eyes. The light overhead cast deep shadows over his face. When he saw he had company, he quickly tried to smooth out his ruined and bloodstained clothes. He was a piteous sight.

"Hello Mr. Toker," Jahari said as he shook Cameron Toker's clammy hand. "I realize you've been through a lot-"

"You must believe me! I loved my wife more than anything! I know it sounds unbelievable, but it's true." He sounded too weak to continue speaking, but with every syllable, his eyes pleaded with Jahari, who needed little convincing.

Jahari spoke in a clear and confident voice.

"I believe you Mr. Toker. I've dealt with beings like the one you've described to the FBI and we're going to make sure the murderer suffers the consequences of his actions. Now, I need some information from you to help me with my investigation. That means you have to focus. I know it's a lot to ask of you right now, but it'll be worth it. Trust me."

Cameron gave a deep, rattling sigh. "I don't know how I can help you, but I'll do what I can."

"I appreciate your cooperation. Now I'm almost certain the creature you saw in your house was a vampire. That's very easy to spot; the difficult thing here is understanding why your wife was its target," Jahari said. "What you have to understand about vampires is that they're very deliberate creatures. They have societies and rules. You can't just kill and eat anywhere; there are regulations. What your vampire did was calculated. He stalked you until he found what he wanted: your wife. If the vampire wanted to kill you, he had every opportunity, and if he was trying to get you through your wife, he would have told you why. Or at least, that would've been the logical thing to do. That's why I believe this really had nothing to do with you. It was all to get to your wife. Now, the way he went about it was sloppy and conspicuous. This leads me to believe that it was a purposeful move. This is a message for someone else. I'm just not sure how it connects back to you or your wife. Has your wife done anything unusual in the last week or so?"

Cameron Toker rubbed his temples and spoke in a low, shaky voice. "Uhhhh, I mean, this time of year is always hard for her. She struggled with depression a while back and her twin sister Ellen died around this time 3 years ago."

"Did she do or go anywhere out of the ordinary? Do anything that might've seemed odd?" Jahari pressed a little this time. He was trying to be gentle, but he needed more than just the sister story. The FBI could've looked that up.

"Nothing unusual, but she went upstate. My wife is an event planner. Well, I guess now she was an event planner... she took a job from some hippie group or something. They were into spirituality, I think."

Jahari tried not to smile in anticipation. "Does this look familiar to you?" He pulled the amulet of the eye from his coat pocket.

Cameron Toker's eyes focused, and finally, after what seemed like an eternity, showed some recognition. His voice trembled as he spoke. "I've never seen that necklace before, but the symbol is the same as the movement she was organizing the event for. I think it was uh, it was on the flyer! Yes, the flyer. I can't remember the name of the group for the life of me." Cameron Toker sank into his chair. Jahari could see that was all he'd get out of the man. But it was a good start, and it was barely even lunchtime.

CHAPTER TWENTY-SEVEN
The Amulet

Jahari took his leave quietly, but his mind was buzzing. He needed to get home. The amulet might've been bugged. He found Mario in the hallway. "Mario, I think I've got something. The amulet you found in the Toker house might be the thread to tie this vampire situation together."

"I need something concrete, Jones. I know you do good work, but you just walked in there and showed evidence to this guy who may or may not be an accomplice. We aren't even close ta that stage of the process. What if he planted the necklace, or if the necklace was dangerous? We have procedures for a reason."

"Oh please, we both agreed he didn't do this. Spare me the bad cop routine. This ain't Dirty Harry and I'm not law enforcement. I'm taking the amulet home and I'm gonna do some research, aight?"

Mario wiped sweat off his brow despite the mild weather. "At least give me a heads up when you pull stuff like that. I hafta cover my own ass, so I look good too, okay?"

"If you wanna look good, stop wearing boot cut jeans," Jahari called over his shoulder as he hopped into a blacked out vehicle that would drop him home. He turned the amulet over and over in his hands like he was trying to commit its features to memory. The streets were busy, a gentle rain adding to the gloom. Steam rose from sewer grates, obscuring the eyes of passersby. Images blurred in the raindrops, creating prisms out of the lights in people's eyes and darkening shadows. Sometimes they'd approach the car, but didn't get too close. They knew better, or maybe Jahari's condition was improving.

Not only could Jahari see and communicate with dead spirits and the otherworldly, but he attracted them. They were mostly harmless, just souls who'd lost their way. Jahari had to be careful. He found that they were attracted to negative emotions and his powers amplified that attraction. It was something he learned to control very early in his life. He had to remain vigilant to protect himself. He wore silver necklaces to help ward off dark spirits, kept small things in his pockets to occupy his mind in case he became afraid, angry, or sad, and avoided whistling. Whistling was like a dinner bell for ghosts. Usually, he kept a domino or something similar, a small object that had a distinct feel, or maybe something that made noise. It was ironic; he used bones to ward off the dead.

The ride took entirely too long because of rush hour traffic, and Jahari's legs had fallen asleep by the time they'd pulled up to his apartment building. His legs sang the gospel as he got out, finally stretching out from the backseat's tyranny. He walked up 5 flights of steps to his apartment and fished his keys out of his pocket. He could remember hundreds of incantations, but couldn't remember if his key ring was in the top pocket or the inside pocket. Then he heard a stumbling noise. Jahari tensed. He turned around slowly; if his enemy thought they had the element of surprise, it would help.

Clearly, they didn't think much of me with that clumsy maneuver. The underestimation works for me, though.

He turned to find a petite woman, around his age, dusting off her pleated mini skirt and picking at a small rip in her stockings. She was wearing a large bomber jacket the color of pine needles, and an embarrassed expression on her face. Jahari looked at her as she grinned nervously.

"Hi," she said, straightening her skirt some more. "I definitely wasn't stalking you. I just want to talk. Are you Jahari Jones?"

Jahari noticed the slightest hint of an accent. He also noticed that the hallway was narrow. There were no windows and the only escape was inside his apartment. It was a good place to pick a fight, depending on what your skill set was. Jahari decided a little conversation would buy him some time.

"That depends. Do I owe you money?"

She chuckled good-naturedly. "No, my name is Moriko Miyazaki. I was told to meet you by your uncle Dominique. I think he said he was going to let you know?"

Jahari frowned slightly; it was believable. His uncle might do something like that, but he still wasn't sure. "Must've slipped his mind."

"He said he might forget. He told me to give you this if he did. Does it mean something?" She gave him a single domino, a deuce-five, which definitely gave her claim more weight. It was the same type of mother-of-pearl domino his uncle used, and the numbers were his calling card. "I don't mean to bother you, but your uncle told me to speak to you. He said you could help me and I could do the same."

Jahari let out a small sigh. "Aight, come inside." He figured she was probably telling the truth, plus it'd be a lot easier to fight in an environment he was familiar with than in the narrow hallway, if it came to that. "Don't follow right behind me. I gotta turn off the booby trap."

"Your apartment is booby trapped?"

"Yeah, it's good for if someone tries to bum rush me. It's worth what I spent on it because the fire only burns the intruder and not my rug. That's the tricky part. I got it in the Middle East." Jahari worked the traps as he spoke. "It's off now; you can come in."

"Ummm thank you..." She took in his house and all of its organized mess in stride. His apartment was filled with strange and marvelous things, like little dancing sculptures made of blue glass, books that glowed in the bookcase, and creepier artifacts like shrunken heads chattering in glass jars. He told the heads to shut up and invited her to sit down on the side of the couch that wasn't covered in old tomes.

"So let's hear your story."

CHAPTER TWENTY-EIGHT
The Sight of the Third Eye

"…and when I woke up, your uncle was there. He told me about BRAHMASTRA and how my father was working with the organization and then he sent me here. He said that there was some kind of connection with what happened to my dad and incidents that happened years ago?"

Jahari swallowed hard. "Yeah, they call themselves the Sight of the Third Eye. As far as we know, a man named Aleister Crowley founded the organization towards the end of the 1930s. He was known as 'The Wickedest Man in the World', but to be honest, I've seen worse. They started out as a bunch of mystics who were experimenting with yoga and martial arts. They were very interested in the reincarnation cycle: how people are born, go through their lives, die and are reborn. It wasn't anything new. Societies have known about this for centuries. The public just doesn't care or dismisses it as myth and legend. But the Sight started trying to tamper with how the cycle works; it's complicated. They wanted to harness the power of the soul, but that's impossible. They tell us that the soul is part and parcel of God. It's got limitless power, but it's not of this material world. The Sight spent years trying to manipulate the soul, but they couldn't even perceive it, no matter what they tried. Instead, they developed spiritual abilities to attempt to create new bodies after they died. It was probably the most intelligent way to achieve immortality. Create a perfect body to put your consciousness in after death, control where you go when you die, escape what's waiting for you on the other side. Anyway, they never really got anywhere. They were disorganized to begin with, but more so after Crowley died. After that, it's difficult to track what happened. One thing we know is that they've been doing strange rituals in places that have very strong spiritual energy. Places that are sacred or where a lot of death has happened. Anyway, we have pictures of the aftermath of these rituals; it's not pretty. We're not sure what they're for, but they're like summoning spells and usually involve human sacrifices. Apparently, I was part of one of those sacrifices."

Her eyes widened. "How are you alive, then?"

"They found me as a baby in the fire pit, not a scratch on me. They screwed up the sacrifice somehow. I'm not exactly sure what happened, but it didn't work."

"But why babies? And you never answered my question."

"As to the question of why babies, we know that the body, the spirit as in a ghost, for instance, and the soul are three separate things. The first two you can damage, can decay over a period of time. They've got expiration dates and are made of material energy and elements. But the soul sticks around, it never changes, it can't be polluted. That's where reincarnation comes in, but I don't have time to explain it all now. Suffice it to say that death releases energy as karma, and that karma can be used to gain power far beyond what a normal person could achieve. There are people that fast and perform austerities, even self-mutilation, as a sacrifice to gain power. The reason you'd use a baby is that there's more potential karma. They just started that particular life. Also, karma can be, for simplicity's sake, positive and negative. Killing babies creates negative karma of a much larger magnitude than your run-of-the-mill evil deed. How I'm alive is anyone's guess."

She took a second to absorb all the information. Jahari couldn't really get a read on her. She appeared way too shaken up to be lying, and she accepted everything he told her without questioning it. It was a strange situation, but he wasn't suspicious yet.

"My father died trying to stop these people. Stopping them was so important that he gave his life up. Let me help you! I know I don't have all the experience you do, but I survived that forest." She had a hard, defiant look in her eyes. There was a spark there. It was the opposite of what she saw in Jahari's eyes. Jahari's wily, calculated look held desperation; his look was that of someone daring their opposition to try it. It said I'm prepared to go, but are you? It scared her when she first saw it. Now it made her feel sad for him. Funnily enough, it reminded her of the ghosts in Aokigahara. He had that same look, like he was drowning.

"I won't get in your way and I'll try to do things your way, for real!" She said. Jahari's silence made her nervous. "Listen, we can do this together or I can do it on my own, but... yeah, no matter what, I'm in this. I need answers." Mori wasn't sure how to end her ultimatum, but she thought she'd made her point. By this time, Jahari had taken a seat on the couch opposite her and was scratching at the back of his head absentmindedly.

"I've been searching my whole life for a reason any of this happened, and I have little to show for it. In my short life, what I've learned from doing this kind of work is you never get exactly what you want, exactly how you want it."

"What do you mean by that?"

"I've seen people sacrifice everything, do unspeakable things, and they're still left wanting. I've done everything in my power to save people and death still slips in through the cracks. What I'm saying is, there's still time for you to get out of all of this. You survived. You can live your life. I don't think my uncle should've gotten you involved in any of this."

Mori furrowed her brow. "I don't mean to be rude, but I was already involved. This is my life now. Whoever killed my father could come after me and my mother next. There's nowhere to run. My dad died and I don't know how or if it even affected the world. I need to find the meaning of it all. Please try to understand me. "

"Oh, believe me, I understand," Jahari said with a grimace. He paused, gathering his thoughts, and then spoke, "Give me your phone number and I'll call you tomorrow."

"So, is that a yes?" she said as she took his phone and held it much too close to her face.

"Yes, but I need you to be careful. What we'll be doing isn't a game, so be for sure."

Moriko handed his phone back with a foxlike grin. "I'm nothing but serious, my man."

They exchanged goodbyes and Jahari sank into the couch to think. When he looked in his phone, he saw that she'd set her contact name as "Drew P. Weiner."

CHAPTER TWENTY-NINE
The Long Dreaded Process

There were no dreams that night, which Jahari appreciated. The sacrifice was almost like watching a rerun of an awful movie. Unfortunately for him, he could feel that long dreaded process beginning yet again. It started with a bloated feeling in the pit of his stomach. Then the feeling traveled up his spine slowly to his crown as his spirit overflowed through the confines of his body. Like a spider molting, his ghostly body tore itself from the tethers of his physical body. One thing he'd discovered over the years was that the sacrifice had damaged him. His spirit was much more powerful than most people's. Because of this, he could move things with his mind, sense emotions, he could see the dead and use other abilities that involved the subtle body and the mind. Unfortunately for him, sometimes the output of power was uncontrollable and he would drift out of his body without using the proper care. It happened frequently when he slept. Thankfully, tonight he was just in his room and not somewhere downtown. He looked around the room, getting his eyes used to his surroundings. When he was out of his body, everything looked as if there was a negative filter over it. He called his excursions "strolling" to keep the melodrama to a minimum. At the same time, he was caught in between the realm of spirits and the corporeal world, where he could still influence things on the physical side, but could also interact with spirits. That interaction was rarely a good thing.

Jahari let out an exasperated sigh. He didn't need this shit. Not tonight. He navigated his apartment, which always seemed more spacious out of body than in. He looked over the railing of his staircase to see a familiar figure floating in his living room. It was nice to see a friend. He gave a casual greeting as he made his way down the stairs, even though he knew he wouldn't get a response. The figure didn't move. Jahari couldn't remember an instance where he had. Jahari plopped down on the sofa, if spirits could plop down on sofas, so he was facing the specter. This ghost had been hanging around Jahari's apartment for 8 months now, appearing on random nights and doing absolutely nothing. Jahari's apartment was spirit proofed, but that was more for harmful spirits; every once in a while a benign one would slip through the cracks. The ghost's hair was long, blond, and ragged, like it'd never seen a comb before death. He was thin and dressed in unremarkable clothing that hung from his ghostly frame. His most striking feature was the sizeable chunk of neck that was missing from his body, along with his lower jaw being mostly gone. The first time he'd appeared was late at night, floating over Jahari's bed. It was terrifying. But after 3 appearances, it was clear that he was harmless and probably just lonely. Jahari wasn't going anywhere, and neither was this spirit. So, after a couple months, Jahari decided maybe he could get some peace for this wandering soul. He'd begun investigating how this poor guy had died, but all

that he could find was that his name was Earl
Englund and that he was killed in the 70s by a
gunshot wound. The murder happened in the
hallway outside Jahari's apartment. The case
wasn't investigated for whatever reason, and Jahari
suspected politics were involved.

Earl floated around doing nothing, but it
seemed like an expectant nothing. Jahari scratched
his head. "Wassup Earl? How's it going?" More
nothing, although Jahari could see the slightest hint
of possible joy when Earl heard his name. Most
spirits don't know why they're still hanging around
instead of moving on to another body. They feel
pain, or rage, or loneliness but can't remember
why. That's why they became dangerous. Earl
hadn't gotten to that point, and Jahari didn't think
he would. It would've happened already, if that
was the case.

"I found out that you have a sister. I'm gonna
talk to her soon and find out more information, I
promise. She lives in the Bronx. You can finally fix

your face. Let's just say you've got a face for radio right now." He usually made jokes to lighten up Earl's stay, and they usually got no reaction. This time, Earl's eyes narrowed. Jahari was actually frightened for a moment. He'd been around this spirit for some time, but was unsure how powerful it was. He tensed; a strange, wheezy, sucking sound came from Earl. He was... laughing. It was so unexpected that Jahari had also started laughing. Earl floated away, still laughing, and Jahari almost had enough time to appreciate it before his spirit was vacuumed back into his body.

CHAPTER THIRTY
Late the Next Morning

He woke up late the next morning, with the grogginess and slight headache that came with strolling. He showered, threw on some clothes, and started sorting through the clutter in his apartment: a dream catcher that had turned out to be fake, some not quite stale donuts, his pencils that needed sharpening. Finally, working his way up to an important task. He inspected the amulet that was taken from the Toker house meticulously. It was a simply crafted oval, with two circles inside one another, the first one thick, the second thin. He looked at the unpainted side of the eye, the back of it, and noticed that there were ten numbers engraved on the thick side of the iris. It was obviously a phone number. He called another number instead, his cousin's.

"What's going on Jahari? How'd things go with Toker?"

"Eh, as well as well could be expected. There is one thing, though. You know that amulet we found in the house? It has a phone number inscribed on it. I'm not dumb enough to actually call, but I was wondering if you could use the number to get some information, hopefully an identity of some kind. Whoever this number belongs to could have something to do with the murder of Evette Toker. It's definitely connected to The Sight Of The Third Eye. I'll send you a picture of the writing to confirm, but it looks like it might be Evette's handwriting. I think it matches."

"When have you ever seen her handwriting?"

"There was a shopping list on the Tokers' refrigerator. They needed to buy tomatoes."

"Ok, so we have the number and possibly a suspect or informant in whomever the number belongs to. Anything else?"

"Nah, that's about it."

"Sounds good. Hey, are you busy tonight? Want to grab dinner?"

"Only if we can have something other than pesto. You ran that into the ground."

"It was only twice."

"It was four times in one week!"

"Calm down. You have to stop yelling so much. The last time you got loud, you that annoying coughing fit. You were coughing up a storm."

"Hmm. Coughing... coughin? Hey, wait a sec, Aisha."

"What is it?" He could tell she was ready to get off the phone and her tone had already become absent minded. He moved to his laptop; this had to be quick, otherwise she'd hang up and then be useless. She liked to say she was 'bad with her phone,' a lie that irritated Jahari.

"Did you hear about that robbery on the way to the museum?"

"Yeah, it was part of a WWII exhibit opening. Some Italian artifact. Well, it was found in Italy, but it's obvious it was African when you look at the architecture."

"Well, get this: it wasn't just an artifact. It was a coffin." Jahari smiled. Now they were getting somewhere. "Do you happen to know if it'd been cataloged by BRAHMASTRA?"

"Not off the top of my head, no. You think our bloodsucker was in that coffin?"

"That's exactly what I'm thinking, Cuzz." Jahari tapped on his laptop. "And a quick search has revealed that this artifact is not in our databases. This coffin could be very important. Has anyone investigated that case? Can you check for me?"

"BRAHMASTRA is taking care of that one. It's still open. An agent was sent early yesterday morning. Veronica Cifra. You know her?"

"I mean, I don't know her like that. We operate in the same area. We don't cross paths that much, but she can be pretty helpful."

"Oh yeah, sure, Mr. High-Profile Cases gets help all the time, I'm sure."

Jahari could imagine the air quotes on "High-Profile Cases" from the other side of the phone. "She doesn't help me like that, c'mon."

"Well, have fun getting your help," she said with maximum smugness.

"Suck a lemon."

Jahari got off with Aisha and then called Veronica setting up a meeting later in the afternoon. Then he called Moriko.

"Hello?"

"Ay, this is Moriko, right?"

"Yup! How are you?"

"Uh, I can't complain...thanks for asking. I have a lead we can investigate."

"You found those jerks from the cult?!"

"Um, no, I've only been working on it for a couple of hours. But my lead does seem to connect with The Sight. I'm gonna send you a breakdown of what's going on here. Meet me outside of my apartment around 4."

"Well, look at you."

"I'm sorry... what?"

"You just call up and order people around, huh? What if I was busy around 4?"

Jahari was still confused, but now he was also irritated. "I mean, if you have something going on-"

"Hahaha, I'm just messing with you. See you soon!" And with that, she hung up.

Jahari scratched his head. She was something else.

CHAPTER THIRTY-ONE
Moriko And Jahari

Moriko arrived right on time, which surprised Jahari. Not because she was on time, but because he was late so often, he just assumed everyone else was too.

"Hi! How're you doing?" She was so perky.

"As good as one can be, hunting a dangerous vampire. You?"

"I'm pumped up! We're going out on the prowl, right? Do I get to ride shotgun, or is someone else tagging along?" She said as she pointed to the black Toyota Camry parked out front.

"You can do better than riding shotgun, and no one else is coming with us; we're a dynamic duo." Jahari got into the passenger seat before Mori could protest.

"Wait, why am I driving?"

"You gotta trust me. I have good reasons for the things I do."

Mori frowned, "I trust you on like, spooky ghost stuff or whether your apartment is going to make me spontaneously combust; wait, is this car booby trapped?" She opened the door, but didn't get in, and continued talking to Jahari through the driver's side window. If anyone had been around, the two of them would've looked like either a couple arguing or an extremely polite carjacking.

"Of course not. How else would I get anywhere?"

"If I'm not here? Not by driving, apparently."

"Don't be ridiculous. I've had other people drive me. You just got here."

"Wait," Mori said as it dawned on her, a sly smile creeping towards the edges of her face. "You can't drive, can you?"

"Psshht, of course I can. Well, like, I mean, I know how to drive. Theoretically I suppose."

Mori couldn't help but giggle. "How old are you?"

"I'm exactly shut the hell up and two months, thank you very much."

Mori finally got into the driver's seat. She

turned to Jahari, her tone going from teasing to curiosity. "So why can't you drive?"

This annoyed Jahari. Not the question, or even the way she said it; he wasn't even sure if he found her irritating or not yet. But there was something about the way she approached him, how she seemed invested already, that made him want to tell her things like that. His everyday life was being on guard, 24/7. He'd trained for years to keep his emotions under control, to be as calm as possible, to deal with things on his own, without fanfare. He wondered why she cared so much, to be honest. It made him paranoid. She asked, but the way she asked was more than just polite conversation. Jahari wasn't a fan of polite conversation. Most times, it was a waste of time. Still, he gave her an answer, the full answer, because the question felt sincere: "It's because of the way my abilities work. That sacrifice changed me. I'm powerful, but there's always a catch. Sometimes I'm in a lot of pain and I can barely breathe. Ghosts are attracted to strong emotions. I have to keep calm, otherwise my powers are hard to control, plus I get visitors. When road rage might kill you and everyone around you, you shouldn't really be driving, ya know?"

"Do they... do they hurt you?"

"Not usually. But they want to have a body. They want to live again, to eat, to touch things. Most of them are driven by jealousy. Some try to make you do something stupid, to hurt yourself. I remember one time, maybe four or five years ago, I was driving right after a job, so my adrenaline was pumping. Next thing I know, I started seizing up because three spirits latched onto me. They made me drive into a pole and the accident knocked me out. For 15 minutes, I was trapped in the car, fighting for control of my body. Shit wasn't fun." Jahari scratched his head nervously. The only people that really knew about that incident were Aisha, Mario, Uncle Dominique, and a few BRAHMASTRA agents. Jahari didn't like all this sharing. It made him feel vulnerable. "Anyway, we should dip."

Moriko started the car and followed Jahari's directions as she thought about what he'd said. "When I went into Aokigahara, I saw terrible things. Things that shouldn't exist. I wouldn't wish anything like that on anyone. I'm sorry you have to deal with that regularly."

"Left."

"Huh?"

"Oh, you gotta make a left here. I almost forgot how to get us here," Jahari said sheepishly. "I appreciate your sympathy. It's just my life though, nothing I can do about it besides learn as much as I can."

"Hey, why can't we just use a GPS or something? Why do you have to guide me to this place?"

"Come on now, you really think a BRAHMASTRA warehouse is gonna be on the Maps app?"

"You never told me where we were going! You just made me drive."

"It's a place where our local branch of BRAHMASTRA catalogs and processes the artifacts we deal with. You ever look at Egyptian crap in a museum and wonder how you're not cursed?"

"No."

"Of course you don't. So this is one of the places where we check everything that's going to go into the public eye. We also have offices."

"Do you have an office?"

"I mean yeah, everyone does."

"So we're going to your office?"

Jahari frowned. "Hell no, I'm never at my office."

"Okay, why are we going there?"

"There was a robbery during last week's shipment, and I'm thinking if we get a little more info, it might help us tie everything together."

"You think it has something to do with the

murder? It seems a little obvious. A coffin was stolen and now we have a vampire running around."

"I mean, Evette Toker was away from home during the same timeframe as the robbery, so it's possible she got into something she shouldn't have. What I really want to find out is the reason they stole the coffin and killed Evette. When a vampire first wakes up, they don't stalk their prey and they wouldn't target someone that wasn't easily accessible. Our bloodsucker not only tortured Cameron Toker psychologically, but killed and fed on his wife. He never touched Toker. It makes no sense. He should've fed ASAP."

"So, what will we find out from visiting this place?"

"You're gonna tell me. You've gotta put in work if you wanna find The Sight. This is practice." Jahari said with a smile. He rolled down the window to let the cool fall breeze into the car. The Harlem River glittered in the sun of the late morning, stretching out like a gigantic green serpent. They took the FDR Drive downtown, passing huge buildings supported by nothing but concrete columns, with Brooklyn watching them from the other side of the water. Jahari liked highways like this; he could cruise by and almost forget the beings that loomed around him. The only shapeless forms to see were the gray monoliths of the city whizzing by. It was so funny to Jahari; if you looked closely, even the average person could pick out the energy bubbling up to the surface from the water, or the faint skeletal forms clinging to the legs of the docks. But no one ever did. That wouldn't last. There was a shift coming.

They made it to The Battery and out of thin air, there was a stately building of three stories that looked like an old-fashioned post office or maybe a courthouse. The white exterior, supported by four pillars atop a wide staircase, looked weathered with paint peeling from age. The building appeared simultaneously regal and also unassuming, like you wouldn't even notice it if you weren't paying attention. They entered through wide revolving doors. The lobby of the building was much larger than the outside indicated. In contrast with the outside appearance, the inside was clean, modern, and well maintained. There were plush chairs, with well-dressed people waiting patiently in them. The back of the lobby was painted a tasteful gold, and a ceiling fan whirred pleasantly. A receptionist sat behind a well-burnished desk. An older lady looked up from her crossword puzzle briefly, but made no other acknowledgement of their presence. Jahari motioned for Moriko to follow him as he walked past the desk and the people waiting.

"She's with me, Margaret," Jahari said, pointing at Moriko over his shoulder with his thumb.

"Mmhm," was the receptionist's only response. The people waiting grumbled as they watched Jahari and Moriko pass.

The interior was almost bank like in its

characteristics, with a thick marble floor and a high ceiling, but with cubicles set up where the tellers would've been. Hustle and bustle, and the occasional noise like that of an animal, reverberated off of the walls, but despite the activity there was an air of peace around the place. Most of the noise was coming from the left side of the hall, where conveyor belts, the kinds you would see in airport security, and lines of people in protective suits were inspecting objects. They weren't going that way. Mori immediately noticed that people started whispering when they walked in. Jahari and Mori moved with purpose, and even though they were at a distance from the workers, the workers seemed to shrink back from them. Jahari seemed oblivious to this as he led them towards the closely set cubicles, which created a claustrophobic maze as they weaved in and around the white walls. It was almost disorienting, zipping through the mass of monochrome. The only glimpses of life were the occasional curious faces

peering above or behind the cubicle walls until
Jahari came to an abrupt halt. They'd stopped in
front of an empty cubicle.

"Damn, I guess she's not in today. That's
weird. Maybe she's at her shop?"

"Where? And who? I'm lost."

"She owns an auto shop. Sometimes she's
there."

"Who are we talking ab-"

"Oh great," a voice said, answering
Moriko's question. "And today was going so well."

"Aw Rock, you're gonna hurt my feelings,"
Jahari said with a smirk. But it wasn't his usual
smirk. It was charming?

Rock was a tall woman, about 5'8, if you
were estimating, plus about three more inches for
the heels she wore. She looked impeccable in a
sand colored pantsuit that complimented her dark
mocha skin nicely, along with a pair of matching
leather gloves. Her hair was short and jet black,
styled in finger-waves framing her beautiful face.

She'd cocked a thin eyebrow above her almond-shaped eyes at the two of them. She had a beauty mark underneath her left eye, and features like that captured in Tobias Andreae's masterpiece.

"I want to hurt more than your feelings, fool," she said, with a frown as she passed them with the type of style and grace in her gait that you would find on the runway, or maybe the dance floor. She sat down in her cubicle, crossing her legs, and leaning on one of the meticulously organized stacks of papers in her space.

"Come on, don't be like that. I brought you a lil' somethin' somethin'."

Rock gave him one of the most wicked side eyes Moriko had seen in her adult life.

"What is it?"

Jahari pulled a small takeout box from behind his back. "I was uptown, and I just happened to pick this up."

"Wait... Harlem Cheesecake?" she asked excitedly. She got up quickly and in the process knocked over almost everything on her desk. Jahari caught everything before it hit the floor with his psychokinesis, papers, pencils, a mug, and lip gloss, before Rock could even gasp.

"Sugar!"

Jahari winked at Mori, who frowned, having just figured out what was going on.

By this time people in the surrounding cubicles were standing at the ready as Rock's yelp had put them on edge, and although her screaming didn't seem to be an alarming occurrence, they all seemed wary of Jahari's replacing all the fallen work material on her desk with his mind.

"Grown ass woman saying 'sugar' instead of cursing like a normal person, it'll never fail to make me laugh."

"Hush. Cursing isn't ladylike, but what would you know about manners?"

Jahari moved a little closer to Rock, resting his arm on the cubicle wall, blocking anyone's view of Rock herself and making it so that he could use a tone of voice that wouldn't be easily overheard in one smooth move, "I mean, I just brought you a gift, that's pretty gentlemanly right?"

"What do you want, Jahari?"

"I was just in the neighborhood and I had to stop by, y'know. Oh, and I also wanted to ask you for an itty bitty teeny tiny favor? Somethin' light," he said, flashing her a smile; Mori tried not to vomit.

Rock had just started to eat her cheesecake and held her hand in front of her mouth as she spoke. "Of course! What do y…" she frowned halfway through her sentence. Her eyes narrowed as she looked at Mori, then back at Jahari, then back to Mori. "Who's this?"

Jahari snapped his fingers gently. "I need you to focus right quick. Sorry, but I really need your help," he said, stressing the "your" to make it clear she was his personal savior in this situation. This seemed to break the death stare that Rock had locked onto Mori. He continued, "You know about the robbery last week, right?"

"Of course, we lost four items, and the warehouse suffered minor damage."

"Cool, so do you have the titles and descriptions of the items taken, or were they not catalogued?" Mori watched as Jahari's charming persona shifted slightly and gave way to the intelligent, methodical, and driven person that she'd been around for the last day or two. He was still friendly. None of it was an act, but now the task at hand had taken precedence.

Rock scanned her screen. "Yes, we lost a minor Djinn lamp that was discovered somewhere in the Saudi area. It's a relatively new lamp, a lot younger than many we've found. Nothing exceptional about it, although it requires an incantation and blood sacrifice to activate. There were two small statues stolen. The effects and origins of these statues were unknown. They were headed for further investigation, not the museum. And lastly the big item, a coffin piece, from northern Italy. It was dug up by looters in the area near the old ruin. They'd submerged the coffin in a river, with the word 'forbidden' scrawled all over the chains that bound it. Locals avoid the entire area. Part of the reason it was being brought into the country in the first place was to determine whether it was safe enough to be kept or if it needed to be destroyed for public safety. That's all the info we have."

"And can you tell me about the positioning of these items during transit?"

"All adjacent or in the immediate vicinity. Here's the layout of the warehouse with all the items' locations."

Jahari scratched his chin and thought hard. To his surprise, Mori spoke up this time, "Excuse me, Veronica, do you guys have your own warehouse crew? BRAHMASTRA I mean."

"She goes by her middle name Raquel," Jahari said under his breath.

Rock scrunched up her face as if a large toad

had asked the question and sprayed her with mucus in the process. "We have a mixed staff because it is easier and rouses less suspicion. Mixing in civilians with our workers helps us blend in."

Mori seemed to be onto something, so Jahari stayed quiet and listened. She continued, "so what happened that night?"

"There was a crew of 8 men that night and they'd worked a little more than half the 12-6 shift before the incident occurred."

"So that means, sorry to interrupt, that it was roughly 3am when the theft took place?" Jahari asked as he wrapped his head around the story being told.

"Roughly, yes, the crew was taken by surprise. They heard the commotion. There was a lot of smoke filling the room and 5 of the crewmembers woke up the next morning with migraines. The other three men disappeared. We interviewed the rest of the workers and their stories lined up."

Mori spoke again, and this time she sounded more confident. "Can you give us information on the workers who were working with the stolen artifacts in question?"

*No one says 'in question' in real lif*e, Jahari thought, but her enthusiasm was refreshing. Veronica gave them copies of the files containing information on the three workers who weren't affiliated with BRAHMASTRA who worked that night.

"Oh wait, Jahari, you have to make an official request for these files? You know I'm not supposed to release the information until there's an official request."

"Rock, Rock, Rock, I'm working the case. It's totally okay."

"You play too much. This happened last time, and I had to do a bunch of the paperwork retroactively. Do you have the request, Jahari?"

"I'm requesting 'em from you right now, aren't I?"

"So then, you don't?"

"What I do have, sweetheart, are these files. See ya later, buh bye now," and with that, Jahari zipped back to the car, leaving the two ladies standing there awkwardly.

Moriko was the one to break the silence. "I'm sorry about your name. I was just going off what I saw on your name plate. My name's Moriko."

Raquel shook the proffered hand politely. "Raquel. Although our little friend over there calls me Rock."

"Are you usually in an office like this?"

"I'm actually not in the office very often. Usually I do field work. I'm called in to clean up messes. I don't really do investigative work unless it's absolutely needed. Jahari is mostly the same, except he does more investigation."

"Have you been doing this," she said, gesturing around the office spaces, "for a long time?"

"Since I was 16. It's not uncommon for people to join young. Jahari has always been in the life. It's easy to join if you have a close family member vouch for you. My grandmother used to be a part of all this."

"Did you join because you wanted to be like her?"

"You ask a lot of questions, don't you?"

"I guess that's my cue to go. I didn't want to leave without introducing myself. It was good to meet you."

"Mmhmm."

CHAPTER THIRTY-TWO
Work Wife

Moriko had to jog to catch up to Jahari's long strides. He was leaning up against the hood of the car, zoning out by the time she reached him.

"So how often do you ask your girlfriend to bail you out when you need info?" she said with a devilish smile.

"She. Is. Not. My. Girlfriend. She's just an acquaintance at work." Jahari got in the car, but he couldn't escape the roasting that was coming his way.

Mori exaggerated her laugh. "Ooh, right. Mister Loner, Jahari Jones has no friends I forgot." She started the car without breaking the conversation or their eye contact. "Probably why you always ask her for favors, right? Work wife?"

Jahari countered her laugh with his own, a wry sound that made Mori feel bad. "I rarely ask anyone for anything. We're cool, and shorty's kind enough to help me from time to time. That's it."

Mori paused for a second before continuing. She didn't want to pry or make him uncomfortable, but she asked anyway. "You're really good at your job. Why was everyone so jumpy when you caught all that stuff that Veronica or Raquel or whatever knocked over?"

Jahari flinched at the question. "What do you mean? They were probably on edge because Rock was yelling. Hey, what the hell?!" he said as Moriko pulled them over into a parking spot.

She looked at him dead in the eyes. "Look, I haven't known you for very long but I can tell you're not someone to be afraid of. I also know that you bottle things up. You use your powers as an excuse to do that, and it's valid, but it's also not healthy. I think you should tell me. Raquel isn't your only friend, okay?"

Jahari sighed. "So you're my friend, huh?"

"I'd like to think so." She said defensively. Mori sat there, brow furrowed, not budging. "You can correct me if I'm wrong."

"I'm not sure if you're wrong or not, but I'll tell you. They're afraid of me. Or maybe afraid isn't the most accurate word. It's more... unease. I've got a weak connection to my body and people can feel it. You notice that little draft sometimes when I'm around? That tingle that goes up and down your spine? It's almost like being around a ghost."

"That's it? People who spend all their time fighting the darkest evils are scared because you make the thermostat act up? I'm not sure if I buy it."

"I'm gonna come clean. I'm glad you didn't buy it. If it was that easy to fool you, you might have to stay on driver duty."

Mori smiled at him. "So what is it? No bull this time. And another thing, how did you catch all those loose bits of crap that flew off whats-her-face's desk? Must've been hard?"

"Not particularly. I've been practicing for a long time. I can handle objects with my mind just as well as I can with my hands."

"Can you fly? Just how powerful are you?"

"I can float. Flying is never really a practical option. If we're just talking about my psychokinesis, I can produce enough force just by concentration to shatter concrete. The thing is, my powers get amplified the more intense my emotions are. The organization has put my upper limits as unknown."

"You Hulk out?"

"What?"

"You know, like, Hulk, stronger as you get madder, grrrrrr."

"Oh yeah, I guess," he said with a chuckle. "Also similar to the Hulk, my powers get really hard to control. Plus, they attract spirits. It's a strange cycle. The spirits amplify my power and the more power I use, the more spirits I attract."

"So, how do you deal with it? All those people, knowing you're the most powerful guy in the room? What do you do about how they treat you?"

Jahari paused. It wasn't something to which

he'd given too much thought. "I give them what we both want: a wide berth."

Mori pulled back out onto the road. They'd come to a red light and Mori played with the heating absentmindedly. "You ever think you should stop avoiding stuff?" The words came out before she could stop them. She had a penchant for bluntness that worked to her detriment just as often as it helped. "Hey look I'm sorr-"

"It's fine. Don't worry about it. I know you didn't mean anything by it." But he was quiet for the rest of the ride.

CHAPTER THIRTY-THREE
Clive Hennings

Clive Hennings was tired of the bullshit. He hadn't slept in almost two days and his partner wasn't answering his calls. They'd lost one of the amulets, no doubt in the hands of the feds, or worse, BRAHMASTRA. He stopped pacing around his dusty Connecticut motel room, only to peer through the blinds. Afternoon sunlight filtered through the slits, slicing through the dim room like a knife. He felt like a man on death row. The pacing was good. The repetition became comforting after a while. He needed to keep busy, otherwise he'd lose his mind. Unfortunately, nothing could distract him from what had been going on in his life recently. It was supposed to be a simple job: pinch the casket, test the incantation, then bring their sister back. The heist itself was fairly easy. Eddie, his baseman, was already working part time as a warehouse worker, and it was fairly easy for him to slip in on the shipment detail. Neither of them had any known history of being involved with the occult, and they'd practiced so they could stun the other workers for long enough to buy them the time to escape. They grabbed the casket and some other crap and made it to the van Evette was waiting in so fast, you'd think they'd sprouted wings. They all had alibis. Evette had told her husband she was going upstate with the rest of them to an event, an event that had already happened weeks prior. Everyone else thought Eddie and Clive were working at the warehouse. If only the rest of it had been so easy. Clive blamed Eddie. Eddie was the one who had discovered the spell. They were new recruits for the Sight of the Third Eye, and after doing some research, they thought they'd do something major. Clive wanted to bring his sister back; Eddie wanted to show the Sight that they were worth something. Now it had all blown up in their faces.

He remembered it all so clearly. Eddie was performing the spell; it was almost sunrise. They were by the docks, trying to keep the sacrificial fire going. The spell was supposed to raise the dead and rejuvenate the body, no matter the subject. He'd barely finished chanting when the creature started screaming, the most horrid, blood curdling sound you could imagine. It was a scream of pain, fear, but most of all, it was a sound of disgust. The emaciated creature tried to rip Clive's face off but Evette had pushed him out of the way; her sleeve was torn, but she wasn't hurt. The sun had peeked over the horizon by then and golden light started seeping in through the windows. That was their saving grace, because the creature fled as soon as it saw the light. They'd raced away from that rotten place, cursing, crying, and counting their blessings. Evette had saved his life. And now she was...

A knock at the door startled him out of the thoughts. He grabbed the handgun off of the dresser and steeled himself. He wasn't exactly a marksman; years of partying had left his grip a little shaky. Still, it was all he had. Clive cracked the door open and poked the barrel of the pistol through the opening in one swift movement. A dispassionate Eddie stared back, looking impatient, short and built like a bag of laundry.

"Hey numb nuts, why weren't you answering your phone? I thought you were... I thought I was alone in this."

Eddie frowned and pushed his stringy long hair out of his face. "No cell phones, remember? I don't want to be tracked. That was the plan, wasn't it?"

"That plan went out the window the second we woke up some kinda demon or some shit. Come on Eddie."

"Look, there was a reason the three of us were supposed to have no contact. This whole plan was supposed to be to impress the Sight. Last thing I want is those bastards we stole from on our asses. Can you please let me in now? Or do I need a password?"

Clive opened the door with one hand, tossed the gun on the bed, and yanked Eddie through with the other. "Are you trying to piss me off?"

Eddie ignored this and moved about the room like he was looking for something. "Where's Evette? We all need to be on or P's and Q's for this to work. Did you contact her?"

"SHE'S DEAD YOU DENSE SHIT!" All the emotion erupted from Clive at once. The death of his sister, the paranoia, the feeling of guilt mixed with fear and adrenaline to make him want to bash Eddie's head in. "I went to Evette's house the other day and there were police everywhere! She's gone. She... that... that thing got her!" His vision was getting blurry from all the tears welling up in his eyes. He turned away so Eddie wouldn't see.

"Clive, brother, I didn't mean for..."

"I know you didn't. But now both of my sisters are dead, and I'm being followed. Eddie, I'm being followed and I can feel his eyes on me. I see the face that was in that coffin every damned night."

"I saw it too. In person. Two nights ago I was driving on the highway and that creature appeared in the middle of the road. It looked different this time though, but somehow I knew... shit. It's coming for us next, isn't it?"

"Probably." Clive wiped his nose. "What are we gonna do?"

"You said the police were around?"

"Yeah, they'd swarmed Evette's place. By now they must've told BRAHMASTRA. I don't know what we're gonna do."

Eddie's face darkened. He pulled out his amulet. "I haven't been sitting around twiddling my toes, you know. I spoke to that guy, the guy who recruited us. He helped me. Listen, Clive, if we can get the spell to work like it's supposed to, maybe we can bring both of your sisters back. Maybe it'll work this time."

Clive glowered at him and spoke in a short, controlled bark, "We. Cannot. Bring. Anyone back if we're dead. We are being hunted and everything that happened to Evette is going to happen to us unless we destroy this thing."

Eddie smiled a bit and held up an ornately engraved oil lamp. "I think I have a solution."

CHAPTER THIRTY-FOUR
That Night

That night, Jahari called Moriko over. She plopped down on his couch for the second time that week, and Jahari inhaled a deep, exhausted, and self-satisfied breath. He pointed to a complicated and extensively detailed cork board with strings all over it, like the kind you see on detective shows. "So, here's my little conspiracy. First, we look at this vampire. What do we know about vampires that have just awoken from a rest period?"

"That they have crust in their eyes? I don't know much about vampires. You kept saying something about feeding." Moriko slouched in her seat; she could tell this would be a long explanation.

Jahari ignored the wisecrack and continued. "So, boom. Here's some useful information. I've been reading up on bloodsuckers," he said, spreading three worn and especially thick books out on the coffee table: Dealing With The Undead by R. Belmont, Vampirism: Ancient Enemies In A Modern Age by Akila Kamal, and High Stakes by

E. C. Brooks. The covers were nondescript and Moriko could see Jahari had riddled them with sticky notes.

"First off, vampirism is a curse. Vampires are created when the blood of a vampire is mixed with a living human's blood. Now vampire blood is very volatile by nature; it attacks living tissues. The shock of vampire and human blood mixing almost always kills the human. It only takes a tiny amount to end a life. This is where blood comes into play. Vampires drink blood because their bodies are decaying very slowly. By drinking the blood of living creatures, they are literally absorbing the life force of that creature. This is how vampires live and grow more powerful: by drinking and by growing older. What's more is, animal blood is almost useless, and really only staves off the thirst for very small periods of time. Experts think the higher level of consciousness that humans possess is the deciding factor. Now, when vampires have been deprived of blood for long periods of time, their bodies start to decay. They experience extreme pain, their bodies morph and become inhuman, and they turn into feral predators. You've noticed how certain animals' bodies change according to environmental effects, right?"

"Like foxes and their winter coats?"

"Yeah, that's a good comparison. With vampires, it's closer to locusts, physiologically they change their bodies to suit their need to feed. This is important, because our vampire hadn't been awake for what, half a century? Let's use that as a rough estimate. Being without blood for that long, he'd be thirsty as hell. So why stalk Cameron Toker? He could've killed any number of innocents, healed himself and made this whole process easier on himself. I think we can conclude our vampire would have to be pretty powerful to not only maintain his intelligence, but to stave off the thirst for that long; he must've had a score to settle."

"Ok, that makes sense. How does this get us

closer to stopping the vampire, though?"

"Well, it lets us know that the people who woke this vampire up are being hunted, so-"

"If we find them, we find the vampire!" They were both smiling now. But Mori was still a little doubtful. "But how do we find them?"

"I'm working on that. Here's what we know. I'm guessing that out of the three men who weren't regular warehouse workers, our guys were Clive Hennings and Edward Allen."

"How do you know that?"

"I don't. But, the possibility is very strong and here's why. Records show Edward had freelanced in warehouses in the past, so it's feasible that's how he got himself and Clive in. Clive has no history in that line of work. But the thing that convinced me was when I found out that our boy Clive is Evette Toker's older brother. On top of that, he was at the crime scene the same day I was there. I only saw the bottom half of his face, cuz he was wearing a hat, but it works with the mugshots we have of him. I've looked into Clive, mostly because it could've been either of the other two men. I didn't have enough evidence to say for sure. Eddie is a hunch. Clive has been arrested twice, once for possession and once for common assault. He served a year and a half all together. He's never been taken in for anything occult-like, though, so he's either smart or not very ambitious. If you look at the way they stole this coffin, I'd say he just wasn't ambitious. Remember what they took from the scene of the crime?"

"Something like a lamp, some amulets, and the coffin?"

"Exactly. Let's think about it. BRAHMASTRA didn't know what those amulets did. What are the chances that these guys did? Then they grabbed something extremely unpredictable and dangerous in that lamp. It doesn't make any sense."

"So they grabbed those other objects as a distraction?"

"That's the only explanation that I can think of. The question is, why revive a vampire? That's what I'm still trying to figure out, and it's bugging the hell outta me. Anyway, chances are, if the vampire killed Evette Toker, Clive might be his next victim."

"So, what's our next move? Find Clive?"

"Seems like our only option at this point; he's the only definite lead we have. The problem is, I'm not sure how to find him." Jahari sat on the couch and rubbed his forehead, his face scrunched up with thought and frustration. "There has to be a clue somewhere where they tipped their hands."

"Let's think about what we do know. If you were a dummy with a vampire hunting you, what would you do?"

Jahari's skull massage paused for a second. "I'd probably end up making it worse."

"How would you do that?"

"I dunno. They have those amulets. I assume they know about as much about those as we do.

They don't seem especially skilled in the dark arts, otherwise they would've tried something to control the vampire. I guess I'd try the lamp."

"Okay, so how would we use a lamp?"

"Hmm, the lamp they stole was an Ifrit class, so you'd need blood or ashes for the ritual. The issue here is, blood and ashes don't really narrow anything down, they could get stuff like that from anywhere. That's probably the easiest part of summoning an Ifrit. Plus, we're on a time limit. This isn't a helpful clue."

Mori got up and took a moment to study the web of information that was woven in the middle of Jahari's living room. "What are Ifrit like? Maybe that'll help us."

"Uhhh, they're evil beings, spirits born from collective greed and then bound to an object someone would covet. They grant wishes in a way specifically designed to punish the greed involved in actually gaining and using the lamp. As far as we know, they can grant any wish with no limitations.

But mostly they try their best to cause pain and suffering, so all the wishes they grant backfire. They're extremely selfish and they sustain themselves on the suffering of others. They grant three wishes, and they require a proper summoning rather than just rubbing the lamp like Djinn. Certain environmental factors make it easier to summon them too. I gotta look that up." Jahari stood up wearily. "Hey, I'm gonna go to bed. My head hurts. You can chill here if you want. The couch pulls out and there are blankets in the brown cabinet under my workbench."

"You trust me in your home around all this stuff?" Mori asked, half flattered, half incredulous.

"Honestly? Kinda. I'm confident enough that if you tried to pull something, my defenses would get you. I mean, if I don't first. But you move too sloppily to be an enemy."

"Thanks?"

CHAPTER THIRTY-FIVE
Eddie And Clive

They'd taken side roads mostly, cruising on narrow asphalt, their dark blue van scurrying across the dusky cityscape like a roach on a kitchen floor. It was nippy outside, and at this time of night, the streets were deserted. Eddie was driving, tapping on the steering wheel to a barely audible song playing on the radio. They'd said little to each other in the time it took to drive from Connecticut to New York. Eddie and Clive had always been a team. They'd met at summer camp in middle school and bonded over comics. Flaming skulls and red capes, demons and magicians had brought them together. The same beings now threatened to tear the life from their bodies in the night. It felt like they'd known each other from the cradle, and now the grave was calling. The silence between them broke when Eddie hit the curb outside of a derelict meat packing warehouse near Chelsea. It was well past midnight, and the loud banging sound of metal on concrete put Clive on edge.

"What the hell is wrong with you?! Why

don't we just kill ourselves now and save the vampire the trouble? Or worse, turn ourselves in. If we get caught, we're done for." Clive couldn't hide his nervousness.

"We're not gonna get caught. It isn't a crime to drive badly. Get a grip; you're making me nervous."

"You should be nervous!!! We don't know how much time we have. I feel like that… thing is hiding around every corner. Every dark corner hides those bright red eyes."

"Don't worry. I don't think the vampire has a bead on us, otherwise we'd have seen him again." Eddie said in a hushed tone as they exited the vehicle. "It was good that we kept moving. I dunno how this bastard found Evette, but we have the advantage."

Clive clenched his jaw and stayed silent. He just had to trust Eddie at this point. There was nothing else left to do. He kept a lookout absentmindedly, wondering how his life had gone to shit. He wasn't answering his family's phone calls. The authorities had his sister's body, so she wouldn't even have a funeral. As far as his parents knew, they had no children left. And then there was that *thing*. What he was feeling wasn't just fear; he'd feared for his life before at concerts and seedy little festivals. Something else was growing in his heart, a dread so much worse. A sense that it was all futile. Everything he'd worked for or tried in his life was a waste, a moth two wingbeats ahead of the bat. It felt so unfair; Every time he'd find purpose, find something he wanted, it would always slip through his fingers. His existence was cream, sweet, fluid, and, most of all, perishable.

"Clive! I think this is it. This is a good spot. There's a lot of energy to manipulate. We can leave the inconspicuous stuff here tonight and perform the sacrifice the day after tomorrow."

Clive exhaled deeply. "Do you think this will even work? What's the point?"

Eddie's face contorted into a mocking mask.

"Do you want to ask the bloodthirsty monster nicely to leave us alone? Maybe we can get the band together and play him some music. Maybe BRAHMASTRA will have us play at their company picnics."

Clive grabbed Eddie by the collar of his black overcoat. They were breathing the same air; Clive could see every furrow of disdain on Eddie's face, how his patchy stubble framed his scowl. Clive growled, but neither of them spoke; their eyes were locked, sweat forming on their foreheads from the work they'd done. Clive made a big deal of letting go of Eddie's jacket, and Eddie made a big deal of dusting himself off.

"Listen, I need you to focus right now. We're not in a garage band anymore, we're about to die. This shit has to work. You and me, man, we're going to live. If there's one thing we're going to do, it's live. That's always been us."

Clive heard an unfamiliar note of doubt in Eddie's voice. The warehouse had gone cold, and

Clive couldn't tell if it was the weather or the fear trickling down their spines. It was a large building, with an open ground floor and metal walkways criss-crossing overhead. Chains with large metal hooks for hanging slabs of meat hung from the ceiling, and stacks of crates created a maze of sorts below. All the corners made Clive nervous; there was broken glass and vermin running around, but he couldn't help but imagine turning a corner to find the monster that killed his sister waiting. He could tell Eddie had imagined the same scenario because he was inching around corners laterally like a crab. They stuck close together, just in case, and continued their drudgery in silence, hauling bags of salt, boxes of chalk, clay, and a small bag of silver into the lonely building. The plan was to bring in the stuff that could be passed off as construction materials and then come back with the rest to perform the ceremony. They didn't see or hear anything or anyone, but this only heightened the fear that bubbled in the pit of their stomachs.

They left the warehouse feeling like eyes were on them.

Jahari watched them leave and couldn't help the feeling that eyes were on him as well.

CHAPTER THIRTY-SIX
Perps, Suspects, Sussies

Jahari's night was anything but restful. He'd started strolling almost immediately after he fell asleep. Jahari bolted upright just as the sun had peeked over the horizon, not with alarm, but with satisfaction. He put on a shirt and raced downstairs. Mori had passed out on the couch. Jahari wasn't sure how comfortable she'd be if he touched her, so he used a spoon from a takeout box and started poking her arm with the end. She shifted slightly without opening her eyes.

"Hey whathehellman?"

Jahari poked more vigorously as he spoke. "I know where to find them. I know what to do to find our guys!"

Moriko's eyes flew open. "You found our perps? Do you call them perps? Suspects? Sussies?"

Jahari smiled with triumph. "When we catch these bastards, you can call them whatever you want." He began shuffling through the things on his workbench, throwing some items, carefully displacing others, pouring liquid out into a trashcan.

Mori scratched her head and frowned; she was still waking up, but there was a question nagging her. "Hey, but how did you figure out where to find these guys? You were stumped yesterday."

"Remember when I said sometimes I drift from my body when I sleep?" Jahari said as if he was asking her if he told her what he'd had for lunch.

"Um, you mentioned it. You kinda ran through a laundry list of weird powers you have. Some seem more useful than others, to be honest."

"Excuse me, they're all extremely useful! And I don't see how you can even comment. You don't have any powers!"

"I don't need powers. I'm like Batman, I'm so cool I can do everything; no powers necessary." Jahari flipped her off and Mori laughed, having gotten under his skin to a satisfactory degree.

"Well, I was strolling last night, and I saw the ghost of Evette Toker. She looked like she had something to tell me, but when I spoke to her, she wouldn't answer. There she was, with her hand out, like she was pulling me to her. I grabbed it, her hand I mean, and all these images flashed through my head. I was getting dragged through the city right to this warehouse. It was old and creepy looking and somewhere in the meatpacking district. It was by the river. I remember hearing the water. I saw Clive Hennings walking out of the building and getting into a van."

"Wait, how do you know it was Evette's ghost? What if it was something else disguised as her? What if it was a trap? It would make sense to throw you off and lead you into a dangerous place. We have to be smart about this." Mori tied her hair away from her face and stared at him boldly. Jahari wasn't used to being challenged. The Bureau left him up to his own devices as long as there wasn't too much collateral damage. So this was...

interesting. Now he had to consider another person's opinion, and it was an odd situation for him.

"You're right, but this is our only lead. I think we should find the warehouse and wait them out. There's a full moon the day after tomorrow. Full moons are always ideal times for doing anything supernatural. It's a complicated ritual, so I don't think they'll chance it on any other day; they need all the help they can get. I'm gonna search the area and see what I can find today."

"So what should I do?"

"Get some rest. We're gonna be staking the place out tomorrow, and we need to be alert. Finding the place is the biggest concern here, and I should be able to figure that out pretty easily." Jahari picked through the things on his workbench to determine what would be useful later.

Mori groaned as she stood up and stretched her legs. "Sleeping in jeans must've been a medieval torture method."

"Sorry, all my clothes are really long and I didn't know if it'd be weird or not."

"This whole situation is kinda weird, isn't it?" she said as she gathered her things to leave.

"Yeah, I guess it is. You going home?"

"Well, I have to pack for our big stakeout, right?" She flashed him a smile. "I'm looking forward to it. We'll get some answers and save some lives, right? It's a big thrill!"

Jahari chuckled, but he had something else on his mind. "Can I ask you a question before you go?" She gave him an expectant look, so he continued, "how did you survive in that forest? I'm asking just because I've been in situations like that before. Talking about it is hard. It makes me feel like I'm complaining or something. I'm good with just thuggin' it out, like it is what it is, but sometimes it feels like my whole life has been a big trip in the forest, and I'm curious to know how other people deal with stuff like this. Maybe you tried something I haven't thought of, ya know?"

Mori took a second before she spoke. "Well, I was in that forest and I felt so alone. I've never felt isolation like that before. That place played with my mind and made me feel like no one else cared and that I would never be anything but alone. It made me feel like I fell into a hole that I could never climb out of. And somehow I could feel all the other people who'd died there, and they were all experiencing that same isolation. But by the end, I knew I just had to live, and it had to be my life. The forest gave me a choice, and I made it."

Jahari could tell she was looking at him to see what he was thinking. He kept his face blank and thanked her for sharing. It was sincere; she didn't really have an answer, or at least not one for him. Still, it comforted him that someone could relate. Jahari walked her downstairs to her cab. And then just like that, it was just him and his thoughts. Out of the corner of his eye, he noticed one of his neighbors, an older Puerto Rican lady who lived in the building next to his, smirking at him. She'd seen Jahari put Mori in the car and was watching under the pretense of taking out her garbage.

"Finally, some action! You never have anyone over, so I wasn't sure whether I should set you up with my daughter or my nephew!" She cackled. Jahari frowned at her, but called out, "but what's your daughter look like?" as he went back inside.

He reflected on his conversation with Mori briefly, hoping he hadn't made it awkward for her. He felt like the whole interaction had reached its natural end and she seemed ok with it. Jahari got himself ready for the day and made his way to Manhattan on the train. The subway bustled with activity as the morning commute hit its peak. He weaved in and out of the crowd and found a seat towards the back of the train car. People gave him his space. He dozed off a couple times, but the trip was uneventful. It was a dangerous situation, sleeping on the train. The darkness of the tunnels attracted spirits, and Jahari's guard was down when he slept. Under normal circumstances, he'd never do it, but he was just so damn tired from all the recent strolling and late nights. He tried not to stare at the few spirits he encountered, the man with the raw, bloody face sitting opposite him, the skittering gray thing that he saw in the station's corner. He came out of the subway a half an hour later and the harsh, cold air hit his face like a brick. It was gray and gloomy, and the sunlight hadn't broken through the clouds despite the early morning's best efforts. The air had that taste that comes with being near the water, and a light fog drifted over the sidewalk. He avoided the puddles that had formed during his transit and tried to follow the path he had taken last night. Even though it took some time, he found the warehouse he'd envisioned. It was slightly less depressing in the daylight; it made the chipped dull paint less flat and gave the seagull droppings that covered the roof some romanticism.

It's probably better if I don't go inside. I

don't want to mess anything up and tip our hands. Plus, who knows what traps they've set, he thought. Jahari kept low to the ground, just in case they'd set up some kind of surveillance. He edged along the warehouse and looked in a window to find... nothing. There were a few bags of rock salt and some other crap that wasn't important at first glance. The warehouse looked like it had been out of use for a while. Chains hung motionless in the gloom. The only movement Jahari could see was dust motes floating in the beams of sunlight that filtered through the windows. It was warming up as the morning sun intensified and broke through the clouds. So warm that someone could drift off without even realizing... Jahari massaged the bridge of his nose; the investigation was getting to him. *Maybe it's the lack of sleep, or Michael's death, but I can't take anymore,* he thought as he tried to wake himself up again.

Suddenly, he got that feeling, where the hair on the back of his neck stood on end, that eerie static. He looked around frantically. *Something is here!*

Perched on the wall like some kind of obscene frog was a spirit. Its neck was long, coiled, and mottled blue and purple, a sharp contrast from the dead shade of gray on the rest of its skin. Its eyes were shut in tight slits, but its mouth was open beyond the dimensions of any natural creature. It was slowly sucking the life out of Jahari.

He looked around to find the alleyway closing in on him, and his vision got wavy and distorted. It was already dark in the alley, and he had no actual means of escape. Jahari felt fear creeping up his spine and crawling up his brain stem. The spirit's mouth tilted upwards slightly when it sensed his fear. It closed in, its neck elongating and pulsing.

There's nowhere to go and I'm running out of time.

Jahari tried to communicate with the spirit. Generally, he couldn't speak to someone mentally without them being open to it, but he could always make them understand his emotions and intent. Despite this, he still tried to use full sentences: *Listen, I don't want to hurt you, but if you don't stop, I'll have to defend myself.*

The spirit's mouth opened wider in response, as if it were mocking him. His whole body felt numb, like he'd just been electrocuted. His vision started flashing, and he could see there was no use trying to reason.

Jahari released every emotion inside him in a burst of energy that dispersed the spirit. The entire area smoked from his power but was no worse for wear; his control was almost as fine tuned as his power was vast.

Well, that woke me up, he thought as he rubbed the back of his neck. The spirit wasn't particularly strong, but defeating it left him feeling like he needed to sit down. He made his way towards a bar across the street from the warehouse.

I've got to pay attention. I didn't even notice

the spirit's energy in the area and could've ended up possessed for hours if I hadn't taken it seriously.

The thought chilled him to the bone; if it were up to him, that'd never happen again.

He stood outside the bar door for a second, a flamboyant little place painted hot pink with fire engine red trim, and tried to compose himself by taking a deep breath and focusing on the sign that hung outside the bar. He looked at the burnished wood, at the dead neon around its edges, at the curvy female demon pouring beer that was the store's logo. Right as he went to open the door, it flew open. A tall woman came out of the place mid conversation.

"-it's your last chance. I hope you know that." As she said that, she pushed past Jahari and looked directly into his eyes. Hers were a shade of green you only saw in emeralds. He was hypnotized, but it was only for a moment. She left in a hurry, and Jahari walked into the bar with a strange sense of déjà vu. The bar was hazy with spliff smoke, the cloud only cut through by the neon lights struggling to illuminate the small room. There were only three patrons, two seated in a booth at the back of the bar, and one sitting at the bar, staring into his glass, with his head resting on the counter. Jahari sat next to him; the man didn't stir.

Jahari cleared his throat politely. "Pardon me. Can I get a glass of water?"

The bartender, a small hairy man with beady eyes, turned. "You came to a bar to drink water?" he asked with raised eyebrows.

"I dunno. What else you got?"

"Beer, but the beer tastes like the water," said the guy sitting next to him, "but then again water doesn't get you drunk, does it brother?" He lifted his head off the dingy bar and looked at Jahari with unfocused eyes.

Well, I'll be damned. It's Clive Hennings. Jahari tried to keep a neutral expression, not that it would've made much of an impression on Clive; he was a little past tipsy. Jahari gave his most convincing fake laugh. "Lemme get a lemonade, if you have it, otherwise I'll just have some water." He turned to Clive casually. "The beer's that bad, huh?"

Clive half belched, half chuckled. "Yeah, tastes like piss, but it's doing its job. What's your name?"

"I'm Joe. What's yours?"

"Clive. What are you doing in a bar at 9am if you're not getting drunk? That's uh pretty uh," he belched as he searched his mind for the right word, his eyebrows scrunching together until he got it, "weird. It's weird." He pushed his long, greasy, black hair out of his face and scratched his scalp. He looked like a mess.

"I'm... trying to forget something."

Clive looked at him and his bloodshot eyes focused, like he was really seeing for the first time. "I know the feeling," he said with a tremble in his voice. Jahari bought Clive a drink before he left.

Lord knows he'd need it.

CHAPTER THIRTY-SEVEN
The Calm Before the Storm

It felt like the calm before a storm. Mori came over first thing in the morning. They met outside of his apartment. She was wearing the same green jacket, blue jeans, some canvas sneakers, and a dark purple knit sweater. She'd tied her hair back in a ponytail and she was chewing gum. "Good morning," she said in a husky voice. You could tell she was still half asleep. "Why are you dressed like a burglar?"

Jahari looked at her like it was obvious. "First, I'm not dressed like a burglar." He was kind of dressed like a burglar, sporting a dark blue tracksuit and a matching beanie. It was a getup that was a little too thick for the brisk but sunny weather they were experiencing. Jahari looked down at himself and gave his outfit some thought. "Ok, maybe I do look like a burglar. But this is my stealth suit for today. Usually I wear a stocking cap but I can't find it. Also, it might be cold," he said sheepishly.

"Well, you definitely won't be cold in your stealth suit. What's up with the color? Did they run out of black ones?"

"If you wear black at night, it makes your silhouette visible cause your clothes are darker than the night sky. Navy blue blends better."

Mori yawned and stretched. "I should've brought some navy clothes then. I'm gonna be a stealth risk."

"Nah, you're good. We don't need you sneaking off anywhere. Here, take this," he said, handing her a hand sized object wrapped in a washcloth, "just in case you have to handle business."

"This feels like a gun."

"Funny how guns often look and feel like guns."

"Can we stop saying the word 'gun' in broad daylight?" she said, unwrapping the small handgun and turning it over.

"Sure. Let's also stop waving the damn thing around. NYPD don't play that shit."

"Is this a magic gun or something? Does it

shoot silver bullets? Or sunlight? Or garlic?"

"I'm not Blade, it's just a gun!"

"Shhh, okay, I get it! Anyway, why do you assume I know how to shoot this thing?"

"I don't, but if you hit someone, that's good. If you miss, you distract them, and that also might be lifesaving. If this were a movie, I'd give some basic tips, shit like 'line the sights up, let the front sight get clear and your target go blurry, and then apply even, rearward pressure', and you'd magically be a markswoman with zero practice. Too bad for you, we don't have enough romantic tension for that to work."

Mori laughed as she rolled her eyes. "Great, another thing I have to work on."

"Nobody's perfect Mori, don't sweat it."

"Well, I'll try not to shoot you. What else are we bringing?"

"Just some wire cutters, a knife, some first aid, these granola bars I got in Mexico, my phone charger, and stuff like that."

"You think we'll have to fight them?"

"Depends on if the vampire shows or not. This is probably the most vulnerable these guys have been in a while. Usually they're safe because they can move around in the day and throw the vampire off, but now they have to stay put for hours in the middle of the vampire's active hours. They might have enough common sense to quit while they're ahead; they probably realize they screwed up. Maybe they'll just accept that we know better and let us protect them."

Mori scoffed. "Yeah, most people are great at admitting when they don't have everything under control." Jahari couldn't help but think she'd directed that comment at him, but he said nothing. She continued, "So if they don't surrender, we have two fights coming our way?"

"Seems that way. You gonna be okay?"

"I can do it. Vampires are easier than ghosts. At least you can touch vampires, right?"

They packed up the car and were out and

about before the sun had fully risen. There was electricity in the air, and Jahari couldn't help but feel a little excited. This was his element. It was an environment he thrived in, and hostile as it was, he was like a coyote in the desert. Jahari thought about Mexico briefly. It was a rough mission. There had been more than a few times in his life where he felt close to death, and even more where he knew it was impossible for everything to turn out in his favor. Pyrrhic victories were not an alien concept to him. He tried to push these thoughts out of his mind. It was a recurring theme of his life: get things under control, push the memories to the side, bury them. This mission had awakened something in him, like a starving man who'd been given a little food. In every mission, he gave everything he could for the people he was tasked with protecting because they needed him. They couldn't deal with whatever was haunting them, so he did. Now, with a lead on The Sight of the Third Eye, he could finally direct all that pent up energy towards a goal.

He was a man on a mission.

Mori wasn't a morning person, and so they were quiet on the way there. Jahari bought them breakfast from a deli, and their stakeout began. Mori kept herself awake the best she could by drinking the cup of coffee he'd brought her.

She stuck her tongue out. "Eurgh, I never liked this stuff. Why didn't you get one for yourself?"

"I don't really drink coffee. Or alcohol. Or anything that messes with my mental state. Alcohol is the worst and makes me an easy target for spirits. Coffee just makes me edgy. Makes me tweak," he said, widening his eyes and sticking his tongue out like a ghoul.

Mori cracked a smile and looked out the window. "Hey so if they're gonna need the moon to do this ritual, why are we here so early?"

"Honestly, I'm not exactly sure what kind of people we're dealing with. I figure they might be smart enough to set up beforehand. They're on a clock, so unless they've prepared perfectly already, they're gonna need time or they'll create mistakes. If they wait, the moon being full will help lending the ritual energy, but not if they spend all their time setting up. If they share this mindset, we can get them in broad daylight. So we're watching to see if they show."

"So we'll probably be here awhile?"

"Yup."

"Then I think we should do something to pass the time?"

"What are you thinking?"

"I Spy?"

CHAPTER THIRTY-EIGHT
I Spy

They couldn't spend hours playing I Spy, and around 3 o'clock, Jahari took a nap. It wasn't the best idea. His dreams came in muddy waves, feelings, colors, and sounds coming to the shore of his consciousness and mixing. He saw a hallway, a red streak, a bee falling off a leaf, a blanched face, a rotted cell. He felt warm embraces and being plunged into frigid waters. None of it was enough to wake him, but his sleep was uneasy. He woke up to Mori's face directly in front of his.

Her eyes were wide, and the tone of her whisper was alarming. "Jahari! Jahari, wake up, wake up! They just pulled up to the warehouse. Look!"

Jahari sat up immediately with a level of focus that was surprising for someone who'd just been asleep. The two of them froze, peering through the windshield at the two men getting out of a midnight blue van.

"Should we get 'em? They're right there," Mori whispered. Jahari could tell she wasn't the cool and composed type. He could hear the waver in her voice and see how wide her eyes were. She was out of her element, as brave as she was. It was a good thing. It meant she'd stay on her toes.

"Actually, 'we' are not doing anything. I have to go in there and make sure they don't summon that djinn."

"Very funny, Jahari. What are you gonna do alone, Mr. Hero?"

"Please, come on, I've been doing this my whole life. I'll be fine solo. We have to diffuse this situation before the vampire gets here. We're on the clock."

"Listen, you have a better chance of stopping them if you have help. I can distract them or I could be the one to ambush-"

"Mori! Listen to me. We're wasting time! You can help best if you stay here and I'm not going back and forth about this."

Mori stared him down for what felt like a week. Jahari didn't give an inch. Finally, she turned away and mumbled through gritted teeth, "Go."

"I'll call you if I really need help. If I'm not back in an hour, come and get me, okay?"

She said nothing, but nodded. Jahari left without another word, jogged to the fence that lined the warehouse and took a small device out of his pocket. It looked similar to a Geiger counter, except the antennae were made of a special wood that detected concentrations of spiritual energy. He scanned a roughly human sized portion of the fence for traps and when the device failed to pick up anything suspicious, he got to work. Focusing on that area of the fence, he used his psychokinesis to slice a hole big enough for him to crawl through. He entered the interior of the fence and, after scanning the area, flattened himself against the warehouse's exterior. He peeked through the window, but it was tinted and so dusty that the tint made little difference and he couldn't see anything. With his mind, he blasted the padlock with just enough force that the lock separated, but not so much that it rattled the door. He slipped inside, closing the door behind him and watching the light from the street lamps get swallowed. Now all he could see was the red light radiating from the weak bulbs inside.

Jahari moved cautiously. *No time left for scanning. I need to move*; he thought. The warehouse was hot and before Jahari knew it, beads of sweat had strung themselves around his neck like pearls. A labyrinth of crates and racks stretched out in front of him overbearingly. The light stung his eyes, and after the fifth turn he made through the maze, the room swirled. The chains above him swayed like the gallows in the sultry air of the warehouse, and not even the passage of time could mask the smell. It was the smell of old carnage, blood and offal that not even all the rinses and washes and outside air could mask. Sometimes that stink of violence never leaves. Jahari hated the meatpacking district.

He tried to sense any small sign of life and

find the two men, but it was almost like looking for something with a blindfold on. He probed further, but a force countered his own so hard it sent him reeling. Disoriented, he lost his footing and noticed something strange. He had stepped on a panel in the floor that gave way and sunk about an inch into the floor. The floor creaked as a small door opened out of what looked like a storage crate to the left of him. Jahari stood motionless as three creatures ambled out of the crate. They had naked, gray, sinewy bodies, hairless and smooth like porcelain. They barely came up to his knees, but Jahari knew what they were and what they were capable of: Homunculi.

I'm not sure how Clive or his friend created these in this short amount of time, but this isn't good. Homunculi are extremely strong and much smarter than they let on. They're either gonna waste my time or they're gonna make me give away my position. Jahari slowly edged towards the opposite side of the enclosed area, but found his back against more crates.

Almost as if its patience had run out, the first Homunculus leapt at Jahari's face and opened its mouth to reveal a mouth full of teeth that looked like broken glass. Jahari snatched it out of the air with his psychokinesis and dashed it onto the ground as hard as he could. In a flash, he scanned the room for a weapon. His eyes darted across the room until they settled on a large pole protruding from one of the cracked crates.

"Perfect," he said with a smile.

With the force of a missile, he launched it through the second Homunculus, which drove the pole and it through the wall. The creature writhed for a second, and then slowly peeled, like wood in a fire. Then, after a moment, it turned into ash.

Watching this process turned out to be a mistake, as one of the other Homunculi wrapped its arms around his neck from behind. Jahari felt his windpipe contract as the powerful creature jerked his neck back and clawed at his face. Razor sharp talons whistled by Jahari's ears but never quite made contact; Jahari willed the blows away, but he knew he couldn't be defensive.

These things don't get tired, and I have to make sure I'm not gassed for later. I can't play around anymore.

Jahari directed a small blast of force at the little monster, but it was just as quick as it was dexterous; it contorted its lower body and dodged the blast while it swiveled to Jahari's front. Now it was choking him, with its legs wrapped around Jahari's torso, and its maw inches from Jahari's face. It opened its mouth wide and lurched forward.

"ENOUGH," he bellowed, using his line of sight to direct his psychokinesis and tear every tooth and the top part of the Homunculus' head clear off of its body. "It would be great if I could have just one night without fangs in my face," he said while he dusted himself off. "Now, where's the third one?"

He heard a creaking noise from above him.

As he looked up, he saw the third Homunculus smiling at him as it pushed a mountain of crates on top of him.

CHAPTER THIRTY-NINE
Trapped

Eddie and Clive raced to the source of all the racket. It sounded like a war was going inside the warehouse. Eddie knew their trap had been sprung, so they were both on edge. "What the hell is that thing?" Clive said with a tremble in his voice. He was pointing at the remaining Homunculus, which was standing on top of the mess it had made like a dog. Packing material, pieces of wood, and ice littered the area. The Homunculus cocked its head to the side, but it was looking at Eddie, awaiting instructions.

"Search through this mess and find the body. If he's alive, don't hurt him any more than you already have."

On the one hand, Clive was happy Eddie could keep a cool head in a situation so dire, but he was horrified at the latter half of Eddie's statement. "Why wouldn't we kill it? It's the vampire. Just finish it off, for God's sake! I'll do it myself if I have to! This shit has to stop." Clive looked around him for anything he could use as a weapon. He picked up a metal rod that had fallen out of one of the crates and started swinging it into the pile of debris.

Eddie walked up to Clive calmly and slapped him so hard it echoed. "I need you to listen to me very carefully. This man might be from the police, or even worse, he might be from BRAHMASTRA and the last thing we need is to attract more attention with a murder. Get a grip." Clive spit at his feet, but said nothing else. They stood there in total silence, with their hearts crashing in their chest, like thunder from a distant place.

The Homunculus broke the silence, letting out a sharp whistle. It had unearthed a man from all the rubble. The man's presence was just as horrifying as birth. The two men rushed over and looked at an unscathed Jahari Jones, who was unmoving except for the gentle rise and fall of his chest, almost in sync with the dust that drifted with each step.

Clive swallowed hard, but it didn't clear the hard lump of fear that had collected in the back of his throat. In a state of total amazement, Clive did something uncharacteristically brave and poked his unconscious foe with the rod in his hand. There was no response. He looked at Eddie, who returned his wonder-struck expression with interest. Then, as if they'd read each other's minds, they lifted Jahari, putting their arms under his, and his arms on their shoulders. He wasn't especially heavy, and there was something vaguely spiritual about lifting up someone who could very well be their downfall. Deep down, perhaps not killing Jahari Jones, registered in Clive's subconscious as an act of kindness, an act that may save whatever was left of his soul. At the forefront of Eddie's mind was how they could best detain Jahari. They settled on wrapping him in chains and using the thickest padlock they could find to secure him. Then they dumped him off to the side of their little project.

Clive swallowed like he had a porcupine

quill stuck in his throat, "So… what now?"
Eddie looked at him as if he'd said 1+1 equalled 6.
"Maybe we should find a couch in this damned
warehouse and prop him up? Maybe we can play
Go Fish and get milkshakes from the diner across
the street! Good last supper, huh? Why am I always
the guy who has to find the solution?"

"You caused the problem!" Clive hissed
through gritted teeth. "You wanted all that reading
and practicing you did to pay off and we hit the
jackpot, woo hoo! Hooray for Eddie the Great and
Powerful!"

"Shut up!"

"No, no, no, I'm not finished. You-" Clive
was interrupted by a faint scratching noise to their
right.

CHAPTER FORTY
No Useful Answers

Jahari had let his ruse go far enough. Shielding himself from the falling debris had been easy; listening to two idiots squabble was not. He shifted loudly, purposefully, into an upright position and pretended to be disoriented. The color returned to both of their faces and with it was a dappled mix of confusion, relief and happiness, all on the palette of their expressions. As usual, Eddie was the first to react.

"Who are you?! Were you sent to stop us? What are you doing here?"

Jahari looked at him square in the face. "I'm minding my fuckin' business."

"What?"

"Look, none of your questions are gonna have answers that are useful to anyone here, so let's skip the foreplay."

"You're definitely not the person in control here, Mystery Man," Eddie sneered. The Homunculus crept to its master's side to prove his point.

"Neither are you. The moon's up, and your scent is getting stronger by the moment."

The two men blanched again. This time Clive spoke, but his attitude was much humbler than his companion. "He's right. He's taken care of, anyway. Let's just finish this, Eddie." His pleading hand found a place on Eddie's shoulder.

"Hurrying might not be exactly in your best interests. You guys have already forgotten to salt around the circle and your diagram is off," Jahari said, gesturing with his foot to all of their purported errors.

Eddie threw his hands above his head. "Oh please, why should we trust you? You snuck in here, and you've probably been tracking our movements."

"Think about it. I killed two of your homunculi. If I had really wanted to kill you two, you'd be dead. If I had wanted to arrest you guys, I could've done that too. Chances are, what I'm telling you is gonna help more than it'll hurt."

"I'll get drained by that undead bastard before I listen to you!"

Jahari shrugged. "Stuck on stupid. I respect that."

Clive grabbed Eddie by both shoulders, gently. "We're wasting time. I believe in you, brother, but we screwed up when we woke up the vampire. I don't see how listening to him could hurt us more than what we have coming."

"Let's say he saves us; where do we go? On the run again? Do we get locked up? What if the other option is worse than death?" For the first time throughout this ordeal, Clive saw naked fear in Eddie's eyes, fear finally pooling like a bruise forming, unsightly and full of shame. They had run out of places to run, run out of tricks to try. It was pitiful. He looked like a child who'd lost his father in the grocery store. This vulnerability was not lost on Jahari.

"Look, I'll help you and you don't even have to do anything. Lemme ask you a question. Do you know anything about the djinn you are about to summon?"

"It needs blood and ash to summon, and it grants three wishes," Eddie said triumphantly.

"Give yourself a pat on the back, but here's my advice. Be very careful how you phrase your wishes. Djinn thrive on chaos. It'll use your own words against you," Jahari while shrugging.

The effect was immediate; he'd given enough information to make Eddie afraid of his own ignorance, but not enough to know what to do on his own to fix it. Eddie's jaw flexed. "What'd you say about the circle?"

CHAPTER FORTY-ONE
Beep, Crash, Beep

For all his bravado, Eddie followed instructions well. He corrected the circle, re-salted the area, and followed Jahari's orders to the T. Clive worked diligently as well, handing ingredients to Eddie when needed, monitoring Jahari, and looking less fearful. Jahari felt that he'd done enough after a short while and only offered his help if asked or if he saw something wrong. Everything was going according to plan in all three men's minds, but there was one enemy they weren't monitoring, and that enemy was time. The timer on Jahari's watch beeped, signaling that an hour had passed. The shrill sound seemed far away as the blood rushed in the three men's ears. Their heartbeats sounded like peals of thunder.

Beep **CRASH** *Beep* **CRASH** *Beep* **CRASH** *Beep* **CRASH** *Beep* **CRASH**

"Will you turn that damned thing off?! I can barely hear myself think. What the hell is that noise?" Eddie bellowed over the din, covering his ears, and shut his eyes like that would mute the sound.

"Wait… you can hear it too?" Clive said. "I thought it was in my head."

"Of course *Beep* I can *Beep* hear whatever the hell that is. I bet he did this. What are you doing, you little shit?!" Eddie rounded on Jahari and grabbed him by the collar.

Jahari gave him a curious look. "Dawg, how do you expect me to do anything with these chains on? You should be worried about putting the finishing touches on the ritual."

Eddie was starting to lose it. His frustration had boiled over into incoherent groaning and Jahari could see flecks of spittle forming at the corners of his mouth. As Jahari slipped from his grip and fell to the floor, he thought about ending this whole charade right then and there. He hadn't signed up for dealing with crazy. Then he noticed the pale fingers wrapped around Eddie's throat. The vampire had arrived.

He looked much different from what

Cameron Toker had described, but that was to be expected. After decades without feeding, the hunger had sent his body into overdrive. The vampire was physically impressive, standing slightly shorter than Jahari, not stocky, but no longer emaciated and corpse-like, with sandy blonde hair in a sloppy buzz cut. He was, however, wearing the same faded, black, bloodstained burial shroud draped around him like a cloak that he'd been wearing when he had killed Evette. The vampire lifted Eddie close to his face, screaming about something Jahari couldn't quite make out in a language he didn't quite understand. His mind was racing, and he needed to focus so he could make his move. Crawling on his belly like an inchworm, he scanned the room quickly until his eye snagged on the dim glint of light reflecting off of the lamp in Clive's trembling hands. And like that, he had a plan.

In one deft move, Jahari peeled chains off him with his psychokinesis, shattering the padlock and unfurling the chains. Then he hurled his bonds like a bolo at the vampire's legs hard enough to draw blood. The vampire hissed in pain, lips drawn back, allowing anger to pass through his vicious fangs. Jahari saw the vampire hit the ground hard from the force of the chains and turned to focus his attention back on Clive. Unfortunately for him, Clive was nowhere to be found.

Jahari swore, shaking the ground with the force of his frustration. Determined to get his bearings, he turned over on his back to find the bleeding vampire standing over him. "Dammit."

"That… hurt!" the creature said in a voice just louder than a whisper.

Beep Beep* Beep* Beep* Beep* Beep* Beep*

The vampire stared at his watch in confusion, and Jahari smiled at him. A sudden rumbling unsettled them both, but only for a moment, then the company car crashed through the warehouse wall so fast the vampire didn't even have time to gasp. The car struck him, dragging him through a dozen racks and even more crates. Mori walked through the gaping hole in the warehouse wall as if everything was normal.

"It's been an hour…" she said with a shrug.

"Well, shit, thank you very much. My car is busted, but your timing was perfect; I was out of ideas."

"You can't drive anyway, so it's not that big of a loss?"

"When you put it like that, it's actually more annoying," Jahari said as he got up and dusted himself off, "but we don't have much time. He's not gonna be down for long. What we really need is that lamp."

"Are you going to wish for a way to kill the vampire?"

"Nah, you gotta remember that Ifrit are manipulative. If I wish for a way to kill the vampire, it might create a situation where one of us gets hurt, too. They operate on the principle that you can't get something for nothing and will twist your words to make sure they harm you just as much as help you."

Mori pulled out the gun from her belt. "So, are we fighting or what?"

A smile crept onto Jahari's face. "Nah, I've got a plan. But first things first, the lamp." Jahari called out into the darkness. "Eddie! Clive!"

An arm popped out from under planks of wood and dust and Clive's voice answered, "I'm here. I'm fine. I don't know where Eddie is."

"We'll find him, Clive, but if you want to live, you have to help us." Jahari turned to Mori. "I'll distract the vampire. Can you help him out of the rubble and find the lamp?"

Mori frowned. "I'll do it, but if I see you need help, I'll be right there with you."

"If you can get me the lamp, we won't need any more help than that, trust me." Mori started freeing the entombed Clive while Jahari turned his attention to his foe, keeping the sacrificial circle behind him.

The vampire had just finished tearing the car to scrap metal and smiled when he saw Jahari was ready to fight. In a flash, the vampire was rushing forward, but much slower than last time.

He's not really a fighter. He's so strong it makes him sloppy. The only explanation for him moving slower is that he's being cautious. That moment of over-analysis proved to be a mistake for Jahari, however. A telegraphed swipe came hurtling towards Jahari's head. Jahari blew it away with little effort, smirking, until he realized what was really going on. The vampire's other fist shot out like a missile, leaving Jahari with a split second to concentrate, meaning his force blast wasn't necessarily the strongest. The vampire drew away his hand, which was mangled, fingers bent at crooked angles, forearm damaged, wrist broken. Jahari pulled his bruised left arm away; the vampire had drawn blood, and he knew it.

They skidded three paces from one another,

eyes locked.

Dammit! I got too cocky. I have to compose myself. He's crafty, attacking my weak side and feinting like that. But he's still being cautious. I can do this! He knows I can hurt him. All I need to do is outmaneuver him, use his strengths against him.

Jahari's thoughts were shattered like glassware by the vampire's sudden scream. The arm Jahari had blasted had turned a deep purple and become bloated as the blood pooled into it, knitting flesh and bone back together. In a flash, his hand was fine, if a little red, and the vampire was flexing his fingers with a fanged grin on his face.

Jahari swore.

A blur of a vampire barreled forward, but this time Jahari was ready. Jahari shot a focused stream of force through the floor, raising the boards and tripping the vampire. He stumbled, and Jahari pressed his advantage. Using the momentum from the vampire's dash and his own psychokinesis to steady himself, he grabbed the scruff of the vampire's coat and threw the vampire over his shoulder and onto his back as hard as he could. It wasn't enough; the vampire was up just as quickly as he was downed and swinging even faster. Jahari watched his waist, avoiding and parrying the strikes that rained down on him. He weaved under two hooks and, using his mind to create a hard shell of force around his arm, launched a counter that landed squarely on the tip of the vampire's chin.

Scrunch

Blood poured from the fanged maw, and the vampire was stunned. Exactly how Jahari had planned it. There was no time for the vampire to react. Jahari kept punching him, aiming at his jaw specifically. It was a sickening symphony of impact and dull groans of pain, one that Jahari had learned how to tune out long ago. The concentration of the act made it feel like it was going on for eons, but after a few seconds, he heard Mori's voice cutting through the noise.

"Here it is!" She said as she sent the lamp

sailing in his direction. Jahari blasted the vampire away and then chased the lamp's arc. He slid on his belly like a penguin to catch the lamp, just for it to fall right into his hands. But as he held the warm metal in his hands, Jahari's neck tingled. He sensed a presence looming over him.

"Hand. It. Over." The three words were almost spat out of Eddie's bloody mouth. His eyes had a manic clarity to them and his hand held firmly the gun Jahari had given Mori.

"You gotta be kidding me."

"I don't care! Give me the lamp before I paint the floor with your brains." Behind Jahari, the vampire was groaning dully on his knees, but fortunately for the two of them, he wasn't moving.

"Worry about snaggletooth over there, not little old me."

Eddie fired a round into the vampire, sent the Homunculus to follow the bullet, and then turned the barrel back to Jahari. "Problem solved. Now, please, the lamp."

Jahari sighed, slowly rolled onto his back and raised his hand and the lamp, but hesitated.

"Oh, what is it now?"

"*Tuo tempo è scaduto!*" the vampire roared. He'd already torn the Homunculus to shreds. Things were becoming dire quickly. The vampire hurled fragments of wooden crates and rubble at them.

Jahari stopped the debris in midair with little effort, but in doing so, he'd diverted his attention away from Eddie. Eddie rushed him and whipped the muzzle of the gun across Jahari's face. Jahari blocked it with his uninjured arm, but couldn't use his power to cushion the blow.

"Argh, I just saved you, asshole!"

"I'll thank you with my wish. Don't worry."

Eddie tried to gain positioning and put his entire weight on Jahari, but Jahari wouldn't stay still. Jahari created space by extending his leg and kicked up a cloud of dust with his mind. The dust bought him some time, but when he got to his feet, the gun was still pointed at his face. To make matters worse, the vampire was within a few steps distance from the two of them, holding Moriko by her neck.

"*Finito.*"

They were at a standstill. Eddie wanted the lamp in Jahari's hands, but Jahari couldn't really make a move without the vampire hurting Moriko. Worse still, Jahari wasn't sure what the vampire wanted to accomplish. The trio stole furtive glances at one another; Jahari was worried about Mori. Eddie, fearing his time was running out, watched the vampire, and the vampire warily watched Jahari, the first being that had posed a threat to him since his past life.

Jahari broke the silence. "Here's what's gonna happen. Eddie, I will pass you the lamp. Vampire, please, just don't hurt her, she's an innocent here. Let her go and I won't interfere with you any longer."

"Why can't I just shoot you and grab the

lamp."

"That's a fair question, jackass. The only problem with that plan is that I'm what's making the vampire think twice about killing you right now. There's just something we gotta tweak to make this work."

"What could you possibly want to do right now?" Eddie said, the muzzle of the gun trembling as he adjusted his aim.

"It's just that the lamp should be over there," he said, yanking the lamp out of Eddie's hand with his psychokinesis. "I should be there too," and he slid himself over to the summoning circle, "and you should be way over there," he said with a blast of force that sent Eddie flying.

Jahari rubbed blood from his injured arm on the bronze and felt his stomach drop. He could see everything around him slow to a snail's pace; a bullet crawled lazily through the air from Eddie's direction. Moriko pulled a blade out from God knows where and stabbed the vampire in the thigh.

Jahari looked at his hands and noticed he was still moving in real time. The lamp was glowing as if someone had thrown it in a furnace and belching thick red smoke. The smoke enveloped the room in a syrupy haze, and it obscured the scene that was playing out in its sloth. Soon Jahari was left alone in the dark.

"Moriko?!" He called out. His voice echoed out endlessly, but what responded wasn't Moriko. Whatever it was just barely had enough form to be seen. The smoke quickly coalesced as the lamp grew still. The heavy cloud was in the center of the space and black, glittering eyes shone from deep inside of it. Icicle-like teeth with points like darts lined a mouth that led to nothing but a void. The Ifrit's massive form spilled out, expanding over the entire room like the ocean rushing through a broken levee, but it spoke in a high whistle.

"Ah, dear Jahari Jones, greetings and salutations. I am the Almighty Djinn of Bronze and Rubies, Warden of Smoke and Embers. I congratulate you, for you have successfully summoned a being such as I." It made a big show of this greeting, bowing deeply with billowing paws and giving Jahari that uncanny, toothy grin once again. His face had no solid quality to it, so the features shifted with the movements of the air, becoming too close to each other, or longer than they should be. Jahari could see brilliant rubies set into each tooth. The Djinn waved its hands in elaborate circles, smoke and sparks flying as it picked up the pace and continued its introduction. "Now, I give you the rules. You are now the exalted inheritor of three wishes, with no restrictions on what your desires may acquire. You must take full advantage and use all three, for these gifts are hard to come by." On the surface, it was ostentatious, but Jahari knew better than to show any expression besides interest. He watched, wide eyed, as the gears in his brain turned.

"O great and powerful djinn, I am honored to be in your presence. Thank you for lending your immense strength to a small mortal such as myself," Jahari said, stalling for time. The Djinn's brow cocked, amusement creeping on the corner of his face, like a parent watching their child do a funny dance. "For my first wish, I humbly request that any effect of a wish that I make during this ritual that would cause physical, mental, or spiritual harm directly or indirectly to myself or anyone I care about, or even any effects I deem negative or would be deemed negative by anyone else, those effects should be experienced by you tenfold."

The air became thick with the pressure of the Ifrit's rage. Heat radiated from the rolling eyes and teeth floating in Jahari's face. Jahari smirked; he knew a djinn could cause no direct harm to its master, and the circle would contain any other chaos that might result from his wishes.

"Impudent insect! You have the audacity to make such a wish and... and..."

"Enough. I have two wishes left and I have things to do today," Jahari said in a steely tone.

"Your master is ready to move on."

"Fine master, your first wish is now granted and I eagerly await my continued service." Each word was spat out as mockingly as possible as red bands of light snaked around the Djinn's arms, binding them. Jahari's wish had been granted.

"Now for my second wish, I want you to render the vampire in this room unconscious but unharmed until 11:59 AM our time. After 11:59 AM, he can regain consciousness, but he will remain physically weak for another hour."

"Child's play for one such as I, although such a simple wish seems puzzling following your first."

Jahari sucked his teeth impatiently. "I thought you were here to grant wishes, not ask questions. Is how complicated my wishes are your concern?"

"It isn't master, but you know, your wish hasn't been granted just yet. There's still time if you want something else. I see that you're looking for some information; you could always ask for the knowledge you seek. Fix your body and mind, perhaps? You could wish for peace in your life. The world is at your feet, Jahari Jones."

The smoke that blanketed the room started rolling and forming shapes, dreams, ideas, treasures, power, and knowledge. Fortune billowed into his brain, black and promising like the banks of the River Nile. Jahari saw his uncle, his parents alive and well, his body healed and perfect. Anything and everything appeared at his fingertips.

The Djinn wafted into Jahari's ears, filling his head with its voice. "You could wish away those nights of waking up as a child in a cell." Jahari's mind flashed with memories he couldn't quite place... the cell? That thing that was in there...

But Jahari stayed firm. "That is enough. My second wish is gonna be exactly as I stated it and my last wish will be that I will survive a situation of my choosing, totally unharmed. Got it?"

A frown formed on the djinn's face, as if someone had ruined the punchline of a joke he was making. "So be it. All you have wished for will come to pass, master. Farewell, and good luck. You'll need it." With that, the smoke siphoned back into the lamp, which was glowing with the heat of the djinn's energy, but the image of that contorted face with the glittering eyes lingered. The lamp scorched the floor underneath it and, impossibly, melted into nothing. A sweet breeze carried the ash away, and the events around Jahari resumed.

CHAPTER FORTY-TWO
We're Dead Meat

Jahari turned to see the vampire collapse onto the mangled Eddie. Clive was struggling to stand, and Mori was a pace away, knife drawn. Jahari hoped Clive wouldn't try to pull anything, not with him and the girl who just ran over a vampire with a van.

"What the hell just happened?" she asked breathlessly. "Did you do that?"

"I used the lamp. I'll tell you about it later. Watch Clive while I get Eddie." Jahari said, prepared for the worst. Eddie's chest had been raked so badly that he looked like a zombie. Deep gashes criss-crossed over his abdomen and chest, exposing his ribs, and his pinky and ring finger on his left hand were bent at an unnatural angle. It was a piteous sight, but when Jahari bent down and whispered in Eddie's ear, the mangled man found his tone to be terse and authoritative,

"Listen up. Your wounds are not beyond BRAHMASTRA's ability to treat. If you want to live, it's not a problem at all. I'll make sure you're taken care of. You probably won't even have lasting injuries. All you have to do is give up all the information you have on the Sight."

Eddie spoke in a soggy, pained growl, "I'm... I'm supposed... to believe you won't do worse? We're dead men." He rolled on his side so he could see Clive. "Hear that Clive-y Boy? WE'RE DEAD MEAT! It's all over, but no one is going to clean up my mess but me."

"Just cooperate Eddie. You're hurt and we're in over our heads. It doesn't have to be this way man, enough people have died." Clive pleaded. Eddie spat at Clive feebly. "We get what we deserve."

With a speed that seemed impossible given his condition, Eddie pulled what looked like a homemade hand grenade from the inside of his coat.

"I'LL SEE YOU IN HELL!" he said as it detonated it in his hand.

Everyone felt heat swell and a blinding light

grew, but just as soon as their senses picked up the blast, it was gone. Jahari was panting slightly from the effort of suppressing the explosion.

"I'll probably see you before that, as a ghost," he said mournfully. Jahari turned away from Eddie's steaming remains and focused on the living. He could see that the events of the night were finally sinking into Mori and Clive's heads. Mori's hands trembled, and Clive's face was ashen and blank. He needed to get them thinking otherwise shock might set in. He pulled out a piece of paper from the pad and pen he kept in his pocket and started jotting digits down. "Mori, I need you to take this, and call the number, say my name, then recite the second set of numbers, then your name. Repeat it back to me."

"Call the number, Jahari Jones, second set of numbers, my name." The response was swift, clear, and unfaltering.

"Make sure they send the medical unit and ask for the FBI plus the usual response team from BA, and ask them to bring another truck and make sure they set the up the Bank. Make sure they bring vampire containment equipment, silver chains, garlic spray, anything and everything. They'll know what to do." Jahari turned his attention back to Clive as Moriko turned away to make the call.

"Clive, think. Are there any traps left around anywhere?"

"N-no, I don't think so."

"Okay, so now we're gonna make sure. Show me anywhere and everywhere you and Eddie went." Jahari had Clive sling his arm over his shoulder and carried him to his feet. He sobbed silently on Jahari's shoulder. "I know it's hard, but you'll get through this. I need you to focus because I need some information from you."

"What do you need from me?"

"What do you know about The Sight? Did they choose you for something? How did you get involved with them?"

"We were looking into the occult as a hobby,

me and… me and… yeah."

Jahari cleared his throat. "And then?"

"We found out about a gathering on the internet. It seemed like a fantasy type of thing, for enthusiasts."

"Clive, I need you to speed this up. How did a gathering for nerds turn into a paranormal terrorist group?"

"On the surface, it was a festival, but it slowly became more and more intense. They had us do these exercises, like holding our breath for long periods of time, standing on one foot in the elements for hours and hours in the heat and cold. They tortured some people and tested our aptitude for mystic arts, then picked 12 of us based on our talents, but I don't know what the hell any of our talents were. We were given all kinds of books, artifacts, and resources, and were told to prove ourselves. There was a ritual that could rejuvenate the weak, maybe even raise the dead. We were going to test on, on the, on the vampire. But we didn't know it was a vampire in there, man. I just wanted to bring my sister back."

"Do you know any of the other recruits?"

The arrival of BA's response team cut Clive's answer short. Four agents promptly shut down the warehouse and the streets across a four-block radius. One agent stayed to give Clive medical attention while the others swept the area for anything important. Jahari narrated the events of the night to the medic. Mori sat and wondered what she'd gotten herself into. She'd never even scratched her beloved Corolla back in Japan, and now she'd totaled a car, colliding it with a vampire. It was far from an average night for her.

The FBI showed up 11 minutes after BA did, which was a little slower than usual, considering Jahari was involved. A call from him was like a five alarm fire. A severe man in a slate gray suit walked up to the little gathering and spoke.

"Good evening, I'm Agent Constantine Ketchum."

"Evenin'. I'm Special Agent Jahari Jones from BRAHMASTRA. This is Moriko Miyazaki. She's a deputized agent."

"Yo." Jahari called out.

The medic briefly looked up. "Special Agent Lauren Howard, emergency medical response team. The rest of the BA team are my subordinates," she said in a bored tone. It was late. She hadn't bothered flashing her badge and I.D. like Jahari had; he was probably going to do whatever he wanted in the next few minutes and would catch the resulting flak. She would let Jahari deal with the Fed and hopefully get back to bed before sunrise. It wasn't her first rodeo.

Agent Ketchum was a thin man with sharp features, a pinched nose, and lips thinner than mountain air. His facial expression was just as cold. "So can someone, uh, fill me in on what's going on here?"

"Well Mr. Ketchum, I-"

"Agent Ketchum, Mr. Jones. Agent."

A sardonic smile crept onto Jahari's face. "Ah Agent. Well, the case of the theft of an occult artifact and the murder of a young woman in cold blood have both come to their dramatic conclusion tonight. Spooky shit. Good thing we were equipped to contain the situation. Can't expect you to catch them all right? Or any of them, for that matter. Now my question is, respectfully, why were you sent instead of Mario or Aisha?"

"If it's all the same to you, respectfully, I'll be asking the questions here." Agent Ketchum said with profound disrespect, "and what I really need right now is a detailed breakdown of the events that transpired here tonight. I need statements from everyone involved, and I need arrests made."

Jahari and Lauren looked at each other with amused expressions. Lauren gave Jahari the "he's gonna be very mad when he realizes he is out of his element" face, and Jahari gave Lauren the "he must have lost his damn mind" face.

"Aight, here's what's about to happen, I am

going to take the vampire to a safe place where he'll be questioned and possibly destroyed and Lauren's team will probably patch Clive up and get command to figure out what will be his fate. Eddie is pretty dead, so my guess is you guys will deal with him. And then we'll call it a night," he said, patting Agent Ketchum on the arm patronizingly. "Sound good Connie?"

"And you just make rules up as you go along? Did you consult anyone before you pulled that action plan out of your ass?"

Lauren piped up this time. "Well, actually, he consulted me, but he didn't really have to, considering he outranks everyone here. We belong to an organization that doesn't answer to the government. Our action plan is completely up to his discretion. Usually, he does what he wants to do, and it works out for the best. So, I think you can both zip it up. The lady's given her opinion."

"Welp, I think everyone's up to speed, Agent Howard, would you mind passing Moriko over here the keys to the truck, and I'll be out of all of your hair, or lack thereof," he added looking at the pathetic wisps covering Ketchum's head. He said his goodbyes to the agents at the scene and checked on Clive one last time. "Stay up, okay?"

"Thank you for everything. I hope I can help you in the future." They shared a lingering handshake and then Jahari was off. He lifted the vampire with his psychokinesis and put him gently inside the back of the truck. Then he used the silver chains to bind the vampire, sat him up on one of the benches, and locked the loading doors.

When both he and Mori were seated and ready to go, Jahari prepared himself for the really hard part of the night.

"You good? Tonight was some crazy shit, yeah?" He asked the questions lightly, as if they were nothing. He thought it might help, or at least disarm her. It wasn't her first experience, but it was still intense.

"I'm not sure if I am okay. Can I be honest

with you?"

Jahari said nothing. He just nodded, and she continued.

"Part of me feels strange saying this to you, considering everything that you've experienced, like it's small in comparison, but there's so much carnage, so much death. There's so much that I've seen in what? Less than a month? I would've never imagined this kind of darkness in the world, even with what I know. I'm not a naïve person; I know there are horrible things happening every day, but this," she paused for a moment to gather her thoughts, and when she spoke again she was defiant, aggressive almost, "I'm not asking for pity or for you not to judge me. This is probably normal for you. It's probably a regular week! But it's a shock to me, a shock that I can deal with and beat just like I beat everything in the forest. It's still shocking, though."

"I'm not judging you," Jahari said softly. "I'm still scared."

"I never said I was scared!"

"No, but I can feel it. And it's good. The fear keeps you alive. And it keeps you human."

"Well, then, how do *you* beat it?"

"Beat what?"

"That darkness."

"I'm not sure you do. It ain't really about beating anything. The darkness is always there, looming. It's a part of you, like your shadow. You just acknowledge it and accept it and, I don't know, but ain't control. Control means struggling. Many people try fighting their demons. I try to persuade 'em to behave."

"Thank you, Badass Sensai."

Jahari chuckled. "Maybe that was a little much. I pray about it sometimes."

"Oh, really?" Mori said, her eyes widening, "I wouldn't have guessed you were the praying type. So that must mean that you believe in God, then?"

"Yup."

"So despite all the terror you've seen, you believe someone all powerful is looking out for each one of us?"

"Beats the hell outta the alternative. Plus, I've actually seen stuff from the Vedas in action. That creates faith. There's more in play than just bad stuff happening to good people. There's so much we can't see or even understand. And through all that, I'd like to believe someone is looking out for me. There's a Creole saying, 'lespwa fè viv'. It means 'hope makes one live'. The idea that someone cares, that hope might be all we have in the world, even if it's just another person."

"And what happens when you fail? Do you pray then? Do you still believe someone is looking out for you?"

"Failure isn't an option I've had the privilege to enjoy."

"What happens when you can't take it anymore? When the darkness eats you up?"

"I don't know, but I know I'm a helluva lot better suited for this than regular people. Someone has to do it, so that everyone in the world can have peace of mind. That feeling you have in the pit of your stomach? It destroys normal people. We've got more of the stuff, I guess. I don't know exactly what the stuff is, but regardless of whether it's a blessing or a curse; that's the hand they dealt us."

They sat there for a moment, staring out the windshield at the busywork of law enforcement unfolding in front of them.

Finally, Mori spoke in a small voice. "How do you know that I have the stuff?"

"Hitting that vampire with the car was pretty cool, that's when I knew," he said. "It seems like you're built for this, but again, if you ever want out, you don't have to stick around."

"Oh enoughhh, I don't know how you've survived without me this long."

"From what I remember, you almost had your windpipe crushed."

"Whatever you want to tell yourself," Moriko said with a laugh. "Honestly though, with what happened to my father, it might be safer for me doing this. Like compared to trying to live a 'normal' life. At least I know where the monsters are coming from."

"So it doesn't have anything to do with my psychic ass keeping you hale and hearty, huh?"

"I've been taking care of myself just fine. I told you, YOU need ME. Now, what are we doing next?"

"Now we get to work. We gotta go to the Bank."

"I'm not even going to ask what that means?"

"Good, I'm too tired to explain." Jahari opened his palm and unfolded the small piece of paper he had been clutching.

"What is that?"

"Clive, put it in my hand when we said goodbye." In neat, block letters were 10 names, and at the bottom of the small paper it read "The other recruits. We used the amulets to keep in contact." An amulet identical to the one he'd found in Evette Toker's house was wrapped up inside the paper.

And so, giddy at their discoveries, they cruised to their next destination, with dawn nipping at their heels.

CHAPTER FORTY-THREE
Piñata Head

Enzo woke up feeling like someone had used his head as a piñata, which wasn't far from the truth. He rolled over onto his back to see Jahari and Moriko looking at him with amusement and healthy caution.

"He's awake." She said.

"It's about time."

"Are you sure he can't hurt us?"

"Only one way to find out, right?"

Enzo tried to lunge at the two of them, but he found moving his arms to be almost impossible. All he could manage was a weak hiss and a lame movement of his hands. He had no such trouble speaking.

"*Che cazzo*?!"

"Ooh, potty mouth." Jahari was enjoying this.

The vampire snarled, this time in English, "Where are they?"

"You must be talking about the two bozos you've been chasing around the Tri-state like Tom

& Jerry?"

"You waste my time, *cretino*!"

"Hate to break it to you, big dog, but your time is my time. Look around you," Jahari said as he put his arm under Enzo's shoulder and hoisted him upright.

"Welcome to the Bank! It's BRAHMASTRA's multipurpose room! Designed to house and neutralize several kinds of dangerous creatures when necessary! Check your local Bank out, in every major city of the world." He gestured to the layer of metal, vertical blinds that covered the walls, running from a track attached to the flooring and ending in a track on the ceiling. The blinds overlapped, like the bottom of a colander.

"See these? I can collapse these blinds with a thought and the noon sun would come in here through the plexiglass windows and fry your ass. I'm making you aware of the situation you're in because we need your help."

"Why would I help you two after you ruined

my chances of finishing those two 'bobos' or whatever you called them?" His face was inches from Jahari's, and had he been able to move properly, Jahari would've been in serious trouble. Jahari could feel the anger boiling in Enzo's spirit.

"Because we aren't your enemies. Our job was and still is to make sure you aren't running around willy-nilly killing people in the most blatant ways possible. We only fought with you because of that. The common thread in all of this activity is this," he said, pulling out Evette Toker's amulet.

Enzo's face darkened. "Where did you get that?"

"It was in the house where you murdered that woman."

"They were fools with more power than they could control. They turned a monster like me loose on the world and got what they deserved!"

"Well, I agree with you, on the first part at least. There's more to it than those three, though. This symbol has been popping up all over the world: Japan, Latin America, Europe; there's even been whispers of activity in India. We think The Sight of the Third Eye is prepping for a resurgence. So the real question is, what do you wanna do?"

"I want to go back into the river they submerged me in, where I can't hurt anyone and I can rest. I have nothing to do with this world anymore, nothing that isn't bloodshed. I don't want to hurt people anymore."

"Trust me, I know what that feels like. You live so far outside a normal person's experience that no one can relate. It gets so lonely that you believe it's better for everyone if you just keep to yourself. But not everyone gets the luxury of rolling over and dying. Some of us have a responsibility to shoulder these burdens for the rest of the world. If you choose to go back into that river in Italy, I can't guarantee your safety. Vampires have rules about territory and feeding and you're definitely a liability, not to mention the organization I work with might destroy you before you even get across the border. Fact is, you wouldn't make it out of the United States."

"They can try! I have my strength back now!"

"Do what you gotta do. I have no dog in this fight, but I will protect myself if I need to, and that won't go well for you, believe me. And if by some miracle you can kill me and Mori here, then BRAHMASTRA will come after you. This time they'll have even more people and information on you. I know you have little choice here, but I really want to help you. In order for me to do that, you gotta fill me in on a few things. Got it?"

He meant what he said about wanting to help. Enzo could see it. So Enzo told them his story, from his birth to his gruesome rebirth. Moriko listened carefully, as if she were memorizing his every word. Jahari was listening for something different. Enzo could tell he was more interested in how the story was being told, rather than the content itself. He had deflated, and as all the words came out, so did the emotion, the energy, the fear. After he finished, silence filled the room.

"So now what?" Moriko said with uncertainty.

Jahari gave them both a devilish grin. "We've got all the pieces on the board. Now you guys can take it easy while I finesse this."

"How can you guarantee my safety?" Enzo couldn't shake the feeling that it was all a trap, and the thought buzzed around in the back of his head like a mosquito.

"You're worried about your safety *now*?"

"I haven't been in my right mind! And you've given me... more to think about," he said with his fangs bared. "I want my mother to be avenged. I want all of this madness to stop, otherwise this curse I'm living with is a random act of cruelty. My death cannot be a waste, soldier boy."

"If all of that is true, then you have nothing

to worry about. We're all gonna get what we want out of this. And I'm not a soldier."

"I should hope not. I've had to do away with quite a few of those."

"Okay guys," Mori said, breaking the tension in the room, "tonight has been hard on all of us and, according to Jahari, our next move is going to take time. Perfect opportunity for everyone to take a step back and collect our thoughts. You just have to trust us and in return, we're going to be kind to you, right, Jahari?"

It wasn't a question. Both men nodded.

Eating For Two

CHAPTER FORTY-FOUR
October 1, 2021

It's been quite a long time since I did this. Honestly, it feels a little silly, but what with everything that's been going on, I feel like this might be good for me. I used to journal when I was a kid, so this feels like an extension of that in a way. I found an old tape recorder in the attic; it didn't even need any repairs. Pen and paper feel a little old-fashioned, and this a good little place to bitch and moan about Scott. *chuckles* It's been exactly 2 months since we lost you. You never had the chance to see the world, so I'm going to tell you all about it here! Scott, your father, and I had never settled on a name for you. Maybe you'll tell me later, somehow. You'll have a lot of tapes to reply to. I'll try to record you something every day. God will deliver it straight to you in heaven.

I will always love you, Daughter,

Francine

CHAPTER FORTY-FIVE
October 2, 2021

Today was a good day! They offered me my job back at the hospital and they gave me about two weeks to decide because that's when the current cardiologist is leaving. I don't leave the house much anymore, but this might be good for me. This house is starting to feel like a prison, and I've gone to the grocery store quite enough, thank you very much. It's just so strange. I've worked in hospitals my whole life. They're like a second home to me. Now I can't even stomach driving by the hospital. But everything changes slowly. There were so many days where I just didn't want to do anything. People would come by and visit and I could see the pity in their eyes. "I can't imagine how hard this must be for you," they'd say with that look on their face, that annoying look, as if a frown and forehead creases help me. I don't mean to seem ungrateful, it's just sad. The truth is that they really can't imagine. Feeling new life spring up within your very own body, only for it to get snuffed out. The doctors said it wasn't uncommon, there was a genetic abnormality. I'd spent 35 weeks with you, and now I've spent 8 weeks without you. Honestly, it feels like my whole life at this point. It feels silly saying that. I mean, it actually was your whole life. These tapes will be a new life for you. That's a promise.

Love,

Mommy.

You know my name now, so it's kind of weird for you not to call me Mommy.

CHAPTER FORTY-SIX
October 3, 2021

So today I think I'll tell you about your parents! Don't you think that'll be fun? It should take my mind off of things at home; at least, I hope it does. Your daddy's name is Scott Michael Ponce. We met in high school and I was smitten. I remember my parents telling me to take it slow, but we got married straight out of high school. He was the first boy that really liked me; it was intoxicating. Having someone who really loves you, who really wants you, that young, I was flying. Your grandpa gave us a big wedding present, and we ended up going to Alberta for our honeymoon. Those mountains really felt spiritual, like you could touch the beginning of the world. We actually went back to those same mountains 2 weeks ago. Scott thought it might help, the fresh air, the chill, the quiet. I'll admit it worked a little. He practically forced me to go, but it worked out, just like it always does. Your papa has always had a very strong intuition. He's always been an ambitious man, always very headstrong. I trust him, for all it's worth. He's studying to become a minister! He only started about 5 months ago. Sometimes I tease him, because now I can never say, "my God forsaken husband." Well, I hope God is taking good care of you. I miss you so much it hurts. It's so odd, missing a person who was never actually born. I thought maybe I could give you a name, at least in here. How about Wendy? What do you think? I wanted to give you the gift of life, but this is all I have to give. I'm so sorry.

Love,

Mommy

CHAPTER FORTY-SEVEN
October 4, 2021

Hi Wendy! Today I went to the grocery store! I'm really glad that I did. It was really bright and sunny today and it was warm enough that I didn't even need a jacket. I left at around 11am and ran a few errands and picked up some items: cold cuts, canned goods, pasta, rice, and some salmon. There's supposed to be a big snowstorm on its way, so we have to stock up! Your daddy added some things to the list, mainly meat and herbs. He asked for a lot of venison, which was funny because I never knew he liked it. He also had me pick up some candles from the general store. Maybe I'll get a romantic dinner out of all of this! Let's see tomorrow.

Your father was telling me how he feels like he's finally got his drive back. How he feels like he's just opened a new door and stepped through to a whole new world. It's like we're finally on the same page. When I was pregnant, he was going to run for mayor of our little town and now it seems like he's going to try again. He keeps saying, "there's a fire in my belly," and that he feels like he's got his hunger back. I'm just happy for him, that's for sure. It's strange to see him so fired up. I remember, right when I was supposed to give birth, we'd been struggling financially. We won a malpractice suit for a ludicrous amount of money, right after you passed. I wouldn't have traded you for all the money in the world, though. It all feels so hollow. We could live better, fund your father's campaign, but what's the point without you?

Sometimes the day is so normal, and I barely think about you. I feel good and then a wave of sadness comes and everything comes crashing down. It's always worse each time, too, because I feel guilty. How could I go on about my day surviving without you? I don't know how your father does it. It hurts that he can barrel through his life and avoid the pain. At the same time, I envy him. If only I could devote my energy to something, and stave off all of this pain. I want to ask him, but it isn't fair. I guess we all have our own way of dealing with grief. It's hard for me to even tell you this.

Love,

Mommy

Hello again! Today I decided I would do some housework and try some new recipes. Your father has been saving some meat in the freezer, so I thought I would braise some and make him a little something special tonight. He said it was for a special occasion; I think it's beef. Maybe it's Kobe. He's really into meats now. Maybe it's all the fancy dinners, but he's been talking to the local butcher and learning about curing meat and making jerky and all kinds of stuff like that. I think it's because he went hunting with one of his contributors. He's so funny. Anyway, I know he likes to order braised beef at our favorite restaurant. I thought maybe I could practice the technique and then maybe try it with the venison; I don't know. Chicken and beef are the only meats I really cook. Maybe fish everyone once in a while. We had a maid for a long time, and before he was so occupied with work, your father loved to cook. He's a bit of a gourmand, although he lost a lot of weight when you passed. His publicist said it was good for the image. I thought that was in poor taste.

I followed the instructions to the T, but for whatever reason, the meat tasted really off. Maybe I didn't let it thaw for long enough. At any rate, I ate about half a plate and threw the rest out; it wasn't a lot of food. We'll have pasta tonight.

Today was boring. The only other thing of note was a big floor rug your father brought home. He took it into the basement and covered up water damage from a flood we had a couple of days ago. I didn't go down and look at anything. Everything down there was from his campaign stuff, and he'd worked all the repairs out with two handymen. I was just glad that it would look presentable if we needed to go down there. Scott is down there a lot nowadays. Sometimes he doesn't even come up for dinner. He just has me leave it by the basement door. I'm tempted to start my own little hobby. Gardening might be a little much, the winters here are so harsh.

It's almost like I jinxed the weather just

thinking about gardening earlier, because the 6 o'clock news was all about how bad the weather is going to be. There was a severe weather advisory, and it sounded like the entire town would be shut down. I am not looking forward to being cooped up in the house after all I've been through. I'd just gotten into the swing of going out again. This whole thing is giving me a strange feeling. Maybe it was the beef. Well, I'm sure I'll have plenty to tell you tomorrow.

I love you, Wendy,

Mommy

CHAPTER FORTY-NINE
Today

Today was so dull and strange. The whole town went on a weather advisory because of a flash snowstorm early this morning. Scott had insisted on going for meetings all morning, even though the advisory had shut down all the businesses in town. I told him he should just stay home, but he didn't listen. I was annoyed, to say the least, but not because he was being stubborn, that's just your father, he's a stubborn person. But because I woke up with the same strange feeling in the pit of my stomach as yesterday. I took some medicine and ate a big breakfast, but I still felt strange. I called your father to come home, but he said he couldn't leave until after lunch. That's when the storm really picked up.

I sat alone on the couch, listening to the wind scream outside. It was so loud; it sounded almost like those nature documentaries, ones about wolves or hyenas. For whatever reason, I started watching videos like that on the computer. Videos of predators in the wilderness, tearing into their helpless prey. In the past, I had no stomach for that kind of stuff. I fell off a bike and skinned my knee and fainted at the sight of the blood and that was only a couple of years ago. But for whatever reason today, I couldn't look away. The blood, the guts, warm, slick and squirming, spilling out of a living being. They took my guts out when they tried to save you. The thought made my tummy burn a little for whatever reason. I really hope that meat didn't make me sick. There's no way we could get to a hospital.

Time has moved so slowly today. Scott finally got home like 4 hours late because of the weather. The delay hadn't dampened his mood too much, which was surprising, to be honest. Under normal circumstances, he'd get all bent out of shape. He made me some soup, which I really appreciated. It was the most care he'd shown in a while. I'm happy that it was the campaign that took his attention away so often.

Faint snoring

(The tape starts again, static cutting in and out of the recording. The static wasn't there before. Francine is panting into the microphone.)

It's about four in the morning, and everything has gone to hell. Maybe talking to you might calm me down. I hope it will. Where do I begin? From the morning to the night. Okay. Uh, so I'd fallen asleep. I don't really remember falling asleep, but I must've because Scott woke me up and he was so mad, furious. He was saying something about the meat. I can't really remember. It's terrifying. He got in my face and he never does that. He said something I didn't like, and I pushed him and he fell down the stairs. I saw blood. Oh, my god, there was blood. The problem is, I must've fallen asleep again because I don't remember what happened next. I woke up sleeping on a stool in the kitchen. There's a breakfast bar in our house and I was drooling on the countertop. It was so strange; the oven was on and the room was sweltering.

I was so confused; I searched the house for

what felt like forever. I keep telling Scott I want a smaller house. There're so many empty rooms when it's dark, and all the shadows stretch and come alive. I hate it, it's so creaky. Eventually, I made my way to the basement and the blood on the steps was gone. I guess he'd cleaned it up by then, or maybe I just imagined it. That calmed me down a little. So yeah, I uh, I finally found him and he was in the basement. He wasn't too hurt, I don't think, but it was strange. He was a little shaky, and he kept saying, 'leave me alone, it's ok leave me alone' like he didn't want me to see something. I just wanted to apologize to him. It was so dark down there, dark and cold. I couldn't even really see him. My stomach was growling, so I offered to fix us something to eat, but he didn't seem to want anything. I really want something sweet. Or maybe some pickles. What I really need is to just go to sleep. There's too much going on.

Good Night,

Mommy

CHAPTER FIFTY
October 6, 2021...I think

I just woke up and I am sooooo hungry! But I feel better. I had a bit of a headache yesterday. The sun is setting, phew I must've been tired! I'm going to make dinner now. I know you're hungry Wendy.

Yes. Hungry. Very hungry.

Good girl! You're so well behaved and so sweet. Just like this dinner I made. I made sure the sauce had some nice brown sugar in it. Be a good girl and bring the plate down to your father. And you better not eat any of his share! You're such a naughty girl. You and your father are going to eat us out of house and home. I need to pick up more meat already.

(shuffling and scratching sounds come from the recorder, followed by the creak of a door opening.)

No more, please, please no more. Why are you doing this? Stop it! I'm begging you! It's me, it's Scott, your husband.

Husband? No, Daddy, no. You know who

I am. I put food on the table for you. Now it's time to return the favor. Should I save you a piece? Don't move.

(The recording ends with a buzzing sound and a scream.)

CHAPTER FIFTY-ONE
October 7, 2021

Um, hi, hello? I'm starting to worry that this thing doesn't work. Can't really remember the date today so I played yesterday's entry back. I listened to the whole thing and I don't remember... I just don't remember some of the things that happened. And then there was that voice. It sounded like me, but... I can't even bring myself to talk about it. And on top of that, I heard so much commotion from the basement and I heard Scott's voice. I think it was a dream, but it was so vivid. We were actually a family, all three of us. That part was nice, but then again, there was that voice.

I need to go down there, but I feel so weak. The first thing I did when I woke up was rush to the bathroom. I don't remember eating anything but I threw up so much, my stomach was totally full. There were even bones in my vomit. I'm getting really nervous. I'm not sure what any of it means. Ever since the storm, it feels like things have started spiraling out of control. Scott should be here. I have to see what he's doing. We have to find a way to go back into town. We were almost out of meat when I looked in the fridge. I'm going to rest a bit and then go to the basement. I'll record when I get down there.

CHAPTER FIFTY-TWO
Hello Daddy

Hello Daddy.

Ngh, no more. Please, I'm begging you no more. I can't take any more.

(Sounds of commotion, followed by a groan of pain)

You need to hold on tight, Daddy. You aren't finished yet. Sacrifices must be made to keep food on the table. Isn't that what you wanted? Come on. It's not right if you receive but don't reciprocate. Don't worry, we're one big happy family now. Now stop squirming.

Please stop! Please!

(The tape skips abruptly.)

Hello? Okay I think it's on. I'm going to see what's happening in the basement. I haven't heard anything since I woke up, which I guess was about two hours ago. Must be daytime now. I can't tell what time of day it is. The clocks' displays are all flashing different numbers and the snow is blocking out the windows. I can feel you still telling me you're hungry. I can feel you growing in my belly again, but it's wrong, it almost feels like when... I won't say it. I won't say it out loud. I'm just going to get Scott and get the hell out of here.

(Footsteps, followed by a door opening)

Okay, I just need to get to the light. I'm going down the steps, but the motion sensor light only reaches the foot of the steps. Everything below the last step is dark. I really don't want to go down there. These steps are so creaky. It feels kind of like the staircase is swaying. My stomach is starting to hurt again. I'm almost all the way down. Something is buzzing. I hope it's not the light. I never liked replacing the bulb down there. If the bulb is dead, then I'm really in trouble.

(There's a crash, like something ceramic getting knocked over)

Ouch! Ow, I hit my foot on something. It looks like a tray or something like that. It's got sand in it? Maybe ash. I'm not sure. Scott painted something on the floor. It's a pinkish color, it's shaped kind of like a circle. I can't see so well. The light is in the middle of this room; I think. It's on a chain, so I have to be careful. I don't want it to hit me. I don't know why I'm whispering. I feel like something bad is about to happen, but I can't tell what. Okay, here's the light.

(Francine lets out a gasp, followed by a low, shaky wail. Vomiting sounds follow. The sobbing continues for several minutes.)

He's gone, oh dear God, he's gone! Scott, no, God why?! He's only half there, Lord help him. Not Scott, nooooo, not Scott.

CHAPTER FIFTY-THREE
That One Good Eye

He keeps staring at me with his one eye, that one good eye. The man is mocking me. He's just staring and smiling at me, this new lipless smile. Even in the darkness, I can see the white of his teeth shining, making fun of me. He'd been trying to scratch something out on the floor next to him. I never noticed until now. It's too dark to really tell what it was; I just know because his fingers were these nailless stumps by the time he'd...he'd...

He's going rancid now. It's so funny that the stench of my decaying husband is how I'm keeping track of time now. The smell is making me sick, but I, I can't touch him. I can't move him. My stomach is totally empty. I'm so hungry my stomach is growling. It never stops growling. It's so loud in my ears, I can't even think. There's nothing to eat, and I'm starting to feel terrible. Just really terrible. Sometimes I think I hear him breathing, but I know it's just me. I can't get back up the steps. I hate it down here. It's so dark. The only thing I can see is him, what's left of him. He

frightens me so much. He used to frighten me too;
he used to get so angry. Never violent, but so mad.
I used to do everything for him, and he would slink
around and do whatever he wanted. You only ever
thought about yourself! She told me what you did!
Now it's just me! Just me and Wendy! Maybe
that's why you're laughing. Because now I have to
clean up your mess.

(static)

She won't be quiet now, she won't be still.
She's moving around now. Before, I could only
feel her inside. Now she's… everywhere. She
keeps crying, and she talks, but she doesn't sound
like Wendy anymore. She has such a loud voice
now. When she's upset, she growls, but not like
anything I've ever heard; she's inside my head.
She's starting to frighten me. I don't know what to
do anymore. Maybe she'll quiet down if I feed her
from me. Maybe that'll work. You nurse babies to
sleep, right? Right, that will work, that will make
her quiet. I don't know how long I've been down

here. I hope not much longer.

CHAPTER FIFTY-FOUR
I Can't Escape Her

I was able to get up. I must've fallen asleep down here. I can't get back upstairs. She grabs my ankle as soon as I reach the top step. I can't stop thinking about it; her hand is ice cold, and bony, like an old lady. It's so small but so strong. Sometimes I'll get all the way to the top, I'll even get my hand on the doorknob, before she throws me back downstairs. One time, she grabbed me by the shoulder and smashed me into the walls. Other times I can't even get up. I can't escape her. And she won't stop talking to me. I can never see all of her, just parts, here and there, but I know she's there. She's the weight on my back, that thing just out of view when I turn around. I see her, reflected in the blood on the floor. She looks like what nightmares are made of, and she mimics me as I move, as I cry. Sometimes, when I doze off, I feel her on my lap, scratching and biting my chest. She's here right now. Can you hear her? Whoever listens to this, can you hear her? I can barely think. Once she starts, she doesn't stop. Whispering in my ear. I can feel her breath against my cheek; it's like sitting next to an open freezer. She keeps telling me to finish my plate. She's laughing at me. Mocking me. Making fun of what I might have to do. My time is running out.

CHAPTER FIFTY-FIVE
I Can't Do It Anymore

I can't do it anymore. I've fed her everything, everything down to the bones. I did the best I could. I tried to resist. But I can't even tell you how long I've been down here. It's just me in the dark trying to keep her satisfied! You don't know what it's like, Scott! I'm so sorry, Scott, I'm so sorry. My teeth ache from feeding her Scott. I have to fight back tears for every morsel. I don't know how I'm alive. There are ribbons of meat hanging from me. It hurts so much. I don't have anything left. She keeps telling me to find her more. She's not my daughter. I know that now; she can't be my daughter. I gave my body to her and now all I can hear is her screaming, screaming for more food. I have to stop her. Whatever she is. There's still the knife and the plate and fork. Thank God it's a steak knife. It all has to end. I can hear her in my ears telling me to stop. I can feel her hands on my wrists; she's stronger than I am. I don't know how I'm supposed to do this. But I have to do it. She's taken so much from me already. She won't take anything else. I love you Wendy. I love my real daughter. But this is my decision. It's my life, not Scott's, not yours. Goodbye.

CHAPTER FIFTY-SIX
The Recording Ended There

The recording ended there. Jahari sighed. He knew it wouldn't be pretty in that house. Moriko knocked on the window of the town car he was sitting in, which belonged to an agent neither of them knew. Jahari got out of the car and the chilly air greeted him with snowflakes before his friend did with hellos. It was an especially bright day in Albany, almost as if the atmosphere knew of the horrors that had unfolded in the monolithic house that loomed over Jahari Jones and company, and wanted to atone for them.

"Look who I found," she said excitedly. She gestured behind her as his uncle, Dominique Augustin, swaggered up to them. He was wearing a stylish brown and cream peacoat, and his signature straw hat.

"Big Dog!" He said as he drew his nephew in for a hug. "Sak Pase! You look good, all things considered." Jahari frowned, but before he could complain, Uncle Dom continued, "I know, I've been off the grid. I'm sorry I haven't checked in.

It's delicate business, what we're trying to do, remember?"

Jahari simply nodded.

"We're gonna talk about everything soon. Come to the restaurant, okay? Next weekend?"

Jahari tried to keep his face neutral, but he was clearly pleased by the idea. As much as he wanted to resent his uncle's recent absences, they were getting closer to unraveling a mystery much bigger than anything they'd tackled before. But, more important than that, he loved his uncle.

"Yeah, I should have some time next Saturday," he said nonchalantly.

Uncle Dom had a big smile on his face. It was the kind of immaculate, infectious smile that endeared him to everyone he met, and he flashed it then. He was much more personable than his nephew, but there were clear similarities. An onlooker like Moriko would be fascinated to see how much of Dominique was reflected in Jahari.

"They pulled you in for this case, nephew?"

"Nah, this one is open and shut, from what I can see. I think the director wanted to call me in and used this case as an excuse. He shouldn't even be here if we're being for real."

"I'm pretty certain I'm here for the same reasons, but I'll let you talk to him first, nephew. And excuse me, I'm being rude, Ms. Miyazaki, good to see you again. I hope my nephew is looking after you."

"He's been a gentleman! I bet it's because you taught him well. I'm not giving him any credit," she said, punching Jahari's arm playfully.

"Aight, if it's, harass Jahari hour, I'm gonna go. See you two later." Jahari walked away good-naturedly.

CHAPTER FIFTY-SEVEN
You've Been Through A Lot

Dominique watched his nephew go with a proud but sad look on his face. It only lasted for a second, however, and his usual charisma was back in full effect. "In all seriousness, are you ok? You've been through a lot recently. I was surprised you jumped into this life so quickly."

"I'm good, I think. It all comes in waves. Sometimes it gets overwhelming, but right now I feel confident."

"I'm very glad to see that. We're going to have to train you, so you're a little more well rounded, so you have some more ability in the offense department."

"I think I'll do well. I'm a quick study."

"Good to hear. Have you been using your resources as a *yamabushi*? You were trained up as a mountain monk, yes?"

"Well, yes, but I was a child. My grandparents were *yamabushi* and my mother had some training in Shinto shrines as a *miko*. I remember a few of the rituals. I also have a gehobako. There're all sorts of things in there. Here look." Moriko presented the box her father had given her to Dominique. He peered into the box, rubbing his chin in thought.

"Well, this is promising."

"You think this stuff will be useful?" she asked excitedly.

"I hope so. The little jar says, 'in case of emergencies'. There are rosary beads, two *oshira-sama* dolls and the rest just seem like spell tags and charms. You're Japanese, you know better than I do. What do *yamabushi* usually do?"

"Fortune telling, healing people, exorcisms. That could come in handy, right? There's a lot of possession, but it's always the shrine maiden who's possessed. I don't see how that would be helpful."

Dominique took a pack of cigarettes out of his coat pocket and shook it. "You'd be surprised. There's always someone or something out there that's more than willing to lend their power out. Trust me, I have experience."

"Someone gave you power?"

Dominique smelled the pack of cigarettes, as if he was checking to see if they were still good. "Sort of. The difference is that miko are looked after. The spirits Miko have dealings with are all benevolent. Not all gods are friendly."

Moriko wrinkled her nose. This conversation was a little too cryptic for her taste, so she settled on a lighter one. "Are you a smoker?"

"I used to be. I quit for my wife. These aren't for me."

Moriko looked at him slyly. "Sure they aren't."

Dominique put his hand over his heart. "Swear, on my life. Why do you want one?"

"No, I hate cigarettes. I tried one in high school once, it made me throw up. I don't even like the smell," she replied, sticking her tongue out.

Dominique chuckled. "Well, I promise you won't have to deal with them around me. Are you going to come inside?"

"No thanks. From the way Jahari looked, I can tell I'll be just fine out here."

The two parted ways, and Dominique went in search of his nephew.

CHAPTER FIFTY-EIGHT
Down the Narrow Staircase

Mario let Jahari into the large Queen Anne styled house. It was painted a rusty red with cream trimmings, but its innate majesty got lost in the swarm of investigators entering and exiting the house, like ants swarming over a carcass.

"Nice house, ain't it J?"

"From the sounds of that recording? Not anymore."

"Anything you could glean from the audio alone?"

"Nothing I can confirm without seeing the basement."

Mario nodded and motioned for Jahari to follow him. "Good thing that's where we're going then. There's something down there I think you'll be interested in seeing."

Jahari followed Mario down the narrow staircase, parting the sea of silent agents, who did nothing to acknowledge their presence. At the base of the steps, a dusty substance coated the floor, almost obscuring a brightly colored symbol etched into the floor. It was a circle, or maybe a wheel, or perhaps...

"An eye?"

"Exactamente, just like the one in Cameron Toker's house."

Jahari stooped down and rubbed a pinch of the substance that blanketed the floor between his thumb and forefinger. "It's ash. There should be some kind of firepit or receptacle around here somewhere. He was doing a sacrifice."

"We ended up finding a little bronze fire pit on the floor. BA picked it up during decontamination. That was the biggest concern: we had to make sure this place was safe to enter."

"The thing that interests me is, these eyes have all been reddish or pinkish in color. The eyes I remember were all yellow."

"Maybe they got new PR people, I don't know. Let's look at the room before we get caught up in all that, hermano." He walked to the center of the basement and respectfully removed the sheet covering the first body. "Francine Ponce, 33, in the medical profession, if I'm not mistaken."

"Cardiologist."

"Right. Well, she was married to him," he said, pointing at the other sheet, which was a much less solid silhouette, "before all this nonsense. Here's the part we think is weird. If you look at her thighs, chest, and arms, you can see wounds inflicted by human teeth. You can also see very drastic changes in her body. They also said she had the same physical symptoms of someone who'd recently had a miscarriage, but she hadn't been pregnant in months. But she didn't die from any of this. She died from a stab wound in her heart. She definitely killed herself, but get this, the bite wounds are also self-inflicted."

"She was eating herself. The tape... she was eating herself?"

Mario grimaced. "Looks like it. Her husband has almost been picked clean. All the marks are from human teeth, we believe also self-inflicted, because the marks don't match her teeth. Or at least not the ones she currently has in her head. We don't know how any of this could've happened."

Jahari looked at the corpse. Francine's body was rail thin, like she had survived a famine and had grown to be taller than him. Her teeth had taken on a canine quality, with other, clearly adult teeth on the floor in front of her mouth. Some parts of her gums had no teeth and were naked, other places still had their original occupants, and some had sharp, predatory teeth like an animal. Her skin had taken on a gray color and leathery texture, and her hair was graying like a corpse left to dry out in the sun. "It was a possession. The voices on the tape make that clear."

"Why would she want to be possessed?"

"I don't think she did. What did you say the husband did for a living?"

"He was trying to be a politician. They said he was a real social climber. Prior to that, he did energy. Like oil and stuff like that in Canada."

"So we know he had some background in the occult from that sacrifice. He was in too deep."

"But how did she end up icing him instead of the other way around?"

"Google what a Wendigo is and check that freezer. The mystery meat is the answer. And what did you say that guy's name was again?"

"Scott Ponce. Why? Do you recognize the name?"

"Only thing I'm recognizing right now is how ugly this scene is. It's mad grisly. I'm going to go find the director."

"You know you're the most useless, useful person ever!" Mario called after Jahari, who had already gone back upstairs to find his uncle and BRAHMASTRA's acting director, Armando De Souza, sitting on the couch in the living room.

Jahari sucked his teeth. He was hoping he could avoid the director by helping Mario, but clearly, that was wishful thinking.

"Good afternoon, Senior Director."

"Jahari, I've known you since you were a little boy and you've never called me by my title. Speak freely. You always have, regardless of whether it was proper."

He swallowed hard. Dominique had a somber look on his face and motioned for Jahari to continue. "I'm so sorry. I've never had anything like this happen to me before. There were some factors in that mission that we couldn't have anticipated and…"

"You don't have to apologize, Jahari. You and my son were like brothers. I know you wouldn't have let anything happen to him if it was within your power. And we all know the dangers of this way of life."

"You did everything you could and there was almost no loss of life. Don't let the guilt get to you, Big Dog. If there's anything we understand, it's that death isn't the end." His uncle pulled him in for a hug, and the trio was silent for a moment.

Armando lowered his voice. "That's actually

not why I called you here, however. BA is changing hands."

"You're stepping down?!"

"Jahari, please calm down. We have to keep this quiet," Dominique said.

"The frequency and severity of paranormal threats have been steadily increasing and a growing movement within BA has been gaining political steam. The structure of this organization is about to change and they don't want me to be a part of it. I'm telling you two this because everyone knows we're close. That might draw some ill will towards your family."

Jahari scoffed. "We're used to a little ill will."

"That may be so, but they will most certainly try to remove you from any investigation into The Sight of The Third Eye. You two are known for doing your own thing. They will want to control you. I only have a few months left, so I'm going to give you two carte blanche to try to get whatever information you need to finish your investigation. Is that all right?"

"Thank you very much Armando, we really appreciate your help," Dominique said, shaking his hand. Jahari and his uncle said their goodbyes and went back out onto the freshly dusted lawn. It was almost noon, and the sun was high in the sky, turning the snow into twinkling diamonds before their very eyes.

"What do we do now, Unc?"

"Well, we have the resources; we know what comes next. I think we play our cards close to our vests and work hard. If we look like we have nothing to do, BA will make sure we're too busy to do what we gotta do. You make any progress?"

Jahari leaned in close. "One of the guys from the vampire incident gave me a list of names. I'm gonna try to meet all of those people and hopefully I can get some information out of them."

"Good thinking, I've got my own project I've been working on. If everything goes well, we might have everything we need."

"And you aren't going to tell me what you're working on?"

"Nope. Definitely not here. We've never been the most trusting of the BA. Now, we keep them in the dark."

Jahari sighed. "It's kinda wild to me."

"What?"

"Like in that house. I don't know what that man was trying to accomplish, but he ruined everything he had. He gambled his entire life and the life of his wife away and lost. Everything's getting worse. Every day I see something more bugged out than what I saw the day before."

"Nephew, there will always be something or someone creeping around in the dark. There ain't a ghost scarier than the ghosts of the past. We can't help everyone exorcise them, but we can definitely get rid of the ones that go bump in the night," he said, gathering himself. "We still on for next Saturday?"

"Yeah, no doubt, no doubt."

"Love you kid."

"Love you too Unc."

CHAPTER FIFTY-NINE
First Job Finished

Jahari sat towards the back of the 40 seat bus BRAHMASTRA had arranged for them, poring over the photos of the scene. It was strange, looking at the horror that had unfolded in that house, a great, dark, bottomless evil contained in small, glossy squares. The painted eye in the photograph commanded his attention, pulling him into the pupil like a black hole.

"Hey!" Moriko said, popping up from the row in front of him like a spring loaded toy. "Oops, I didn't mean to startle you. I was napping and when I woke up, I noticed you moved to the back. Are you okay?"

Jahari rubbed the nape of his neck subconsciously; it stung a little. "I'm fine. I just came back here to see if there was anything I missed at the Ponce house."

"Do you think there's anything that will help us find The Sight of The Third Eye?"

Jahari spoke in hushed tones, choosing his words carefully. "Ponce's name was on the list. He was definitely at that gathering upstate, where Clive got involved with the cult. I'll see what else I can get from the tapes and the pictures."

Mori's brow furrowed, and she bit the inside of her cheek. "How long have you been looking for these people?"

"Who? The Sight?"

"Yeah."

"Subconsciously, my whole life, but actively, I guess the last five years or so. A lot of it was me gathering information for my uncle. It was low-key, very low-key."

She considered this briefly, but then her expression brightened, as if it wasn't important. "It's a long ride back to the city. Do you want to play a game?"

Jahari shrugged.

"Twenty-one questions? It's a good way to get to know your partner, you know, the person who will probably save your life more than once," she said with a sly grin.

`   "Sure."

"Okay, what's your favorite food?"

"Uh, I like cookies."

"That's funny. I've never heard anyone say a dessert is their favorite food."

"I didn't really try desserts until I was older, so they mean a lot, I guess."

"Your uncle didn't let you have sweets?"

"Eh, it wasn't him exactly."

Moriko could tell there was a sad explanation coming and tactfully changed the subject. "Now you have to ask me a question."

"What's your favorite color?"

"Green! I love it, all shades of green too! My turn now. What's your favorite movie?"

Jahari looked away. "You're gonna laugh."

Moriko blushed a little. "Hey, I won't laugh, I promise. Is it embarrassing? Is it a romance? Are you a romantic? I can't make fun of anyone, my favorite movie is Lilo & Stitch!"

"I like that one too," Jahari said with a chuckle. "My favorite movie is The Sixth Sense."

"Oh, I guess the reasons are kinda obvious there, huh?"

"Yeah, you don't have to think too hard about it. Anyway, do you have any hobbies?"

"Playing baseball. I used to play on my high school team in Japan. I was pretty good, but as we moved around, it was harder to keep up with playing. We lived in a couple of different places in Japan. I still follow the sport, though. I wanted to go to the Women's League when I was a kid."

"When I was a kid, I wanted to be a paleontologist."

"Did you like dinosaur movies or something?"

"Nah, it was really dumb, but I was hoping I could see the ghosts of dinosaurs."

Mori chuckled. "You could've told us if they had feathers or not."

"They will not convince me dinosaurs had

them bumass feathers. That shit is corny. I refuse to believe it. Anyway, speaking of dinosaurs, what's your favorite animal?"

"That's easy, Godzilla!"

Jahari raised an eyebrow. "Godzilla isn't real."

"Jahari, we spent the weekend fighting a vampire and Godzilla isn't real? I believe in him."

"You're not wrong. I've seen some wild shit. I haven't seen Godzilla in person…yet, but who knows? Is he even an animal? He's a mutant iguana, right?"

"That's the crappy American version. You guys ruin everything. He's not really a lizard or a dinosaur, he's Godzilla."

"You got it, you got it. It's your turn."

"So you like my game?" she said triumphantly.

Jahari sucked his teeth and admitted, "yeah, I am enjoying myself. I won't lie. I thought it was a guessing game, to be honest."

"That's twenty questions. This is twenty-one questions. But I'm glad you're enjoying it. Confession time. What's something bad that you've done that you want to get off your chest? No judgement."

"Uh, sometimes I play basketball and I never really had the time to practice as a kid, so I use my powers to cheat when the game starts pissing me off."

"How bad are you?"

"I'm athletic, but I don't really have any of the fundamentals down. I'm not terrible, but I'm not good. What's your confession?"

"Okay, so I lived in Japan from the age of 15 until now. Before that I lived in Queens and in California for a bit, but I would visit Japan a lot. I went to high school over there, and during my second year of high school I joined a sukeban, which is like a girl gang, I guess."

Jahari stifled his laughter. "You were in a gang?"

"It's not exactly a gang, it's more like delinquents hanging out. I always had pretty good grades, but in the gang we would get into fights and shoplift and my friends would smoke cigarettes behind the arcade."

"You don't really seem like the knucklehead type."

"I wasn't. All I did was steal fashion magazines. I did pretty well in the three fights I was in, too!"

"Did you win them all?"

"If you'd seen those girls, you wouldn't even have to ask."

"Now you've graduated to creatures of the night. I'd say your record is pretty clean when it comes to fights."

"You're damn right it is. It's my turn now. Can I ask you a personal question this time?" she said, resting her head on her hands on the back of her seat.

"Go ahead."

"Are you gay?"

"Ayo, what?"

Moriko raised both hands in embarrassment. "I'm sorry! It's just people keep talking about your partner Mike and you didn't seem interested in Veronica or like me and I was just curious!"

"Dawg, Mike was my partner, like BUSINESS partner, like you and me! Like I don't know, cops? Not a fan of cops. Let's go with you and me."

"I'm sorry. I didn't mean to offend you."

"I mean, there's nothing to be offended about. That's not me though."

"But what happened to Mike?"

Jahari's face darkened. "Mike was Armando's son. Remember Armando from the crime scene? He's the current director of BRAHMASTRA. Mike was my best friend. We grew up together. He, uh, he died on our last mission. I couldn't save him. It hasn't even been a week."

"Wow, I'm so sorry to hear that."

"Don't worry about it. You're good."

"Was there a funeral or something?"

"BRAHMASTRA doesn't do funerals."

Moriko chewed her bottom lip. This conversation had taken a somber turn. "Do you ever see people you know? You know, like see them?" She punctuated the word by wiggling her fingers.

Jahari laughed good-naturedly. Explaining his condition to someone he knew was always an interesting experience. It made him feel like he was someone's chronically ill classmate. "Nah, that's the funny part. I've never seen anyone I actually wanted to see. Never seen a loved one or anyone I'd met who wasn't... what's a good word? Antagonistic. Yeah, we'll go with that, antagonistic. I don't know, it's probably for the best, though. You gotta move on at some point. Life is a transition."

Moriko considered that for a moment. She

spoke again in a gentle tone, "Can I ask you a philosophical question?"

"Sure thing."

"Hm, the thing is… I'm trying to help solve the mystery of this cult and everything because I want justice for what happened to my family. I don't want what happened to my dad, my mom, and me to happen to someone else. Is that why you're doing it? To see why your parents were involved?"

A pensive look washed over Jahari's face like the tide over the shoreline. "Not exactly. I never knew them, so I can't say why they did anything they did. It isn't really important either; Unc was there for me. You can't miss what you never had. But that cult and the sacrifice and all of that has made my life hard, very hard. I'm not complaining. I'm sure there're people who have it worse. But the longer these cult members are out there, the more people are going to suffer with lives like mine. I want people to have the peace I don't have, in this life or in the next."

"But what do you want for yourself?"

"Me? That's a good question. I guess all I want is one day to have peace myself."

Moriko smiled as she responded, "Okay, then I have one last question."

"It's not your turn, but go ahead," Jahari said, rolling his eyes and beaming. It was the first purely happy smile she had seen from him.

"Do you wanna go to the arcade when we get back to Manhattan and get something to eat? It'll be fun! Plus, it'll be nice to celebrate. Our first job finished!"

His smile grew. "Loser pays for dinner."

CHAPTER SIXTY
Claws on the Hardwood

Jahari got home at 1:30am. He opened his door to find his stuff strewn about in a slightly more haphazard way than usual. The window opposite the entrance was slightly open, and the curtains billowed hauntingly in the breeze. The hairs on the back of Jahari's neck stood on end. He could feel the static again, faint as it was. Sensing movement in the kitchen, Jahari pricked his ears up. The faint click of pointed claws on the hardwood kitchen floor met his ears. Something was there, but he couldn't sense any negative emotions. A heavy object dropped to the floor and rolled out into the living room from behind the breakfast bar.

A can of dog food?

Enzo's head poked out from behind the corner leading to the kitchen, "Mi dispiace! I'm on a strictly sanguine diet, but they still eat," he said, gesturing to the two gargantuan dogs snapping at each other over a can of dog food. "I had to get some food for them. You don't have any meat."

"I don't eat meat."

"You are a strange man, Mr. Jones." Enzo said with a puzzled expression.

"You just picking up on that?" Jahari replied teasingly. "I'm going to bed. Some of us still sleep at night. Just do me a favor and don't make too much noise."

Enzo nodded, "I'll be silent as the grave."

"Help yourself to whatever. Don't delete the save files on the video games."

"What are video games?"

But Jahari was already up the stairs. He felt good. The past couple of days had been a whirlwind of emotions, exhilaration, confusion, hardship, victory, fear and revelations. And through all of that, Jahari had emerged with a new fire within him. He finally had some direction to finding this cult. Shadows were coming to light. Things were coming together. And he rarely had any time to himself. It felt good to hang out with Moriko. It felt good to have a normal night out with a friend. The last couple of hours were the closest thing he'd had to peace in what felt like years.

He pulled off his clothes from the day and slipped into some shorts and an old t-shirt. As he laid his head down on the pillow, he savored the thought in his mind. *Peace.* It had been a good night.

Had been.

Until he saw the ghost in the window.

Thank You For Reading

Thank you so much for reading Hecatomb Of The Vampire! I hope you enjoyed reading it as much as I did writing it. I also hope that it scared you a little. What would scare me, is if no one left a review! If you could find the time to leave a review it would be a great help. I need your help so as many people as possible read this book! And sit tight, because there's more of Jahari, Moriko, and Enzo on the way. You can leave a review here: www.amazon.com/review/create-review?&asin=B0CJDFHXJCS

Or you can go to the Amazon page where you purchased my book and under where you see the customer review ratings, click the tab for write a customer review. Thank you and be careful out there.

About the Author

Let's see, about me. I'm from Queens, NY, born and raised. I'm very spiritual and have practiced Gaudiya Vaishnavism from birth. Hare Krsna! Studying the Vaishnava philosophy really influenced a lot of the concepts in my writing. My hobbies include freestyling (rapping), writing, reading, biking, watching basketball, and playing video games. I love my bike, my grandpa gave it to me. It's an Italian racing bike, one of those carbon fiber ones. It doesn't have a name but I think it should, I just don't know what the name would be. I've been fortunate enough to travel the world and play a special drum called a mrdanga or khol in a spiritual band of sorts with my wonderful family. If I could fight any celebrity, I would fight T-Pain. I'm a Knicks fan (read: masochist). I wasn't allowed to watch wrestling when I was younger, because I saw one of those attitude era commercials where they were doing the "SUCK IT" thing with the X, and I did that one time in front of my mom and I got in trouble. I just thought it looked cool, I had no clue what it meant. I remember a relative gave me a cage with all the wrestler toys for a holiday later that year, but I didn't watch wrestling, so in my childhood eyes she basically gave me 11 random plastic men in their underwear. This is pretty much all the useful information about me.

You can sign up for my newsletter on my website

https://www.r-complexstudios.com/home

Follow me on Instagram:

https://www.instagram.com/g.n._jones/

Twitter:

https://twitter.com/RComplexStudios

Youtube:

https://www.youtube.com/@reptilebrainstudios1/ playlists

TikTok:

https://www.tiktok.com/@rcomplexstudios?_t=8f
ZuGVNkBWU&_r=1

Made in the USA
Middletown, DE
04 October 2023